Praise for
Charley's Choice

"Charley Parkhurst's life might seem unbelievable, but Fern J. Hill makes it not only credible but fascinating. I really loved this book, read it in one sitting because it was impossible to put down. But Charley's exploits linger—an inspiration, a woman with a mind of her own who did what she wanted and showed 'em all! Thank you Fern J. Hill."

> —JANE CANDIA COLEMAN, author of *The White Dove* and *Tumbleweed*

"The story of Charley Parkhurst does not fall easily into place. Details of her life are scarce, yet Fern Hill artfully weaves them like golden threads among the warp and woof of a tale spun from fact and fiction. The result is a seamless tapestry with the rough texture of the old west depicting a woman's struggle for equality in a world dominated by men. Charley's Choice is my choice for the best fictionalized biography. A must read."

> —JOHN EVANS, author of *The Cut.*

"Charley Parkhurst has long been an enigmatic figure in the Old West. In her first novel Fern Hill has skillfully blended historical research with fiction to give Charley a unique and entirely believable voice. And anyone who loves horses or understands driving them will be doubly rewarded."

> —PERSIA WOOLLEY, author of *How to Write and Sell Historical Fiction*

"A richly detailed, vividly imagined, and sympathetic life of the mysterious Charlotte Parkhurst, who courageously defied her gender's destiny to, literally, become her own man."

> —JOANN LEVY, author of *They Saw the Elephant: Women in the California Gold Rush*

Charley's Choice

The Life and Times of Charley Parkhurst

by
Fern J. Hill

ISBN 978-0-7414-4643-5

Published by:

Info@buybooksontheweb.com
www.buybooksontheweb.com
Toll-free (877) BUY BOOK
Local Phone (610) 941-9999
Fax (610) 941-9959

Printed in the United States of America

Printed on Recycled Paper

Published October 2012

In loving memory of

Jane R. Hill
and
Robert F. Hill

Acknowledgments

This novel has been richly blessed with the kindness and gifts of time from historians, librarians, and fellow writers.

My heartfelt thanks go to: Jack Althouse, Holly Corcoran, Kelly Corcoran, Kathryn Craft, Milt Cunningham, John Evans, Anne Felker, Diane Fleming, Linda Glaser, Josephine Griggs, William Marley, Margaret Murray, Pam Munoz Ryan, and Persia Woolley.

Special thanks for historical information goes to Robyn Christensen of the Worcester Historical Museum, Rachel McKay of the Santa Cruz County Historical Archives, Donna Swedberg of the Santa Cruz Public Library, Jane Borg and Dorothy Wilkerson of the Pajaro Valley Historical Association, and the Bangor (Pennsylvania) Public Library.

And, in belated gratitude to Jane R. Hill who instilled within me the love of reading, and tried to teach me economy of words, and Robert F. Hill whose entrepreneurial spirit pointed the way.

Without you, this novel would not exist.

The End

The last conversations I had with Charley Parkhurst were slow and torturous for her. At the end of almost every sentence, she would take a sip of water or Ayer's Cherry Pectoral, the snake oil remedy she'd bought, but never once did she complain of the pain she must have felt.

I remember well the day Frank Woodward walked up the path to our house asking that my son go to town to fetch Mr. O'Neill, the undertaker. It was Sunday, December 28, 1879, six weeks after I finally convinced Charley to see Dr. Plum, a cancer specialist in town, about her sore throat.

"It's done," Frank said, gently closing the door behind him. The lines on the old man's face had deepened since I saw him last, and, to my mind, his skin had the look of ashes under the grate. The pouches under his eyes were a mottled brown almost matching the color of his sherry-hazel eyes. "Charley breathed his last a half hour ago." A long pause punctuated his delivery of the sad news. He transferred his weight from one foot to the other while rolling his hat between his work-roughened hands.

"It would have been kinder of the Lord to have let Charley pass before the worst set in," I said.

"Yep, he was a good man. A good friend to me for the past twenty years." Frank stood in the doorway blinking back tears, his Adam's apple bobbing with every convulsive swallow he took to marshal his usual reserve. "Guess I should head back and wait for O'Neill to come."

"Charley wanted me to be with you when the time came, so I'll be along shortly."

"Yes, ma'am." Frank bowed his head to put his hat on. I held the screen door wide while he shuffled off the porch and down the front path.

Well, Charley's secret would be out now, soon as the undertaker examined her. Poor Frank was headed for a bit of a shock.

1
The Home
1824

G ee, Charley, a four-horse hitch. Would you look at those beauties? And that carriage."

"Sure ain't from around here," I said, eyeing the reddish-brown four-in-hand as they pranced past our orphanage one rainy morning, their black manes and tails waving in the breeze. "Bet they come from Worchester, or maybe even Boston."

A coachman sat bolt upright in the driver's box decked out in forest green, and a boy maybe two or three years older than me stood on the ledge behind the enclosed carriage. He wore the same rich green livery, but I couldn't take my eyes off the gold braid along the coachman's cuffs as he guided the high stepping matched bays through mud puddles in the road.

"Don't lean against the screen." Matron Tyler stood at the kitchen entryway as she did a hundred times a day. It was her lookout spot, her way of keeping an eye on us orphans.

Fish and I rushed out onto the porch so's we could watch the rig for as long as possible. We had ourselves a good look. If it hadn't been raining pretty steady, we would've followed them a ways.

"Come eat your breakfast, boys."

"That's what I'm going to do when I leave. I'm going to drive horses like that someday, Fish. I swear by my heart. I'm going to wear livery just like them that just went by. I'm going to have gold braid up my sleeve like that driver, and I'm going to work for the rich like them in that carriage."

"You can't, you're a girl," my friend said.

"I can do anything you, or any boy in this orphanage can do. You know I can. I can do it even better than most."

"I'm just saying, they don't let girls do that sort of thing, is all."

"I take care of Dapple, don't I? I feed him, and brush him, and clean his stall, don't I?"

"Yeah."

"Well then, I'm going to do it. You wait and see if I don't."

"Boys come eat your—oh, it's you, Charley. I should've known it'd be you standing out here gawking at horses with Jimmy Bean. What am I going to do with you? Don't go dreaming after horses, girl. How many times have I got to tell you, orphans go into training. They work in a shop, or do maid work for the upper crust, or they settle down and have children. Don't go making it hard on yourself. Come in now and eat." Matron held the door open for Fish and me to go in.

"Don't want no husband or kids tying me down. Don't need nobody," I said.

"Just as you say." Matron let the screen door slap shut behind us.

I knew she was wrong. Nothing she or anybody said was going to stop me from working with horses. It was all I ever dreamed of while sleeping, or thought about while awake. My chin jut forward as it always did when someone told me I couldn't do something 'cause I was a girl. It really ground my oats.

"You want to finish our fort today?" Fish asked as we sat at the long trestle table to eat our watery oatmeal.

"Got to clean Dapple's stall first and feed him," I said, referring to the orphanage's big-boned carthorse. Then in a whisper,
"And I want to try to get a ride in if I can. Will you watch for
me?"

"Yeah."

We both made short work of the tasteless gruel, and headed
out the back door. We got about halfway across the yard when I
spied Billy Todd throwing rocks at Dapple. I ran the rest of the
way with Fish a step behind.

"Billy Todd, you son of a bitch, leave Dapple alone."

"Go to hell."

"You throw one more rock, I'll—"

"Boys, no fighting," Matron's voice called through the back
screen door.

"You wait, Parkhurst. You'll be sorry. You, too, Bean." Billy
Todd and his two friends turned away, but before they were out of
earshot, they began to chant, "Jimmy loves Charley" in low voices
so Matron wouldn't hear.

Fish always got mad when they did that, but I told him not to
mind. We were best friends, Fish and me; I'd venture to say we
were closer than most families. Billy Todd and his friends liked to
taunt us any way they could, and Fish always fell for their
mischief.

Once in the barn, I slipped the harness headstall on Dapple
using an old rope for reins. I'd found the rope years ago, and kept
it hid in the grain room, so's Warden wouldn't find it. I weren't
supposed to ride Dapple, but... well, I just couldn't help myself. I
rode every chance I could even after I got found out and had my
ass switched a few times. Fish kept look out for me, and would let
me know when trouble was coming, but he never took a turn, even
when I told him I'd walk Dapple and help him learn to ride.

"He's too damn big," Fish would say.

"He ain't a pony. He needs to be big to pull the wagon."

"Well, I ain't going to ride him."

"Don't have to, just be on the lookout. Give a whistle if you
see the warden coming."

"Promise to help me with the fort after?"

"Yeah. When I'm done with my chores."

I got to ride the paddock for close on half an hour that Saturday morning before Fish whistled. I slid off, brushed away the short, gray hairs on the inside of my pant legs and seat, and pulled off the bridle. A few of the kids would rat on me, and I didn't know how close trouble was. Just as I straightened, the chief rat, Billy Todd, rounded the corner and gave me a long sneering stare. I met it with my killer look. He looked away first. He always did.

Fish bounced on his toes, while I cleaned Dapple's stall.

"Hurry up, Charley. I don't want to get caught hanging around. You know the warden'll put us to work if we don't skedaddle before he gets here."

"If you're in such a hell-bent hurry, why don't you put a scoop of oats in Dapple's feedbox for me?"

Fish went into the grain room. I heard him knocking around in there, when he give a yelp and darted into the stall where I was working, pale as crushed oats, his eyes wide and wild. He grabbed my arm so tight it felt like he was tearing it off.

"What's the matter with you? Running like that. You're going to spook the horse."

"Rat." His high squeaking voice sounded like the animal itself.

"Where?"

"Coming after me."

Sure enough, a rat almost as big as a cat waddled past the end of the stall squealing with fear. I grabbed the manure fork and dashed after him. Took a couple of jabs before I got him, but I didn't kill him right off. Had to flip him over and bash his head. When the rat lay still, its namesake stepped into the barn.

"What's with you, Jimmy?" Billy Todd asked Fish. "Scared of a little ol' rat? What a sissy."

"Leave him be," I said.

"Gonna make me?"

"You know I can." I'd softened up the sass in him once before for twisting Jennifer's arm up behind her back demanding she give him her birthday nickel. He'd ratted on me, and there'd been hell to pay, but it had been worth it. Billy Todd was a coward, but vicious as a rabid dog. I scooped the rat up with the fork and poked it at Billy Todd. With a short squeal, he ran out of the barn. I flipped the dead rat into the barrow.

I thumped Fish on the arm. "You okay?"

"Yeah. Just don't like rats."

"Me neither."

Fish stepped out of the barn while I hurried through the rest of my chores, and dumped the barrow on the shit heap out back. We spent the day building our fort near a big old maple on the other side of the field that ran behind the barn and along the paddock. Didn't go in for lunch though we heard the triangle rung. Figured we'd be captured for some duty or another if we went back.

Showed up for dinner though. Billy Todd and his two friends were joshing around at the table, casting knowing looks at Fish and me. Something was brewing, but I didn't know what. Warden Tyler was asleep in the haymow with his bottle. Matron Tyler and Dinah served up dinner without him. We'd managed to stay out of everybody's way that day, and Matron didn't seem to be angry at us during dinner, so it appeared Fish and me were in the clear with the Tylers leastways. Still and all, Billy Todd and his friends had me nervous. Something was going to happen, and knowing them, it weren't going to be nice.

Me and Fish spent some time reading before Matron Tyler sent us to bed. Billy Todd and his friends had already gone up along with most of the others. We did as we were told, put our books away and headed upstairs.

I'd just crawled under the covers in the girls' ward when I heard a high-pitched scream. I whipped back the bedcovers, and ran to the boys' ward. I came to a horrified stop across the bed from Fish. His eyes were wide with terror. My eyes were drawn to the sheets. They were smeared with blood, and in the center of the cot lay the dead rat.

Matron no sooner rushed into the boys' ward then she squawked and ran from the room calling for her husband. Billy Todd stood beside me. His tongue peeked between his teeth; his eyes were riveted to the fear on Fish's face. I back-fisted him under his jaw so hard and fast that he fell like a log. Blood began to seep from his slack mouth. I glanced around at the other kids; all of them were looking from the mess on the bed to Fish's tear-wet face. No one saw me hit Billy Todd that I could see, so I went and put my arm around Fish's shoulders and drew him away from the bloody mess on the bed and everybody staring at him.

When Matron Tyler came back with the warden in tow a few minutes later, she drew Fish away to talk with him. I saw her put an arm around his shoulders, but couldn't hear what she was telling him. Billy Todd got up from the floor crying. I inched my way to the door. No one noticed me, so I went back to the girls ward and told the few that hadn't rushed over what had happened to Fish.

I remember watching shadows glide across the floor that night wondering just how much trouble I was going to be in the next day. For certain as I was born, Billy Todd would rat on me, telling the Tylers that it'd been me that slugged him.

Next morning, lucky for me, someone came up with the notion that Billy Todd had fainted and bit his tongue, so no one believed him when he tried to pin it on me. But I knew Billy Todd better than to believe he would let the whole thing pass.

2
Foul Play

A high, thin scream pulled my eyes to the shaking limbs of the chestnut tree as a body thumped to the ground stirring up a cloud of dust.

I ran to the still body, as did the other kids in the backyard.

Two girls screamed. One kept shrieking till someone slapped her face. I would've slapped her myself, but I couldn't move, couldn't breathe.

Fish lay sprawled on the hard packed dirt of the orphanage play yard, his head rested on his shoulder all crooked-like, a bloody piece of bone stuck through the skin of his arm. His right leg was twisted, the foot pointing in the wrong direction. His clear blue eyes stared at the sun without blinking.

Matron Tyler swung open the screen door and rushed toward us, wringing her hands dry on her apron. Warden Tyler lurched out of the barn and ran across the yard. His wife knelt down and pressed the tips of her fingers into the soft area under Fish's chin.

I stared at my friend.

He didn't move.

Matron put her ear to his chest for a long moment. Rocking back on her heels, she looked up at her husband and shook her head.

The children started whispering.

I couldn't look away. I kept expecting Fish to take a deep breath and blink his eyes.

Fish was a champion tree climber. He never would've fallen out of the chestnut we'd been climbing for years.

Then I knew.

Billy Todd.

Generally, he was the first to turn up when there was anything going on. He weren't in the yard, but I spotted him leaning against the side of the house, tucked in behind a lilac bush. His dark piggy eyes hungrily staring at the scene. I rushed at him with murder in my heart.

I knew it was Billy Todd's fault Fish was dead. I hit him everywhere I could with all the strength I had. When he hissed "sissy," I bloodied his nose, but was torn away before I got my chance to kill him like he deserved. Warden Tyler flung me on my ass in the dirt and pointed at me to stay put. He reached into the bushes and yanked Billy Todd out by the arm. I was glad for the scratches on his arms and face, and knew I'd left bruises on his shins where I had kicked him. I only wished I'd kilt him. He weren't so cocky now Warden had him by the shirt. Fact is, he looked a mite scared.

"He kilt Fish."

"Shut up before I lay into you," Warden said.

"You got proof, Charley?" Matron glared at me. "You see Billy Todd do something to Jimmy Bean?"

"Look at him. He's glad Fish fell."

"You do something to this boy?" Warden Tyler yanked Billy Todd nose to nose. Billy Todd grimaced. "You push him out of the tree?"

"No, I ain't done nothing. Wasn't up the damn tree when he fell."

"It was an accident is all," Matron said.

I snorted. I knew what she was thinking. She didn't want anyone from the Presbytery snooping around. Every time something went wrong, Billy Todd was generally in the middle of it. The Tylers didn't want any questions asked.

I got up, dusting off the seat of my britches. This time had to be different. It weren't just a busted arm, or a loose tooth, or a bruised body. My friend was dead, and I knew that somehow Billy Todd had done it.

Warden Tyler let Billy Todd loose with a short shove. I gave Billy Todd a killer look. The warden picked up the limp body and staggered toward the house. Matron trotted ahead to hold the screen door open. When it slapped shut, I looked for that damned snake to have another go at him, but he'd already slithered away.

The rest of the kids wandered toward the house in twos and threes to sit near the back door. I went to the barn to talk to Dapple. While I rubbed him behind the ears, I began to do some thinking.

Yesterday, I'd promised to beat Billy Todd for throwing rocks at Dapple, then not more'n an hour after that I threatened him with the bloody rat, and then I knocked him out for putting the dead rat in Fish's bed last night.

Then come morning, he'd held a shiny quarter to my face and bet me I couldn't climb to the top of the chestnut tree.

I turned down his large bet 'cause I didn't trust him to pay up.

"You'll get yours, Parkhurst," he said as I turned away.

Had he meant for me to be hurt?

I ran back to the chestnut tree and kicked around the busted limbs and twigs lying on the ground from Fish's fall, but nothing looked wrong. I looked up through the branches, but since the tree was full of leaves, I couldn't see much. But I just knew Billy Todd had done something to one of them branches higher up.

Matron Tyler came to the screen door and called Daniel. He got up from his knees beside Penny, the youngest of our home, and went to the door.

"Run into town and get the sheriff. Tell him Jimmy Bean fell out of the tree and is dead. Then go to the undertaker and tell him he'd better come on out here. Run along Daniel and do what I say."

Daniel's long legs sped him over the low fence in the front yard and down the road to Cumberton. Our fastest runner, he'd make the mile-long trip in minutes.

Some of the kids tried going into the house through the back door, but Matron Tyler shooed them away. A few crept to the front and tried getting in that way, but I heard her tell them in no uncertain words to get out and stay out till called for dinner. Matron Tyler could look out both doors while standing at the kitchen entryway. Through the side window, I could see the shadow of her and Warden Tyler with their heads together. Probably figuring out what to tell Sheriff Madison when he came, and the Elders of the Presbyterian board when they came that evening to look into the matter, as I knew they would. The Tylers would say it was an accident, and Billy Todd would get away with what he'd done. Again.

I went back to scuffing through the twigs looking for some sign. Walked around the tree peering up through the branches every which way till I thought I saw a busted branch near the top. Decided to take a look-see. I started shimmying up the trunk, but Matron Tyler's voice pulled me back.

"Charley, get away from that tree. You stupid or something? You want to fall and get killed, too?"

I moseyed away, but I knew I'd be up that tree as soon as her back was turned. All the girls sat around in small groups whispering among themselves. Some of them comforted those who cried, while others just stared off with sick looks on their faces. The boys were nowhere in sight. I decided to keep an eye on things out front.

The sheriff arrived first, only minutes after Daniel left.

"Met Daniel halfway between here and town," he said as he walked into the house. "I came on ahead and let the boy go after Hobbs." The screen door slapped shut behind him. Cumberton's undertaker was always called Hobbs, no one ever called him mister.

The adults talked in voices too low to hear from where I sat on the steps. So I scooted across the porch on my backside to lean against the house under the window. I listened sharp to what they said, but couldn't catch a word. When Hobbs and Daniel arrived about an hour later, the undertaker went straight in, and the whispering started again.

Nobody went out to the tree to see what might have happened. They just stood around the dinner hall while Matron Tyler washed the body. I could hear the water splashing in the bucket and knew she weren't washing floors.

"George, help me get these clothes off the boy," she said. "It'd be a waste if he stiffens up, and we have to cut them off."

"Guess I'd better go tell the Widder Bean about her son," Sheriff Madison said. I hadn't heard him walk across the floor, so was startled when he spoke from just inside the screen door. I stayed put, hoping he wouldn't notice me, or worse, say something about me being under the window. "She'll most likely come down with her eldest boy tonight."

The sheriff let the screen door slap shut behind him. He shot a glance at me before heading down the steps, but he didn't say nothing. He mounted his sorrel and urged it into a slow lope townward. I heard the screech of lilac bushes scraping the side of the house and peeked around the corner in time to see Billy Todd crawl out from under the side window and head around back.

I leaned over the porch rail and threw up into the lily of the valley bed below. My belly always got jumpy when I got real upset. I sank to my knees and leaned my head against the railing, blinking back tears.

I sat there for a while thinking about what would happen next. If Fish's mother decided not to take him home, the burying would take place tomorrow in the church cemetery with the entire orphanage looking on. Me included. I didn't want to watch my friend put under the ground. The sadness and fear in me felt like an anvil sitting on my chest. I could hardly breathe, and my stomach wouldn't stop jumping.

I figured the funeral would be held about mid-morning. Always an early riser, I would have plenty of time to get up the tree to do some checking before the Tylers were up and about. If I found something that pointed to Billy Todd's dirty work, I'd tell the sheriff at the funeral. If I didn't find anything wrong, I didn't know what I would do. Never before had there been a death at the home, but every time something happened to one of the orphans, Billy Todd was involved and each accident was worse than the last. This one was meant for me, but I was still alive. Would he try again? When?

That night we had dinner outdoors though most of us couldn't eat. I tried one bite. The potato seemed to swell in my mouth and made me retch. Everyone pushed the food around their plates and looked anywhere but at one another and the chestnut tree. Matron Tyler excused us all of cleanup duties though Mike and Dinah, the two eldest orphans, helped her anyway. Warden Tyler headed out to the barn to nip at the bottle I knew he had hid there.

The rest of us waited.

3
Murder Evidence

I knew Fish's mother had arrived when a long wail echoed through the house and out the windows into the night. I couldn't make sense of Matron Tyler's low replies, but the tone spoke comfort and filled in where the cries left off.

Mrs. Bean was a careworn woman with no husband and now only one son left. I'd met her many times over the years. Fish's father died a few months before I came, and 'cause Fish was small and sickly, and the Beans were poor, his Ma had put him in the orphanage till he grew up and got strong enough to help with the farm. But that weren't going to happen now that he'd been kilt.

Not ready to shed the tears burning my eyes in front of grownups, I headed back to the barn.

I'd already fed and watered the orphanage's cranky gelding earlier. Now that Fish was gone, Dapple was my best friend. Though the horse tended to flatten his ears and go at the warden and Billy Todd with bared teeth, he never bit either of them much as they deserved it. I'd seen the warden beat Dapple with the buggy-whip, and Billy Todd often threw stones at him. The grownups thought he weren't a good animal to have around

children, but the ugly old nag loved all us kids except, I'm proud
to say, Billy Todd. Must be why they call good sense, horse sense.
Horses know, believe me, they know.

Guess that's why I ended up taking care of him. I loved
horses. I wanted to work for a rich family as a coachman someday.
I ain't afraid of hard work, and don't mind shoveling up horse
leavings, or currying them down. I think they're beautiful and
funny to watch when they're chewing their hay.

As I entered the barn, Dapple nickered his usual greeting. I
looked into his big, kind eyes and burst into tears, burying my face
in his mane. The old gelding stood still and let me cry my heart
out. After today, nothing would ever be the same.

"Charley," Matron Tyler's voice sang out through the gathering dark.

"Coming." I patted Dapple good night and headed out of the
barn.

"Time for bed. Get washed up before you come in, you
hear?"

"Yes, ma'am." I was the last one outside and didn't want to
go in. Truth tell, I was scared. Saw my Papa laid out after he died.
He'd died lying face down, so when I saw him in the casket his
face was half-purple and half-gray. It scared the hell out of me.
When I close my eyes and think on my Papa, I see him as I saw
him then.

I didn't want to see my friend lying on the dining room table
wearing clothes and shoes he only wore to church on Sunday. I
didn't want the still, pale form to wipe out my memories of the
fun, freckled, red-haired, bare-footed boy who was my best and
only friend in the world. And I didn't want to see Mrs. Bean cry
over him.

I dragged my feet to the well and pumped up a shallow basin
of water. Washed my hands and splashed water on my face, then
wiped them on the soggy towel that hung from a nail in the wash-
up bench. I heard a tap at the front door as I entered the kitchen.
Matron Tyler silently opened the door and let the Presbytery elders
troop in. Four of them, like I expected.

Warden Tyler stood in the archway between the hall and the front parlor much as I'd seen him the first day I came. His ruddy cheeks quivered as he greeted each person by name and directed them to make themselves comfortable in the room behind him. Matron Tyler waved me down the hall to her. She put her arm around my shoulders. I shrugged it off.

"You're more like a boy than any girl I ever met," she said, shaking her head. "Do you want to spend a few minutes with Jimmy and Mrs. Bean before you go up to bed?"

I shook my head no, trying to ignore the soft candlelight coming from the dining room where Fish lay and his mother wept.

"Tomorrow then," she said, putting her hand on my shoulder. "I thought you might like to take your leave now instead of with the others in the morning. Charley, you're going to have to say goodbye. It won't be easy, but it'll be for the best."

I shook my head again and went upstairs to the sleeping ward.

I was afraid to close my eyes. I tried, but each time I saw Fish's crooked body on my eyelids.

I lay there staring out the window. The full moon rose over the barn and disappeared from view. Then I watched the last shadows creep along the wall till the moon rose so high its light shone straight down into the yard, snatching the last of the sharp shadows from the sleeping ward.

I pictured Fish alive in my mind's eye. His bright smile. The way he would put his hands on his hips and kick the dirt when he was trying to make up his mind about something. The way he laughed, and the way it made me laugh just to hear it. How he would chew his nails when doing arithmetic, or how he would get so involved with what he was reading he didn't hear me when I talked to him. The way he'd do most anything for a coin to buy candy. Tears slid down my cheeks.

I tried to think of the good times we had, then lit upon the first day I arrived at the home. I was six to his five. His freckled face pressed to the front window, his flattened nose and tongue against the glass while crossing his blue eyes. I couldn't help but smile at the fish-looking smushed face. He uncrossed his eyes, saw me watching, and re-crossed them while puffing out his cheeks and opening his mouth wider.

Fish was the only one who knew how my Papa climbed into a jug of sour mash right after my mama died giving birth to me. And how, after my Aunt Martha died giving birth, and my Papa died on my sixth birthday, my Uncle Zach dropped me at the orphanage seein's I weren't a boy that could work the farm.

Now that Fish was dead, what was I going to do without him? What was going to become of me? How long would I live before Billy Todd tricked me into dying like he done Fish?

4

Orphan Life

When the sun began to rise through a deep red glow along the horizon, I rubbed the tears out of my burning eyes and got out of bed. I dressed, slipped downstairs and out the front door. The morning air cooled my face and made me feel better than I had all night.

I shimmied up the trunk of the chestnut tree out back, till I could grab the lowest branch and hitch myself astride. That was the hardest part. I climbed from branch to branch steadily upward, glad it was not a breezy day that would've had me clutching the trunk.

I didn't put my full weight on any branch till I looked it over and slowly shifted my weight on it to make sure it would hold me. The first thing I noticed as I neared the top was small bits of sawdust in the crotch of a large branch below the busted one whose leaves were already beginning to curl.

"Charley, what you doing up there?" Five year-old Penny stood at the base of the tree peering up at me.

"Looking around. I'll be down in a few minutes. Why don't you go on to the outhouse?"

"You're not going to fall like Jimmy did yesterday, are you?"

"No, I'll be fine. Go pee, okay." I watched her hurry off toward the outhouse and went back to my climbing. I inched up the trunk eyeing every branch before I stepped on it. When I came level with the dangling branch, I froze, my nose inches from the fresh break. The upper half of the branch's break was smooth; the lower half curled back tearing away at the tree's trunk.

My belly took a sickening lurch. I was right, it weren't no accident. I yanked at the branch, but the bark and few remaining splinters would not give. I took out my forbidden jackknife and sawed at the branch till my hand cramped. Carefully, I made my way around the back of the tree to saw with my right hand, my left arm hugging the trunk for all I was worth.

Finally, the branch parted, crashing down the tree. I heard a scream and looked down. Penny stood beneath the tree with her hands over her head.

"Run!" I yelled, but she didn't move. The loose branch landed across two stout limbs and came to rest. I climbed down the tree till I came to the broken branch and called down. "Penny take your hands off your head. Look at me. You got to move out of the way."

She slid her hands off her curly head and covered her eyes before peeking though her fingers up into the tree.

"You're not broken?" she asked, her voice muffled as it came through her chubby hands.

"No, I'm fine. Now move out of the way. Far away. I got to get this branch down before someone else gets hurt." She backed away never taking her eyes from me. When I could no longer see her through the leaves, I called out for her to take three more giant steps backward. I heard her shuffling for a moment, then silence.

"Okay, I'm far away," she said.

I pulled the branch away from the limbs and headed it toward the ground busted end first so's the smaller branches wouldn't catch and stop it from hitting the ground again. I climbed the rest of the way down, swung off the lowest branch, and landed on my feet.

"Don't tell anyone about this, okay, Penny. It'll be our secret."

"Why?"

"I told you to stay out of that tree didn't I?" Warden Tyler roared in my ear, swinging me around by the shoulder to face him. His fist hit my left cheekbone and knocked me to the ground. Penny cried out and ran to the house.

"But look," I said, cradling my cheek. "The limb was sawn half way through. Billy Todd's the only slimy snake who would do such a thing."

The warden drew his fist back for another blow.

"Tyler," Matron Tyler's voice snapped like a shot through the back screen. "None of that now."

"You shut your mouth, boy, or I'll—"

"You're always protecting him. You never beat him when he's mean like you do the other boys. Billy Todd's just like you, same little pig eyes and jackass laugh. That's why you and the matron don't want to report Billy Todd. You're his parents ain't you?"

The warden reached down and yanked me up by my shirt-front till we were nose to nose. His stale whiskey-breath made me swallow to keep my stomach down. "You keep your mouth shut you hear? Don't need nobody like you messing this job up for us. We need that money. One word out of you, and I'll beat you within an inch of your life." He threw me back to the ground where I turned over, got to my hands and knees, and heaved till my guts hurt though nothing came up.

The warden strode across the back yard dragging the branch along behind him.

"Where are you taking that?" I yelled. "Sheriff Madison has to see that. It proves Fish was kilt."

"It ain't going to prove shit. I'm burning it."

"You can't do that."

"Watch me."

"Bastard."

The warden dropped the branch and wheeled around.

Pure hate ripped through me. Had I been all growed up, I would've kilt the warden with my bare hands right then.

He lunged for me. I ran around the house and across the front yard, his heavy footsteps and rasping breath right behind me. I leapt the fence, threw back my head and pumped my arms and legs as fast as I could, leaving that stinking Warden Tyler in my dust.

5
On My Way

I looked over my shoulder and smacked into a sapling that set me on my ass. I hitched myself up and ran deeper into the woods before sliding down the trunk of a sturdy young oak to catch my breath and listen. There weren't no going back now. No reason to. If I stayed, either Billy Todd or Warden Tyler would do me in. I'd always been a little scared of the warden though he'd never slugged me before. Didn't trust Billy Todd worth shit. Never did. That bastard was downright spiteful. I didn't want to spend the rest of my life worrying about being alone with either of them. Didn't want to die from some damn accident like the one that kilt Fish.

Not hearing any sound that might have been Warden Tyler, him being heavy on his feet and all, I got up and started back the way I'd come, keeping an eye peeled for trouble.

I stepped behind an old white oak when the gritty rumble of iron-rimmed wheels and the hollow clop of a horse reached my ears. A bunch of trees stood between me and the road, so's I couldn't see who passed by, but Billy Todd's voice boomed into the quiet and the voices of the other kids began to grow louder as a second wagon drew near. Fish's funeral.

The first wagon must have been Hobbs' hearse and now Dapple pulling the orphanage wagon was about to pass by. I dodged from tree to tree to get a closer look. I wanted to make sure everyone was going to the funeral, leaving the house empty, so I could go back and get some clothes and food. The maple I now huddled behind was not as wide as the white oak of a moment ago, but I was still far enough back in the woods so's no one would see me.

Dapple plodded along, drawing the flatbed wagon with all eleven orphans. I was surprised to see Mike and Dinah, the older two, in the wagon as well. They would probably report to their jobs in town after the funeral. The Tylers sat on the driver's bench with Billy Todd standing behind them like he weren't supposed to. Matron Tyler turned to warn the younger children to quiet down, reminding them what they were about.

"Billy Todd, you murdering son of a bitch. If I ever have a gun in my hand and you're standing in front of me, I swear to God, I'll pull the trigger and kill you dead." Though I wanted to shout my challenge, I only mumbled it, but I meant every word all the way down to the bottom of my soul.

Dapple clopped on by. I would miss him.

When I couldn't hear the horse and wagon, or the children anymore, I moved closer to the road to peek around a tree. When the wagon rounded the curve further down the road and drew out of sight, I stepped out of the woods and ran back to the home.

The front door was locked.

I didn't know it had a lock. Damn the warden. We never locked the doors. No one did. And this time of year, the windows were generally wide open all the time unless it was blowing rain. Everyone hereabouts were neighbors. No one worried about neighbors busting in. Besides, what would anyone want from a church orphanage? Far as I knew, there was never any money to be had.

I climbed over the railing and jumped off the side of the porch into the lily of the valley patch below to run around back. Damned if the back door weren't shut tighter than a jar of sweet pickles, too. Backing away from the house, I looked at each of the windows on both floors. I studied the ones I figured I could climb into. Didn't have any luck. All the latches were fast. There was no getting in that I could tell.

The thought of being on my own scared me. Being without Fish scared me. But living with the Tylers and Billy Todd scared me more. I had to move on. Clothes or no clothes.

I sat on the top stair of the porch and felt my belly rumble. I rubbed it while I thought of what I had inside the house. Nothing really. I would've snitched some food and taken my extra Sunday-go-to-meeting clothes, but that was not to be. Luckily, my savings were hidden safe outside the home thanks to Billy Todd's habit of thieving.

My belly growled so's I could hear it. Mid-day was close on, and I'd been too upset to eat last night's dinner, and I'd missed this morning's breakfast while hiding out from the warden. A sudden thought hit me. I ran to the springhouse and burst through the door. A milk can sat in the spring cooling from this morning's milking. I pried the lid off, scooped out a dipper full, and gulped down the milk, spilling some of it down the front of me. Drinking out of the tin ladle used to dip milk weren't easy. It had deep sides like a large glass, but had a long handle attached to its side that made the side of my face wet and sticky.

I felt the pinching in my belly relax and swallowed some more. I looked around for something I could use to carry some milk with me, but came up empty. I would've checked the root cellar, but last week we'd brought the last of the potatoes, carrots and turnips into the house and swept the cellar clean. I drank as much milk as I could hold before putting the lid back on and heading out. I wanted to be far gone by the time they got back from the funeral.

As I stepped from the springhouse, my eyes slid up the trunk of the chestnut tree. I saw the accident all over again in my mind's eye. How the leaves trembled as he hit each branch. How his body hit the ground in a sprawling, lifeless heap. How his blue eyes stared into the sun without blinking. I shook my head and rammed my fists deep into my pockets.

If only the warden hadn't caught me with the branch, I thought. I could've stopped in town and told the sheriff, but now—my eyes sprung to the top of the tree where I'd found the busted limb this morning, the saw mark was still there—on the tree trunk. I still had proof of Fish's killing to report to the sheriff. Determined to convince Sheriff Madison of Billy Todd's guilt, I headed around the barn and set off across the field.

The corn behind the barn had greened up, but stood only a few inches high. I stepped over each row so no one would be the wiser to my crossing. I needed to get to a certain maple tree on the other side of the field in order to retrieve my savings, and I didn't want to leave a trail that someone could follow and fetch me back.

Early on, I saw Billy Todd steal money from the other orphans and decided to find a place to stash mine. When Fish and I first found the rock, it took both of us to move it. We slid it aside, and I dug a shallow hole. I stashed the few pennies I'd found or earned in a knotted sock. Couldn't use a sock that hadn't been darned and worn threadbare to holes more'n a couple of times, so both ends were knotted to prevent the coins from slipping out. When we got older, I could move the rock on my own, but I still brought Fish along to keep watch. Didn't want anyone sneaking up on me to steal my savings when my back was turned.

After pulling my savings sock from the dirt and pocketing the fifty-three cents I'd hoarded over the past six years, I headed back into the woods to walk out of sight of the road toward town. I stopped now and then to listen for the orphanage wagon, and after I heard it pass, I walked on the road.

When I got to the cemetery, which was just this side of town and out back of the church, the gravediggers were mounding the last of the dirt on Fish's grave. I hid behind two side-by-side grave markers. The men slapped their shovels on the mound to tamp the dirt down. I felt each slap as though it was my body they were beating. They finally threw their shovels on the back of the wagon and one of them pulled out a flask.

"Hate burying kids," he said, taking a swig, then passing the flask to the other man. "Damn glad it ain't one of mine."

"Grave digging's sure a mean way to make a living, especially when it's a kid," the other replied. "Wonder if it were an accident like they say."

"Whadaya mean?"

"Heard one of the little girls ask the eldest girl if Billy Todd killed the boy. Then right quick a big feller next to 'em says, 'Charley did it.'"

Me? There weren't no other Charleys at the home. It had to be Billy Todd pointing the finger at me. Son of a bitch.

"What'd the girl say?" the gravedigger asked.

"Didn't say nothing, just patted the little girl on the back comforting-like."

The men passed the flask back and forth a few times before corking it and climbing on the wagon. I waited till the wagon cleared the cemetery before walking over to the grave.

"They're blaming me for killing you, Fish. That bastard Billy Todd is going to get away with murder and nobody's going to do a damn thing to him. It'll be me they come after." Gooseflesh ran up my arms. I had to hurry and do something, but what?

I stood there damn glad I hadn't looked at my friend too long yesterday while he lay on the ground under the tree. Or that I hadn't made myself look at his lifeless body on the dining room table with his Ma crying over him. I could still remember how he was. Remember the good times. Even the not so good times. But leastways we'd been together.

"I gotta go." My throat wouldn't let me swallow. I took a deep breath. "I'll never have another friend good as you long as I live. I'll always remember you, Fish. Hope we meet up again in heaven."

I turned away from the grave and cut across the cemetery and the churchyard. As I rounded the near corner of the church, the familiar figure of Warden Tyler brought me to a dead stop as I watched him walk into the sheriff's office. I hurried part way down Main Street, turned down a side alley, and ran along the back of the buildings till I reached the back of the sheriff's office. I stopped at the alley that ran alongside and looked around. Nobody seemed to be looking my way, so I crept to the open window behind the sheriff's desk and squatted down, my back to the wall. I wanted to hear what Warden Tyler had to say, and still keep an eye on both ends of the alley so's trouble couldn't sneak up on me.

"I'm telling you, it was no accident," the warden's voice boomed through the opening. "I climbed the damn tree myself and took note of the saw marks. It's that Charley that done it, I tell you."

I damn near jumped to my feet with a yell of protest, but good sense kept me low and quiet.

"Kind of young to be a murderer, don't you think?" the sheriff said. "I remember Charley as a slip of a kid. Always sat in church beside the youngster who died. Quiet. Respectful-like."

"That's the one. I would stake my life on it.

"Didn't see the kid at the funeral. Where you suppose he's gone, Tyler?"

"He's a she."

"Charley's a girl?"

"Yeah, you know how sly females get. My guess is she's on the run. She's a thief, too, stole from us while we were sleeping."

"What's gone?"

"Food mostly and clothes."

It took a lot for me to stay crouched under that window, but I knew I would be thrown in jail, and probably hanged for things I didn't do if I spoke up.

"Does the child have any kin?"

"Only the man you never found six years ago when he dropped the kid off."

"Right. Forgot about that. Never did find which direction he took."

"You going to look for her?"

"Sure, sure. Got to make my rounds now, so I'll keep my eyes open." The sheriff's chair scraped the floor. "I'll be down to the home later to report whether I've found her, and to check that tree."

Seein's how things weren't looking good for me, I scooted along the alley keeping my head down, and high-tailed it away like I had a wolf snapping at my heels. I didn't know the side streets of town since we orphans didn't get much of a chance to spend time here on our own. But I zigzagged down one and up another till I had to stop to catch my breath. I hunkered down under a maple beside a tall, slat-board fence. Good thing, too, 'cause I heard the preacher's voice drawing near. The house sat on a corner, and I could hear the preacher and another man coming down the sidewalk of the cross street. Afraid they might ask questions, or try to get ahold of me, I slipped through the gate into the back yard. Luckily, it was Monday, and Mondays being washdays, I couldn't be seen from the house for all the laundry hanging out to dry in the yard. Must've been a big family, 'cause they had lots of clothes that would fit any size person there was.

"I hear it weren't no accident what happened down at the home," the other man said.

"I'm sure you're mistaken," the preacher said.

"I just had it from Tyler a few minutes ago. He said some kid named Charley sawed a limb causing the Bean boy to fall outta the tree."

"Now, Clive, I remember Charley Parkhurst as a good kid. He's only twelve. Lets get the facts..."

Their voices faded down the road. I stuck my head out the tall, whitewashed gate and looked around then ducked back in. The two men had stopped at the next corner and would see me if I tried to leave. I could tell Deacon Watson wanted to get on— probably to spread his gossip—but the preacher wouldn't stop talking; kind of like he did on a Sunday morning. I closed the gate and leaned back to wait.

A dress fluttered in the breeze, which gave me an idea. It looked to be my size and had a matching bonnet hanging right next to it. I pulled them off the line and stuffed them inside of my overalls. Now I had to move on, or chance being arrested for stealing clothes, and end up being hanged for Fish's murder. I peeked out the gate again. The way was clear, so I hurried on down a few more streets till I saw a blanket slung over a wash line. I snatched that, too, and the strong wash line it was hanging on. As soon as I was out of town and well into the woods, I rolled the dress and hat up in the blanket, tied it with the cord, and slung it over my shoulder before moving on.

I knew it weren't right to steal, but I had nowhere to turn. I didn't have a choice. If I didn't get out of Cumberton, I'd be hanged for sure.

6
Getting There

B irds are damn noisy at the break of day. Once they get going there ain't no more sleeping to be had. I stayed rolled in my blanket for a while and thought about where I was headed.

I'd often told Fish I would head out one day to seek my fortune, but always hoped he'd tag along. We talked plenty about becoming horsemen. He'd get as excited about the notion as I did, but deep down I knew he'd go home to his Ma and brother, and work the farm soon as he was big enough to be of help to them. Always kind of small Fish was, small and lively, but delicate. I slid my shirtsleeve across my eyes and sat up. He wouldn't be coming with me on this adventure and no amount of wishing would make it so. The plans we made were all mine now. Mine alone. But I would remember Fish. I wouldn't ever let myself forget.

I rolled my blanket and headed due east through the woods again. I'd been thinking on finding a job in Worcester. Figured to skirt the small towns on the way, so's nobody would notice a lone kid passing through, and remember on it if questions were asked. I weren't no murderer, but gossip tastes sweeter'n truth, so for me, this part of Massachusetts had become dangerous, making it needful that I stay low.

The next day about midmorning while traveling through some sparse woods skirting a one-horse town I didn't know the name of, I heard the thunk and clatter of splitting firewood—turned out to be a woman doing the chopping. Seein's my belly hurt with hunger, I figured if I offered to help chop maybe she'd come across with some vittles.

"Damn," she muttered, putting a hand to the small of her back.

I started out of the woods and in doing so, stepped on a dry twig. She turned as if startled. Her belly bulged with child.

"Afternoon, ma'am."

"You gave me a fright," she said.

"Didn't mean to scare you none. Heard you chopping and thought maybe we could do a friendly trade."

"Trade?"

"I'll chop you some firewood for food."

"Well, yes, I believe that would be a fine idea," she said, smoothing her apron.

I took the ax from her hand. "Why don't you go on in," I said, not wanting her to see that I weren't much good at splitting wood. I placed a section of a tree trunk on the chopping block as she stood watching me. I tapped the wedge into the cracked center of the chunk and stood back. I spit on my hands and rubbed them together like I'd seen the older boys at the orphanage do before picking up the ax. With a practice swing, I made sure the flat side of the head would hit the wedge, then I swung with all my might. Luckily, I hit true and the log split.

The woman turned away to continue up the back stairs of her home. I weren't so lucky with the next couple of swings, but I got so's I felt the rhythm of it, and my aim got better as I went. I would split a couple of chunks, then stack them up on the back porch, then go back to splitting again. I'd done ten, twelve rounds when she stepped out on the porch and called me to dinner.

She had fixed up some smoked ham steak, mashed potatoes with pan gravy, sliced carrots with honey, fresh milk, and a wedge of rhubarb pie.

After making mention of the weather, she asked my name.

"Charley Par—sons, ma'am." My hands began to sweat. Nobody stumbled over their last name like I just did.

"Where are you heading, Charley?"

I started forking the food into my mouth faster. "To my aunt's house in Worcester."

"Why are you all by yourself?"

"My Papa died last week, and I got no kin hereabouts." She seemed nice and all, but her questions had my belly flipping inside me like to make me sick up.

"I'm sorry for your loss," she said. "But you oughtn't be traveling by yourself. Surely—"

"Aw, I'm all right. Say, where's your husband?"

"I lost my Nick to consumption back in November."

"Gosh, I'm sorry." My cheeks reddened with the anxious heat building up in me. I had to get out of here.

Her eyes began to tear up, and her face showed the gathering of a good cry coming.

"He didn't even know about the baby." She bit her lips together and looked out the window for a long moment. She blinked her eyes a few times and continued, "The bigger my baby gets the harder it is to get my chores done around here. Thank you for your help, young man."

The relief that flooded me at 'young man' had me offering to chop more wood.

"No, what you've done already is fine. You did a good job, and I thank you. I won't have to chop again for a few days."

To my relief, she stood to clear the dishes. "If you don't mind waiting a minute, I'll make a sandwich for you to take with you."

I cleared the table while she did me up a sandwich. A real nice lady she was. I doubted whether she'd be a widder long though. She was young and easy to look at, a good cook, and had a real nice way about her.

Road sign at the crossroads later that afternoon said Worcester was still seven miles east. Figured I could walk that tomorrow without working up a lather and scout out the town some to get the lay of the land, then I would find somewhere to wash up before going after a job. All those years of planning had me getting a job with some rich feller when I went adventuring. Didn't want no job clerking in some damn store. I wanted to work around fine horses, and nothing was going to stop me.

I rolled out of my blanket at the first notes of birdsong, donned the dress and bonnet, and tied my orphan clothes and the widder's sandwich in my blanket like it was a sack of washing to be done. Figured I was a fair piece from Cumberton, so I decided I would be a girl today and walk on the road instead of through the woods like I'd done so far. I headed east reckoning to arrive in Worcester about midday and maybe land a job by nightfall. The day would tell.

Luckily, no one was about when I stepped onto the road. My dress was soaked to the knees and spattered with bits of last fall's dried grass and dead leaves, and a few sticky pickers. I brushed myself off best I could, but it didn't look good. I hoped I would dry soon; my bare legs were cold from the wet, and I'd begun to shiver.

The sun sat upon the edge of the earth and showed through the trees real pretty-like by the time I'd walked about a mile and heard a wagon coming up behind me. The driver pulled his team of sorrel Belgians to a stop right beside me, but I kept on walking. I didn't want no trouble.

"Hey, girl, you want to ride a while?" a deep voice asked.

I looked up at the grandfatherly face above me. The hazel eyes that looked back seemed to be laughing though there weren't any smile on the man's wrinkled face. The morning whiskers that pushed through his sun-browned skin matched his long white hair.

"Would give me somebody to talk to for a while."

"Where you heading?" I asked, rubbing the face of the horse nearest me. The mare's blaze started as a large, almost round white spot that swung out to the right and slid most of the way down her nose, stopping some three or four inches above her nostrils, and finishing off with a oval white snip on her soft nose.

"My farm's about a mile or so short of Worcester."

"Fine pair of horses you got," I said, climbing aboard. "The younger mare's blaze looks like a question mark."

"Yesiree, my wife named her Lady in Question almost soon as she came out. The other is Roxy, her dam. Com'on up girls," he said, with a gentle slap of the reins on their broad rumps.

"Roxy's getting up there, ain't she?" I said, having noted the gray above her eyes.

"I've had her twenty years. It's anybody's guess when she'll give out. She's always been a goer. Lady on the other hand is only about five years younger, but has always been a half a step behind her ma."

We rode in silence for a few moments. The sun reached through the leaves dappling the road.

"I'm returning from a trip to my daughter's home. I made my granddaughter a hope chest. She's a little older than you..."

Quite a talker he was. I listened polite-like, mumbling a word here and there to keep him going. Figured if he was talking about his family, he wouldn't start asking questions about me, but I thought too soon.

"So, where are you from girl? You ain't run away from home now have you?"

"No, sir. Mama is sending me to my Aunt Martha's house to give a helping hand now the baby's come."

"Your Aunt live in Worcester?"

"Yup."

"Long way for a lone girl."

"Pa can't spare the time, nor the horse." I used some of the truth from my past so's I could remember the lies I told. Still, I could feel sweat beginning to dampen my face and hoped he wouldn't take notice. He kept chattering away. My guess was he lived alone by the way he kept talking all the time.

"Well, this here is my turn off, girl. I got to let you down. Ain't much over a mile to town though."

"Thanks, mister."

I climbed down from the wagon none too easily. Girls' clothes hamper a body. Can't get your legs wide enough to do anything. Heard my dress rip as I took the last big step down. That was all right though. I was going to take it off soon's I got the chance. I'd had enough of being a girl.

When I came upon a small lake outside of Worcester, I changed my mind about scouting out the town before cleaning up. I stripped down behind some bushes and waded in. I wrapped my torn dress and hat around a heavy rock and dropped them in deep water, glad to be rid of them. When I saw myself in the water, I realized my hair was a dead giveaway that I came from an orphanage. It was cut straight across my forehead and straight from jawbone to jawbone all the way around. I should have done something about it soon as I left Cumberton. I got out of the water and got my forbidden jackknife, then waded back in to use the water's reflection as a mirror. The fact that I was due for another hair cut helped. My sharp knife sliced through my hair as I shortened a few strands here and there, feathering the straight lines. It didn't look too good when I was done, but I no longer looked like I belonged to an orphanage. I cleaned up as best I could, soaking my hair and slicking it back with my fingers. I never put my hair behind my ears as some did 'cause I had big ears. Maybe it was my wide jaw that made them stick out and look so big. I don't know. I leaned over to check the look of my new haircut and was pleased with what I saw between drips. While I was in town, I would buy a comb, some soap and a towel, and a brimmed hat, if I could afford one.

I donned my overalls and shirt, and walked back to the road to continue on to Worcester. Within minutes, I heard horses approach me from behind. I took a double take over my shoulder at what was coming. Them beautiful bay horses pulling that fine rig Fish and me saw pass the orphanage were coming up behind me at a slow trot. I couldn't believe how lucky I was.

7
Job Hunting

My heart nearly burst with pride just looking at that fine rig. They passed me by without so much as a howdy-do though I waved and called out. They were a couple of lengths ahead of me when the thought hit my mind that I'd better follow them so's I'd know where to find that job I was after. I hurried to catch up, but as I got close, the coachman clucked the team up to a full trot, and I had to run for all I was worth. Before we came to the outskirts of town, the coachman turned the team north. Just as my legs were about to give out, the horses slowed and the rig turned into a private road that lead past the biggest damn stone house I ever did see. The grounds slid away from the front of the house like the skirts of a woman's gown falls from the waist to the floor, full and wide.

I hid behind a tree to watch the coach draw up to the front of the house to discharge its passengers. The unexpected two-mile run had me winded and dripping with sweat.

The footman climbed onto the back of the carriage, and the coachman brought the horses up to a slow trot around the circular drive before continuing on to the stables around back. When the carriage passed my tree, I followed it to the stables where the coachman brought the team to a stop. A pack of dogs set to barking at their arrival, but I couldn't see them from where I stood.

"Shut up, you damn curs," the coachman bellowed.

My heart thudded in my throat, and it weren't from running. The place was more perfect than I'd ever dreamed. I darted behind a corner of the barn and watched from there. Both the coachman and footman climbed down, took off their fancy green coats and handed them to one of the two boys my age that came out to meet them. The footman and two boys unhitched the team and took the horses into the stable to unharness and rub them down.

I was out of breath with excitement wanting their job. There it all was, the job of my dreams. All I had to do was ask for it.

All the while, the coachman shouted directions to the three as they worked. When the coachman started toward what I took to be his lodgings, I hurried after him.

"Sir, sir?" I said. The dogs set to barking again. I glanced at them. Long legged they were. Black with snapping teeth. I stopped at the sight of them.

The coachman turned abruptly to face me with a frown deepening the lines of his middle-aged face. "Who are you?"

"Charley Parkhurst, sir. I followed you from—"

"It doesn't matter where you followed us from. Get off these grounds."

"But sir, I come for a job."

"You think you can just drop in and get a job?" His mean sounding laugh made me feel stupid. "Fool boy. You got to have connections. You got to be recommended. We don't just take someone off the street. You have to have apprenticed two years with someone else before you'd even be considered for working here."

"I didn't know."

"Well, now you do."

"But, sir."

"Get off before I turn the dogs on you," he said, turning away. "And don't come back, you hear?" He looked over his shoulder. When he saw me still standing there, he changed direction and headed toward the barking dogs in their caged run.

I lit out the way I come. I looked back once to see if he let the dogs loose, but only his mean laughter followed me. Rage sped me to end of the private drive, which must've been a good quarter mile.

I headed south scuffing dirt and spitting promises of death for that coachman. When my temper cooled a mite, and I thought about how the rich had rules for picking and choosing who worked for them, I realized that my dreams had just gone up in smoke 'cause I didn't have no connections. I was just some dumb orphan nobody gave a damn about. I started blubbering like a girl. I never thought I'd be turned down. I always thought I belonged working fine horses.

I wound down after a spell, the dried tears left my cheeks itchy. I stopped at a trickle of water alongside the road and rinsed my face. I kept hounding myself to think, to come up with a plan, but I was heartbroken and couldn't think past my first rebuff.

Where could I get the training I needed to get the job I wanted?

How could I get myself recommended?

My belly growled.

How was I going to eat?

Find another well-to-do family and knock on their door? Fish and me should have thought this through more carefully. Planned more. I'd always been one to ride by the seat of my pants, shooting for the best.

By then, I'd reached the Worcester road and turned east. I came upon a livery stable as I entered town. Though a livery dealt in horses, it weren't a place to learn how to drive horses, or learn about training them as much as it was a place to work at shoveling horse droppings and throwing tack on worn out nags. See them ridden or driven by people that used them hard, returning them lathered and winded. Leastways, that was what I'd seen a time or two at the Cumberton livery.

Yet, my belly got skittish with each step I took toward the open barn in search of a job to tide me over. Weren't sure whether it was the thought of not getting this job, or the mess I'd just made of the other one that made me feel sickish. Liveries didn't need recommendations, did they?

I thought I was seeing double there for a minute when I walked into the barn. Two look-alikes a couple of years older than me strolled out of the shadows. Tall and rangy they were, sinewy more'n muscular, with unwelcoming smiles that bespoke trouble, and slitted eyes that glittered despite the lack of sunlight in the barn. The one on the left circled around behind me.

"Uppity cuss walking in here, ain't you?" the one in front of me said, adding a shove that sent me into his brother.

"Hey, watch whose feet you're stepping on," he yelled in my ear, shoving me forward so that I knocked my forehead into the chest of the one standing in front of me.

"I don't want no trouble," I said, taking a step back. "Was looking for a job is all."

"What? You leaving already?" the one in front said.

"I don't want no trouble," I said again, backing away. I figured it was time to skedaddle. "I'll be moving on."

"Sure you will," said the one behind me. Punching me in the back with both fists, thrusting me forward with such force that I tripped over the extended foot of the brother in front. My bedroll went flying, and I landed with my face in the dirt. One of them put his foot between my shoulders, grinding me into the ground.

I tried rolling and bucking.

"None of that now," he said.

Nothing I did dislodged the foot. I struggled, but the weight on my back increased.

"Let me go you damn bullies." I coughed on the dust I inhaled, thinking I might not get out of this scrape alive.

"Let me go you damn bullies," they mimicked in girlie voices. The brother not standing on my back gave me a swift kick in the ribs with his bare foot.

Suddenly, the weight was gone, and the boys were yelling to beat all. I scrambled to my feet to face them. Their father, same blue eyes and brown hair, but beefier in the shoulders, had each by the scruff of the neck, and by the looks of their head rubbing, had come up behind them and knocked their heads together.

"You all right?" the father asked me.

I nodded, but couldn't stop coughing. He thrust the boys away telling them to get me a dipper of water.

"What you want around here, boy?" he asked after his sons brought the water, and I'd stopped coughing.

"Was looking for a job." I threw the warm water to the ground after one swallow. By the taste of it, they'd dipped it out of the horse trough. I picked up my bedroll and dusted it off.

"Sorry, I can't use you," he said, turning away. "You seem like a nice kid."

Sure, I thought. If he had hired me, I would've turned him down flat after what his boys done to me. Too much like Billy Todd they were. Mean-spirited. I weren't going to live in fear of my life here neither.

I didn't speak to anyone else till I stopped in at the general store. I leaned my rolled blanket outside the door and walked in. The welcome bell tinkled, but nobody seemed to look in my direction, so I moseyed around looking for what I needed. Tried on a wide-brimmed straw hat but saw I couldn't afford it. Picked up a chunk of cheap soap, the kind that didn't have any lady's smell to it. After some of the customers paid for their purchases and left the store, the clerk asked if she could help me.

"I need a comb and some toweling."

"We have some nice combs over here in our display case. Which one would you like?" she said, sweeping her hand over the glass top. "Is this for your mother perhaps?"

Some of the combs were for ladies to wear in their hair, but there were still eight regular hair combing combs lying in a row for me to choose from.

"I'll take the cheapest, ma'am." I replied, pointing to the row I was interested in without making mention of my mother.

"That'll be this one," she said, removing a small comb from the case and placing it on the counter. I picked it up and ran my finger down the teeth making them plink, it seemed sturdy enough, so I nodded.

"And you wanted some toweling?"

"Yes, ma'am."

"How much do you need?" She walked the length of the counter and halfway down the far wall to pull down two bolts of cloth setting them on the counter for me to choose.

"One yard," I said, pointing to the lighter weight cloth, figuring the thicker one would be more expensive.

She flipped the bolt over a couple of times spilling the cloth onto the counter before holding one end in her outstretched hand and pulling it taut to her nose. Bless her, she didn't skimp but gave me full measure and then some.

I smiled my thanks.

"Anything else?" she asked, smoothing the cloth bolt before turning away to place it back on the shelf.

"How much is my order so far," I asked, placing the soap on the counter.

"That'll be twenty-five cents," she said.

"Nothing more." Almost half my savings. I dug into my pocket and pulled out my money sock. I would have to wait till I got a job and earned some money before I got the hat I wanted, and the boots I would need for working around horses, and whatever else that cropped up in the way of necessities.

"Where's your Ma or Pa?" she asked, wrapping my stuff in heavy brown paper. "You a runaway, kid?"

"No, my Pa died, and I'm heading to live with my aunt." I avoided looking her in the eye while untying the knot in my savings sock. "She lives outside of town." I counted out the twenty-five cents and thanked her. Grabbing the package, I headed for the door on the edge of a run.

"Hey, kid, wait a minute, maybe I can get you a ride," she said, waving her hand to draw me back.

I waved goodbye to her with a smile and stepped out the door. I grabbed my blanket and hurried down the walk, looking for a way to get off the street in case she decided to come after me. Took a right at the next clapboard alley, which funneled me to the back of the buildings lining the street. I broke into a run and didn't slow till I came upon a brook that ran through town. I slid down the bank and took a long drink after catching my breath.

As an orphan, I'd gotten used to not being noticed by towns-folk. All I'd been was a familiar face, but I didn't have to explain who I was or why I was there. Now that I was in a new town, people would take notice of me 'cause I didn't belong to anyone they knew.

My head felt a little dizzy, so I dug into my bedroll and pulled out the day-old sandwich the widder had made me. My belly made gurgling noises 'cause of the water I'd drunk. I hadn't eaten since the day before and could've gnawed away at a full-grown bull on the hoof and finished it off by supper.

I've seldom eaten something that tasted so good as I remember that stale sandwich. I was used to eating three meals a day at the orphanage—granted they weren't large or tasty, but they were regular.

While I ate, an old man leaned over the side of the bridge right above me. Though all I saw was his face and shoulders, he looked thin and old, like the driver early this morning, white hair and whiskers and wrinkled leather face.

"Boy? You a runaway?" he asked. "If you is, don' do it. Runnin' ain't never served nobody."

"No, sir," I said, hoping he thought I was agreeing with him. My hands started trembling, whether from hunger or nerves, I weren't sure, but I hoped the old man wouldn't notice. "I'm looking for work. Can you tell me where I can find a livery?"

"What you aiming to do, son?"

"I'm looking to work with horses."

"Well we got three liveries in this town," he said. "Each a pretty far piece. Worcester's growing like a mushroom patch, I swear."

He told me where to find them, giving street names and buildings to look for on the way. He had me repeat the directions back to him to make sure I got them right.

"Which is the best?"

"That'd be Eb Balch's place on the east side of town. It's the fa'thest from here, but he treats his animals good. Never heard a mean word about Eb. Well-liked by most everybody. Yes, my boy, Eb's the one to work for."

"Thank you, sir."

"My pleasure, son. Got to be on my way now. Good luck to you," he said before walking away.

Though Balch's sounded real good and a place I would be mighty pleased to work, this morning's rejections and the tromping I'd gotten from those nasty twins had pretty much crushed my confidence. I figured it'd be better to ask at the other livery along the way. Though I felt pretty good now that I'd eaten the sandwich, I knew I wouldn't have a whole lot of spunk till I started eating regular-like again. I slung my lumpy bedroll over my shoulder and trudged up the bank to head north through town.

I found the next livery right off. The sun looked to be about an hour past noon and the sky was beginning to cloud over. I threw my shoulders back and lifted my chin as I walked into the second livery, thinking to make myself look taller. I raked my fingers through my hair and put a smile on my face. I wanted to appear ready and raring to go to work.

A big-bellied man with a wide-brimmed straw hat met me at the door scratching his sides.

"What do you want, kid?"

"Got a place for a stableboy? I work real hard and don't cost much."

His plaid shirt had food stains down the front, green horse slobber on the left sleeve and shoulder, and what looked to be horseshit caked on his boots. He smelled powerful. I took a step back and swallowed. I didn't want to end up like this old coot. I wanted a real horseman's job, but I had to eat, and I needed a place to stay.

It looked to me like he was about to turn me down. I had to do something before the dreaded words were said.

"Hey mister, I need this job. Let me have a go. I'll clean your stalls and groom your stock. Let me show you what a good worker I am."

A deep voice behind me asked whether his rig was ready. The stableman looked over my shoulder.

"Yep, all ready to go."

To me he said, "Sure kid. Pitchfork's in the corner. Shit heap's in the rear."

I walked into the shaded interior of the barn with a lighter heart till I saw what lay before me. None of the stalls had been cleaned in a handful of days. At least they were empty. I set to work with a will. I figured it was my price to pay to earn the job, and when it was mine, I would keep the stalls clean daily as I figured they ought to be.

I shoveled and barrowed my way through the afternoon. The man at the entrance rocked back in his chair and raised a jug once in a while. He gave a grunt of annoyance each time he had to get up to help a customer.

About the time the horses were to be brought in from the corral to be fed for the night, I got light-headed again and had to sit down for a few minutes. The grooming would have to wait till tomorrow. It was too late in the day, and I was too tired. A man drove up in a buggy and started bawling out the lazy son of a bitch whose job I'd just finished.

The man's dark eyes nailed me to the wall, "Who are you?"

"Charley Parkhurst, sir," I said. "Come for a job."

"Don't need you."

"But sir, I cleaned your barn to earn the job—"

"Tough, kid. You got snookered. This old reprobate works for me when he's sober and when I'm here to make sure he does the job."

"But—"

"No buts, kid, move on."

"How about some pay then for the work I did?"

"You want pay? Get it from him," he said, jerking his head in the stableman's direction before striding out of the barn.

I turned to the stableman. "Well? You owe me."

"Like hell, kid. You offered. 'Sides, I got no money. Now beat it. Go clerk at the general store."

"Just as well I ain't going to be working here, probably couldn't stand your stink."

"Why you damn brat." He grabbed my upper arm and shoved me out the door. "Get the hell out of here."

Shouldn't have said what I did, but was glad I had. Sassing back made me feel less squashed somehow.

They say lessons come in all sizes and shapes. Well this one damn near kicked me flat. It was getting on dark. I stopped by the horse trough and pumped some water over my head before taking a long swallow and heading for the last livery in Worcester.

Fat raindrops started dripping from the sky. What if I couldn't get work in this town to tide me over? What was I going to do then? I was meant to be a horseman. I just knew it. Horses were the only thing I cared about. My belly gave a rumbling growl. Well, that and eating. Maybe a quick job clerking at the general store or something in between so's I could eat would be a good idea till I put some money by. I'd only been away from the home three days, but it felt like a week.

By the time I arrived at Eb Balch's sliver-gray clapboard barn, dark covered my world in more ways than one.

No one was about.

Trembling from the lack of food and weary from the day's work, I'd decided that I would wait till tomorrow before asking for a job, so I climbed into the loft and bedded down in what was left of last year's hay. Though it smelled a little dusty, it still held the sweet smell of grass drying in the sun.

I fell asleep thinking that the only good thing that had happened that day was that everyone I met took me for a boy.

Next thing I knew, I was startled out of sleep by someone shaking me. I scrambled to my feet and stood trembling like a newborn foal before a mountain of a man.

8

My First Job

W hat you doing in my loft?" the man looming over me
asked.

"Sleeping, sir. I didn't do nothing, I swear."

"You from around here?"

"No, sir. Came looking for work."

"You did?" A boy about five years older than me peered out
from behind the man. Bright sunlight streamed through the mow
door behind the man and boy. The dust they had stirred up swirled
and sparkled in the sunlight.

"Stay out of this, Tom. I need someone man-size, not some
slip of a kid."

"I can do the work, sir."

"This ain't light chores like you maybe done at home."

"Yes, sir, I mean, no, sir. I want to work with horses."

The older boy stepped into full view with a hopeful look. He
was muscular and taller than me, but not as big as the man. I could
see he had strength by the thick muscle that connected his neck to
the rest of him.

"Ever work with horses before?"

"Took care of our horse at the—I mean at home, sir."

"So you want to pitch hay and shovel horseshit?"

"Yes, sir."

"Let me see your hands."

I extended my dirty hands, and he took them in his large ones. His felt hard and callused as he turned mine over and rubbed his thumbs across the base of my fingers and along the palms.

"They ain't a man's hands, kind of small like a girl's, but they've seen some work, I'll grant you, and some dirt too by the looks of them," he said. My heart started pounding at the way he said 'girl's' with a sneer. Was I going to lose a job before I got it 'cause I had small hands? "Name's Ebenezer Balch. Most folks around here call me Eb. You're a respectful lad, and I like that, but you can put aside saying 'sir' every time you address me."

"You mean I'm hired?" I asked.

"We'll give you a try," Eb said, slapping me on the back. "I expect you to work, and work hard. I don't have time to baby you along. My business is growing, and I need someone who's going to pitch in here and grow with the job."

"Yes, sir."

"Where's your folks?"

"Got none." I looked Eb in the eye while he looked at me long and hard, searching my face for the truth of the matter.

"If you work out, I'll teach you all I know about horses."

"Really? Could you teach me to drive a team?"

"And ride, too, if you don't already know how. I'll make a man out of you, boy. Don't you worry." Eb put his hand on the older boy's shoulder. "Tom here wants to head out West in the worst way. He's been nagging to go, and I've been putting him off till we found a replacement for him. Maybe you're the one we've been waiting for."

"Yes, sir, I am."

Tom's face lit up with a toothy grin.

"To start, you get board and a dollar a week. You'll sleep here in the mow until Tom's gone, then you can have his room downstairs. Any questions?"

I felt all skittery inside, what with waking up scared and being past hungry. I still hadn't taken it all in. I kept telling myself, I got a job, but my mind weren't fixing on it. I knew I needed food, or I would embarrass myself for sure by passing out. So I scraped together some courage and asked, "When can I have my first meal, sir?"

"You look as though you could do with some breakfast right now."

"I sure could, sir. Haven't ate in days."

"Go on up to the house and tell my wife to feed you." The beginning of a smile slid to one corner of Eb's mouth. "Tilly's good at feeding people."

Tilly weren't pretty exactly, but an easy smile of welcome crossed her face when I entered the kitchen. She had roan-colored braids that wound around her head like a crown, and mismatched colors warred at her plump waist. She had a small black mole perched off-center of a rather large nose. But her round flushed cheeks and blue eyes made her look merry.

"Pleased to meet you, Charley," she said after we introduced ourselves. "I'm mighty glad Eb found someone to take over Tom's work. I swear, that boy was close to walking away, leaving my man with all that work to do. It's hard to find good help these days…"

She went on at a full gallop, seeming not to take in air 'cause I never saw or heard her do it. She kept a steady run of talk the whole time she was cooking. Lucky for me, she cooked as fast as she talked.

"Well here, this should hold you till dinnertime," she said, plunking a plate full of eggs, bacon, fried potatoes, and buttered toast down in front of me. She made one more trip from the stove with two mugs of coffee. Pulling out a chair, she sat across from me and ladled sugar and a dollop of cream into each mug, passed one to me, then sat watching while I tore into the food like a house afire. Trouble was, she started asking questions.

"Where you come from boy? Don't you have any folks? You ever work in a livery before? Gee, you're kind of scrawny. You sure can put it away…"

Though she didn't stop for an answer at every question, she wheedled things out of me I hadn't planned on giving out, like my parents dying and Uncle Zach dropping me off at the orphanage. But I liked her an awful lot anyways. I could see us becoming friends, but knew I'd have to be honest with her and Eb, as honest as I could be under the circumstances that is. My pang of conscience had me hoping they'd forgive me if they ever found out I weren't a boy.

Later that morning, Eb laid down the law that I was to be neat and clean in my appearance. "To be prosperous, one must look prosperous," he said. "No slovenly dressing. No day-old dirt or stink. Clean hands and nails at the dinner table. And no less than weekly baths. Not only do I want you clean, I want my barn, stock, and tack clean and looking prosperous, too. Got that?"

When I told him I didn't have any spare clothes to change into in order to be able to wash the ones I was wearing, he gave me a half eagle and told me to buy a change of clothes, a pair of boots and a hat that day.

"Ain't you afraid, I'll take your money and run?" I asked, staring at the half-eagle in my hand. More money than I'd ever seen in my whole life.

"Then you wouldn't have a job now would you?"

I nodded my head.

"Don't ever lie to me. Understand?"

I nodded yes again even as my spirit sank to my toes.

He looked at my face and a small smile lifted the right corner of his lips. "You're on the young side of growing up, but you remember what I say. It's one of my unforgivables."

"Unforgivables?"

"Yes, a rule I hold fast to and don't forgive a breach. Remember, a liar is always a thief, and a thief will steal you blind. I want to be able to count on the honesty of those who work for me."

"Yes, sir." I felt doomed before I even started, but I needed the job and the training. I swallowed to keep my breakfast down. There could be no mistakes.

Eb showed me around the livery and told me what he expected. When we stopped at the paddock, the horses trotted over to the fence expecting a pat or a handout. There was not a rib in sight, though none were fat. Every coat gleamed in the morning sun, and every eye appeared alert and content.

"A sound looking bunch, don't you think?" he said with a smile.

Eb left me in Tom's hands, and Tom, with the devil's own grin, handed me a pitchfork and pointed to a barrow leaning up against the barn.

"You smart enough to figure this'n out on your own, or do I got to show you how it's done? There's plenty to do, get cracking."

After cleaning fifteen stalls, I got to groom a few of the horses, then was put to washing the dust off two buggies and cleaning tack. All the while, Tom hounded me for being too slow.

I was stone tired by the end of the day, but I thought I had died and gone to heaven that night at supper. Tilly set a large bowl of chicken and dumplings smothered in rich gravy before me that gave off a scent of thyme that made my belly rumble. "You look in need of some fattening up," she said with a warm smile. "Got more on the stove, if you're still hungry after making that disappear. No need to stint around here."

Next morning, I woke before dawn and crept down the ladder. I visited the outhouse and washed up as best I could at the pump near the horse trough, combing my wet hair straight back. Returned my comb and towel to the loft and started in on cleaning the stalls. The day before, Eb had made it real clear he expected me to keep the barn clean. Said it gave the place a prosperous look and kept the flies down. Since the horses hadn't been fed, that being Tom's job and him not up yet, I backed the first horse out of his straight stall and tied him in the passageway, so I would have room to work without poking the horse with the pitchfork.

I started on the end of the barn furthest from the shit heap, figuring I would tire as the job wore on. Barrowing a heap of horseshit past twenty-four stalls, Eb's office, Tim's room, the tack room, and the grain room was like running an obstacle course. Cats everywhere. Cats of all colors and sizes. All independent cusses taking their time crossing the passageway, or stretching out to lie in the sun at the doorway. They gave me the 'go around' look. I got so's I would hiss when I approached one that didn't look as though it would move out of my way. Figured it was easier for them to move than me to skirt around 'em.

I'd finished six stalls by the time Tom walked out of his room scratching his rumpled head and grumbled a good morning. When he returned from the outhouse, we fed the horses, and, when they were done eating, took them out to the paddock to roam for an hour or so.

Tilly stuck her head out the back door of their house. "To-om, Char-leey," she strung out the names in a singsong voice. "Come and get your breakfast, boys. Don't forget to wash up."

When I walked into the kitchen, the smell of breakfast set my mouth to watering enough to spit.

Eb was right about Tilly. She was good at feeding people. She served up a heaping bowl of oatmeal and raisins with a dollop of melting butter on top along with a large mug of coffee with cream and plenty of sugar.

I sat down at the kitchen table across from Eb. He had wide shoulders and upper arms that were as big around as my thigh. Freckles peppered his face and arms, while reddish brown hair speckled with gray covered his head and bristled from his chest through the top of his shirt. When standing, he towered head and shoulders above me. His blue eyes most times appeared serious, but I didn't sense any meanness in the man, so my gut feeling was that I could trust him.

I could tell Eb was proud of his livery, so I took pride in my work from the start. I spent my days doing my best to please Tom, who reported how I was doing to Eb. Each evening at dinner, Eb would ask me how everything was going, and I would say that all was fine even if it weren't.

I did everything quick that first week, what with Tom pushing me to hurry all the time, and ended up learning a painful lesson from the school of hard knocks. Got kicked from here to next Sunday by a skittish mare who didn't hear me come up behind her. Didn't break any bones, but I sure hurt like hell for a couple of days. I wore a purple welt on my thigh much longer. Learned it weren't a good idea to do anything quick-like around horses that don't know you. When Tom told Eb at dinner that night, Eb told me horses were often calmed by quiet talk, whistling or humming, and, if I did one of those whenever I was about the barn, the horses would know I was there and wouldn't get startled.

I weren't much of a whistler without sticking two fingers in my mouth back then, so I hummed while I slung shit and pitched hay down to feed, or straw to bed.

All that slinging and pitching blistered my hands. They burned like hell and got weepy when the blisters broke, but I didn't complain. I wrapped them with a strip of old cloth I found in the tack room and kept on working.

Tilly took notice come suppertime and gave me some salve for my hands. They healed right quick after that and soon toughened.

Tom kept me working at a speed he didn't bother to match, but I figured since I was the new pony in the yard, I would have to deal with the nipping order without kicking back.

As I got the pitching under my belt, I graduated to washing carriages and cleaning tack afternoons, and was soon able to include brushing and currying the horses to my morning schedule. By the end of my first month's stay, I had the job of stableboy well in hand, and Eb was telling me what a good job I done. I could tell Tom weren't taking that too well; he started nit-picking my work and pushing me around.

There came a morning that felt like I got my legs knocked out from under me in one fell swoop. I was shoveling and barrowing my way through the morning like I generally did. I rounded the corner heading for the heap with a full barrow, when I pulled up short. Not twenty feet away stood a tall sorrel mare with a question mark on her forehead hitched to a light wagon.

9

Caught

E b, we've known each other since you took your first steps. I trust you to deal with me fairly." The remembered voice grew closer. Eb was talking to the farmer that had given me a ride partway to Worcester, and they were coming right at me.

I lurched for the ladder to the haymow and scrambled up.

"Geez, what is that boy up to," Eb said. "Leaving the barrow in the middle of the aisle thata way. Charley."

I froze where I stood. They were standing right under me.

"Charley... Where is that boy?"

"He's in the mow right above ya," Tom said. "Just climbed up as a matter of fact." I could hear the sneer in Tom's voice. "Looked to me he was in a hurry to get out of your way."

"Charley, get down here. What the hell you doing?"

I had no choice. I climbed down, promising myself to knock the daylights out of Tom for snitching. I stood with head bowed before Eb, trying to duck my face under the brim of my hat so the old farmer couldn't see my face, hoping he wouldn't recognize me now that I wore a shirt and pants.

"This here is Mr. Harrington," Eb said. "I want you to trot Mabel out for him. He's lost one of his team and is looking for a replacement." Turning to Mr. Harrington, Eb said, "Bart, I got a new fare coming. Soon as I get this here feller fitted out, I'll be back, and we'll take her out."

"Fine, take your time," Mr. Harrington said. He turned to me. "Well now, why don't you back that mare out and trot her...Hey, don't I know you?"

"I'm new here." I could feel the sweat start to form on my upper lip.

"I can't place you, but I know we met somewheres. I never forget a face."

"So you lost one of your team. How'd it happen?"

"My Roxy mare was on up in years. I came into the barn two mornings ago and there was no welcoming nicker, like I always got. She lay cast in her stall. Might've twisted her gut early in the night. She was cold when I got to her."

"Sorry to hear that," I said, slipping alongside the liver chestnut mare to back her out of her stall. "They ain't going to match." Shit, shouldn't't've said that.

"Don't know how long Lady is going to last. Me either for that matter. We're both getting on in years. Matching don't make no never mind to me at this late stage. Day might come when Lady'll die, and I'll have to sell the horse I buy today, or buy another."

I brushed Mabel down, slowly circling the mare to keep her between Mr. Harrington and me. He kept walking around us looking her over, but glancing my way, too.

"I'll trot her out for you," I said, untying the mare. He followed me into the sunlight and watched the horse as I walked her down and trotted her back a few times so's he could see how she moved.

"Looks sound, let's hitch her up," he said. "Got my harness in the wagon."

I held the mare while he harnessed her. He'd search my face and look away. I began getting twitchy, like a horse quivering its skin to get rid of a biting fly. I could feel heat flush my face and sweat glue the shirt to my back. We hitched Mabel next to Lady, and I headed for the barn.

"Hey, where ya going?"

"Tell Eb you're ready," I said. Relief began to cool me off some, he'd not recognized me. I headed for Eb's office and met him coming out. Tom was harnessing a mild-mannered dun-colored mare while the new fare waited out front.

"Charley," Eb said, putting his arm around my shoulders. "I want you to ride with us. It's best you know what to expect when someone wants to try out new stock to buy."

Dread made me know that as soon as I climbed up onto that wagon Mr. Harrington would remember who I was. I just knew. I headed for the back of the wagon figuring to stand behind the two men.

"Charley, there's enough room for you to sit up here between us," Eb said, waving me toward the front of the wagon.

When we were settled on the bench, Harrington gave the team a gentle slap of the reins on their rumps and said, "Com'on up girls."

Though the mares eyed each other the best they could with blinders on, they moved out together pretty much in step. The old man put them through their paces, talking to Eb the whole while. Sounded like they were friends a long time. Mr. Harrington drove up and down the Worcester streets and around corners left and right, testing the mare's response to his handling, and their behavior toward him and each other.

"How's your Aunt Martha?" he said with barely a pause from his conversation with Eb.

My eyes flashed to his face. A small knowing smile pulled at the corners of his mouth until a throaty chuckle welled up into a broad laugh.

"What's this all about?" Eb said. "You two know each other?"

"I gave a ride to a young girl last month," Mr. Harrington said between bouts of laughter. "She was headed to visit her Aunt Martha, or so she said."

I felt like my body was afire as fear and embarrassment raced through me. Every place a body could sweat, I sweated. Knew my face had turned red by the way my skin burned.

"It was this here boy dressed up as a girl. You oughta seen him Eb, as clumsy a girl I never did see. Split his dress climbing off the wagon."

I could feel Eb's steady look. "Tilly told me you ran away from an orphanage. What happened?"

"Figured if anyone come after me, they'd be looking for a boy, so I dressed as a girl."

Eb chuckled. "I knew you were smart as a whip. Weren't in trouble at that orphanage were you?"

"Naw."

Eb rumpled my hair.

"I've known Eb here pretty near all his life," Mr. Harrington said. "He grew up within a mile of my place. He's a good man. You couldn't do better in finding someone to train you to horses. He's the best."

I thought better of hauling off and slugging Tom since nothing came of his ratting on me being in the mow. Didn't want to ruin my chances with Eb now that Tom'd be on his way soon, and I would be clear to continue learning from Eb without Tom's flat-eared, teeth bearing moods.

One morning a couple of days later, Tom landed me in the shit heap with a well-placed boot and a hefty shove. I came up swinging. I tucked my head and rammed the bastard in his breadbasket, knocking the wind out of him. I stepped back waiting for Tom to come at me. Had my chin tucked and my fists up in front of my face like I saw done in a fistfight between two men in the middle of the main street back in Cumberton one time. Tom closed in and we threw a couple of blows. All of a sudden, I windmilled backward, as did Tom. Eb had found us and yanked us apart.

"Enough boys." Eb let go our collars.

We stood facing each other. Blood trickled out of Tom's nose. I didn't have so much as a scratch. I stood tall and proud. No one was going to shit on me, I was going to make damn sure of that from here on out.

"Boys, it's time," Eb said, digging into his pocket. He counted out Tom's wages and added a gold double eagle for luck, telling him it was time to move on. Tom and Eb shook hands, and then Eb insisted Tom and me shake.

"Shows good sportsmanship," Eb said. "Smoothes the way for another time the two of you might meet." Tom and me eyed each other up and down. "You never know boys, you never know." We shook, but it weren't friendly, it was more like a bone-crushing squeeze to beat hell.

As me and Eb watched Tom head for the bunkroom to get his things, rubbing his bleeding nose along his sleeve, Eb said, "Glad to see you got some spunk to you, Charley. Don't like fighting, but can't respect a man who won't stand up for himself or his family. You keep in mind I don't like fighting as a general rule, and we'll get along, you and me. Got any questions?"

"No, sir."

"You know what to do 'round here, I seen you handling most of the work for the last week or so. You're a good boy, Charley. If you have any questions, you ask me. Like I said the day you signed on, I'll teach you everything I know about horses and the livery business."

"Yes, sir."

"Eb, just call me Eb."

"Yes, Eb." He seemed to be in a good mood despite my fight with Tom, so I thought I would take my chance and ask the question that'd been playing on my mind over the past few weeks. While I screwed up my courage, he began to turn away.

"Eb?"

"Yeah, Charley?"

"When you going to teach me to drive?"

A slow smile crossed his face. "How about we start tomorrow after morning feed? Can only give you about a half an hour since Tom's no longer here to mind the livery."

I grinned so wide my cheeks hurt.

"We'll harness up old Chester—"

"Chester?" I drew the word out with a moan. My smile faded into a frown. "But Chester is a lady's horse." Tom had called Chester the nanny horse 'cause the gelding would take care of green drivers. Chester was the horse to hitch for the old Eisley sisters, both spry but in their eighties, if a day, and whoever else didn't look to have horse experience.

"Chester is a teacher and a nursemaid." Eb pursed his lips in that way I learned he had of suppressing a smile. "Just what's needed for a green kid."

Eb knew what he was about, but I weren't happy.

As the sun peeked over the horizon the next morning, we harnessed the chestnut gelding. Though I'd helped Tom harness horses while learning his job, Eb explained what each strap did in relation to the rest of the harness, whether it was necessary for pulling or stopping. He made sure I knew how to harness comfortably, so's the horse never returned from a job with a gall from chafing. We hitched Chester between the shafts of a two-wheeled gig and headed into the countryside toward Shrewsbury.

"Here on in, Charley," Eb said. "I want Chester hitched when I come down to the barn on the days we're driving."

"Yes, sir."

Soon as we reached open road, Eb handed the reins over, showing me how to hold them and keep light contact with Chester's mouth, so I would always be in control. He leaned back as though he was just along for the ride and explained the necessity of lightly holding the horse's mouth, making sure my wrists were supple, and I could feel Chester's needs through my fingers.

"Dumb drivers," he said, "think they're being kind to the horse by letting the reins so loose they swing, but they're not giving their horse confidence, and they're not prepared to lift the

horse's head if he trips, nor is the driver ready if the horse shies."
Eb slid the reins through my hands until I could feel a tiny tug as
Chester took each step. "The time it would take to reach the
horse's mouth to gain control could mean life or death for the
horse as well as the driver and passengers. Keep contact."

Tired of Chester's slow walk, I thought to speed him up to a
trot with a flick of the buggy whip. I reached for the whip, but Eb
stayed my hand for another lesson.

"Never use a whip unless you absolutely have to, son. If you
drive with a whip, crack it to get their attention, never lay it across
the back of an animal. The whistle of this buggy whip would upset
Chester. He knows what he's doing."

"Hell, why carry a whip if you can't use it?"

"Charley, you want the animals you work with to respect you,
and in order for you to gain their respect, you must respect them
first. Understand?"

I shook my head.

"Cluck to him. Tell him what you want. Those two big ears
sticking out the top of his head are for listening. A horse is plenty
smart. Think of driving as a partnership, two friends working
together. See what I mean?"

I clucked to Chester, and he sped up a little. I was hoping for
a spanking trot, but all I got was a slow jog. I didn't force the
issue, figuring Eb would deliver another reprimand if I did.

We came upon an overgrown meadow with the gate hanging
open, and Eb told me to bring the horse down to a walk. Weren't
much of a difference in speed that I could see.

"Mind you Charley, I wouldn't have you pull into just any
field. I spoke to Old Man Porter a couple of days ago, and asked if
we could use this here meadow for driving practice. Got to respect
your neighbors."

"Yes, sir." I looked long at him, trying to figure. "How did
you know?"

"Watch where you're going. Don't start driving like a girl,
you hear, or the lessons will end." His words sent a scare through
me. "I knew this day was a coming," he went on. "I saw it in your

eyes, you're hungry to learn. Knew I wouldn't be able to hold you off too much longer."

Eb explained to me how to take a turn without taking the reins from me. Told me to make my turns wide so's the wheel don't catch on the gatepost and bust the wagon's wheel or axle. He had me do large and small circles in the pasture, then figure eights for twenty minutes at both a walk and a slow trot before we headed back to the barn.

We drove that way for a full week before we left the barn by way of the front doors and headed into Worcester. Eb had me driving up and down the back streets of town, rounding corners like I'd done it all my life. Course, we didn't go any faster than a walk, or Chester's snail-like trot, but I gained confidence with every lesson.

Between my early morning driving lessons and sundown, my day was jam-packed with feeding, grooming, shoveling, cleaning harness, and washing our buggies, coaches, and wagons, trips to the blacksmith and running errands on foot for Eb and sometimes Tilly.

Though Eb was a stickler most of the time, or maybe 'cause of it, he was a fine teacher—patient, but persistent as the hounds of hell, expecting me to toe the mark at every turn.

One morning after a week of driving around town during my lesson, Eb instructed me to leave the barn by way of the back doors again. Heading for Shrewsbury on the back road, Eb gave me the go ahead to pick up speed. I gave Chester a gentle slap on the rump with the reins. He lurched into a swinging trot.

"Speak, don't strike, Charley. I warned you about this before. Now bring him down to a walk and start again."

I felt my cheeks redden at Eb's words. I did as I was told, then brought Chester up to his jog trot with a cluck of my tongue. "Now what?"

"Cluck more to increase his speed."

It worked. Chester sped up to what I thought for once was a decent trot, the breeze fanning my reddened cheeks. Now we were getting somewhere. I felt powerful, in control, like the coachman I intended to be. When Chester shied toward the open gate, I checked him with a slight movement of my fingers, and we passed the gate and continued on down the road.

"Nicely done, Charley."

I beamed with pride at Eb's praise.

"You take to driving like a horse to sweet feed."

About a mile down the road, we drew down to a walk and turned around at a crossroads to head back the way we had come.

"Ready for more speed?" Eb's pursed lips spread into a smile.

I grinned and nodded that I was up for it.

"Get him going again and cluck a bit more when he's trotting."

I hadn't suspected the old gelding could float on the wind with a ground covering trot that I felt sure could win races. After a half a mile, Eb had me slow him to a jog and explained the way a horse extended his gait by reaching further with his stride, the back feet extending further than where the front feet had landed.

"Well now, Charley, seems you're ready to drive on your own in town. You have good hands, small as they are, and good reflexes, and Chester'll nurse you through. I got to have your word that you'll not go any faster than a slow trot."

"Yes, sir, I'll take it real easy."

"You are restricted to town until I tell you otherwise. Understand?"

"Yes, sir," I said. "Sir, will you teach me to ride?"

"Don't have time, Charley," Eb said, climbing down from the gig. "What say you throw a saddle on him when you're not busy and practice staying on in the coral, and, when I have a minute, I'll give you some pointers. But mind you, don't go shirking your job. I won't stand for that."

"I'm no shirker."

"I know, but I don't want you going horse crazy on me either."

"No, sir."

"Best get on with cleaning those stalls. Don't want my stock standing in their leavings."

"Yes, sir."

Within three years, Eb's livery business had doubled. We gained new customers, took on deliveries, added new stock and a few more buggies, but it was still me and Eb doing all the work. We had a good reputation and worked long hours every day of the week to keep it up. Christmas day we fed and watered the stock twice and let the barn go dirty for the day. And we took a half a day off for the Fourth of July town picnic. Fun as those days were, it weren't enough time off.

Got to the point where I would fall onto bed late at night and sleep in my clothes. Come morning I would have to claw my way awake. Then came a week where I didn't wake up before Tilly called for breakfast. Generally, I had the horses fed and watered and in the paddock by then, and had started on cleaning stalls. On the third morning I overslept, Eb chewed me out. Told me I was not doing my job and that I'd better straighten up, or he'd find someone else. I damn near started blubbering, but I kept my mouth shut and slammed out of the kitchen without eating breakfast.

To hell with him, I thought as I walked into the barn. No clean shirt today. No slicked back hair. If I had smudges on my face, or my nails were dirty, so much the better. What the hell did he think I was? I did more damn work than Tom ever did. I slammed around the barn all day making the stock nervous, not giving a damn. The only sound during the dinner meal that night was the thump of dishes on the table and the scrape of knives and forks.

I happened to glance up and saw Tilly give Eb a warning look, so I supposed he was going to say something to me. He looked to be chewing saddle leather. He must have taken Tilly's scowl to heart 'cause he didn't say anything. I fed the horses, swept the aisles, and fell into bed.

Eb tore me out of sleep, pulling me off my cot onto the floor in the dead of night. I had no idea what time it was. It being pitch black outside.

"You're fired," he said. "You forgot to water the stock."

As I came to my senses, I heard him grumbling about having to do everything himself as he moved down the aisle. The horses were stomping and a few thumped and scraped the side of their stalls with their hooves. I'm embarrassed to say that I had slept through all the noise. I think the place could have burned down around me, and I wouldn't have woken up.

I dragged my tired ass off the floor and pulled on my pants and boots before shuffling out of my room to see to the chore I'd forgotten. Eb led two horses up the aisle and out the back door. I grabbed the next two and headed out. We alternated back and forth without a word till the horses were all watered and returned to their stalls. Eb went back to the house. I fell back into bed fully clothed not wanting to miss another minute of sleep.

Next morning, I woke to Tilly's call to breakfast. Damn, I was late again. Last night came flooding to mind. Before dropping off to sleep again, I'd told myself I'd better rise early and get a head start on the day as I had done prior to this slump I was in, but the birds had either stopped chirping, or I'd slept through their chatter, again. I didn't want to lose this job, but I was so damned tired. I was bored too, doing the same thing day in and day out, but it seemed my body was three days behind my will to get things done.

I walked into the kitchen and sat down. Tilly placed a plate of hotcakes in front of me. I glanced at Eb. He forked his breakfast in without taking his eyes from his plate. I started in on mine. Tilly poured us all a cup of coffee and thumped the pot on the table.

"All right boys," she said. "We have to talk."

We both glanced at her and continued eating.

"Both of you have been working real hard. The business has grown larger than the two of you can handle. It's time to hire another helper."

We both nodded in agreement, and that was that. Eb and I didn't say much over the next couple of days, but no more was said about my being fired. He put the word out that we were looking for barn help, and I concentrated on doing my job better than I ever had. That is till the day my body betrayed me.

10

Changes

I dragged myself out of bed one morning a couple of days later feeling out of sorts in my belly and hurried to the outhouse. I pulled down my pants to take a seat and saw my drawers were soaked with blood. My heart leaped to my throat almost closing off my air. I stared at the red, hating the smell. I sat on the wooden bench panting, 'Oh, my God. Oh, my God, I'm dying.' My mind kept skittering around so's I couldn't get a handle on it.

"Charley, you better get a move on if you're wanting breakfast," Tilly called out the back door.

"Yes, ma'am, be right there." I shouted back.

What was I to do? I yanked up my drawers and flinched as the cold, wet mess hit my crotch. I washed up at the outdoor pump before entering the kitchen and sat down across from Eb.

Tilly still stood at the cast iron stove scrambling eggs, her left fist on her hip, her long braid gently swinging from side to side in time with her stirring.

"You're late this morning, something ailing you?" she asked without turning.

"The boy's fine, woman," Eb said. "Stop worrying over him.

"Charley, I need you to see to things around here today, I'm going to run down to Pike's to take a look at a couple of horses he's itching to sell me," Eb said, taking a swig of his coffee. "He stopped in again yesterday, asking me to ride down to see them today. Swears he'll sell them elsewhere if I don't get down there.

"The Eisley sisters need Chester hitched by ten…"

I knew the schedule, we reviewed it every night before parting and again the next morning over breakfast in case one of us forgot to tell the other about a job. As Eb went on about the day's schedule, my mind worried on the fact I was dying. I figured I had a day at most and hoped I wouldn't fall down dead in the middle of the livery before Eb returned that evening. I didn't ever want to let him down. He'd become more'n my teacher. I looked up to him almost like a father.

I snapped out of my black thoughts when I burnt my mouth on Tilly's strong coffee and realized that I had eaten half my eggs and bacon without tasting them. Eb had already finished his.

"Tilly, maybe you're right. Charley here is slower than a hobbled racehorse this morning. What's the trouble son? You feeling sick?"

Tilly put the back of her hand on my forehead. "No fever."

"I'll have everything in order Eb. I can do it. I'll be fine."

Eb pushed his chair away from the table, giving me a long searching look. "With any luck, I'll be bringing some new stock back with me. Two geldings and a mare he spoke of sounded promising, so you'd better have stalls ready for my return."

I nodded, still forking the remainder of my eggs and bacon into my mouth as fast as I could, barely chewing before swallowing.

Eb kissed Tilly goodbye and left.

I gulped the last swig of coffee and stood up to go. "Thanks, Tilly."

"Charley what's that all over your backside?"

I put my hand on my behind and felt wet. "Must've sat in something," I said, grabbing my hat and hurrying to the door.

"Get back here Charley," she said. I heard the scrape of her chair a second before she grabbed me by the scruff of the neck and swung me around, surprising me with how fast she could move for a middle-aged lady.

"You ain't what you appear to be are ya?"

"I sat in something is all," I said, trying to shoulder out the door like a horse in a hurry. "I got to get going."

"You ain't fooling me," she said. "I seen how you been protecting your chest when a horse gets rough with you these days. Out with it, you're a girl, ain't ya?"

"I guess it don't matter none now," I said, tucking my chin into my chest to hide behind the brim of my hat. Didn't want Tilly seeing the damn tears that sprung to my eyes.

"What on earth do you mean?"

"I'm going to be dead by the time Eb gets home tonight."

Tilly tilted my chin up till I looked her in the eye. "You ain't dying, girl." She let go my chin and tapped the tip of my nose with her finger. "What's happening to you is natural." She drew me back into the kitchen before continuing into their bedroom. Her voice came trailing back, "I suspected something right off."

"What? Nobody much remembered I weren't a boy for as long as I can recall."

"You got too much hips." Her voice became louder as she returned to the kitchen with some white rags in her hand. "Here, use these between your legs."

"Tilly…"

"What?"

"You won't tell Eb, will you?"

Tilly put her hand to her throat. "I've never kept something a secret from Eb before."

"But you know what he'll—"

"He and I've been through a lot together. We've never lied to one another."

"Please, Tilly, if he finds out, he'll send me away."

"Maybe you could stay on—"

"Not as a girl."

"I would love to have a daughter. And Eb…"

"I would be long gone before he thought twice. You know it. Not only 'cause I'm a girl, but for not being honest. You know how he is."

"You're right, I suppose." Tilly looked torn.

My eyes dropped to the rags in my hand, the symbol of my body's betrayal.

Tilly broke the silence. "He must never know I know."

"I promise I'll never let on if he should find out."

Tilly reached out, put her hands on my shoulders, and drew me to her. I hadn't been hugged since I stayed with the Biddles after Papa died. It felt strange to be that close to someone, and the gesture stirred a feeling deep inside; one I'd kept under control. Though I pulled away, I yearned for more. I searched Tilly's eyes. Was she hugging me goodbye?

"It's our secret then," she finally said, "For as long as it lasts."

"I owe you, Tilly."

"Your acting the part of a boy can't last much longer anyways."

"Why not?"

She nodded toward the rags I held in my hand. "You'll bleed every month. There's bound to be a slip up now and then. 'Sides, men sound different and walk different. They're stronger, too. It's only a matter of time I'm afraid."

"I can do it."

Tilly put her hand on my shoulder, "I'll help where I can."

From that day on, I talked deeper in my throat to lower my voice. When my voice broke, as it did on occasion, Tilly assured me that boys have that problem when they turn into men. I couldn't do anything about not having hair growing out of my chin, but I wore a neckerchief to hide the Adam's apple I didn't have bobbing in my throat. I bought a larger jacket to hide my fat ass, and a pair of wide-cuffed leather gloves to hide the fact that my hands were too small. And I only took them off to wash up for dinner.

When I whined, which I'm embarrassed to say I did from time to time over tenderness and cramps, Tilly would say, "Where there's a will there's a way. You want to be a coachman, you'll have to figure out how to handle this, too."

I got used to acting the part of a man every day and hiding the monthly female stuff. I studied the boys and men I met, their actions, what they said, how they said it. Noticed I'd have to be more careful around women then men. Women watch men longer and look at them with more consideration than men look at other men. Noticed, too, that men take great enjoyment in cussing and swearing 'cause women don't like it. Gets their dander up and sends them off clucking like old hens. So, I did the same.

When my breasts grew bigger, Tilly taught me how to bind myself and made me pleated shirts to hide my lumpy chest. Them bindings got damn hot in the summer, but they hid my gender. Nobody figured me out for a long time.

Along about that time, I started having confusing dreams that haunted me during my waking hours. I sometimes dreamed my breasts got so big, I couldn't hide them under binding any more. Sometimes I'd wake in a cold sweat just as Eb found out I weren't a boy. Too, I had strange dreams that I liked kissing boys and did strange things with them that made my crotch moist and sensitive. I used to blush thinking on those dreams. It got to be downright confusing at times. Just who the hell was I? But when I wondered if I should try being a girl, I'd look at my horses and the work I loved, and knew I'd never be happy doing anything else, especially prissy girl things like sewing and cooking, and wearing long skirts and such. Geez.

When Eb put the word out that we were looking for a stableboy, the idea of having a bunkmate had me pacing back and forth like a corralled horse denied its herd till I hit on a notion I thought would work. Unbeknownst to Eb, I told some of the boys around town that we were hoping for someone that lived close by, so's he could go home every night.

When boys started showing interest in the job, I did my best to be close by when the time came for Eb to trot them through their paces.

Ever work with horses before?

Do you ride? Drive?

How much do you know about them?

How old are you? You live around here?

Let me see your hands, Eb's favorite way of reckoning whether the kid was a worker or not.

Over supper, Eb and I would discuss the kids and their answers. I drove a few out of the race with a well-placed doubt in Eb's mind, but there was one kid I hated that I could see Eb was pretty set on. A smooth character, he was. Talked nice to Eb, acting real friendly-like. A big kid. Bigger than me. When I showed him around the place, he put on a swagger and acted tough, like I was going to be working for him. It got me to wondering if Eb might not like this kid so much as to put him in charge over me. I didn't eat after that. I couldn't. Every time I thought of that tough kid, my insides would knot.

A long week later, the number of kids showing up for the job slowed down to a trickle. Eb announced he was ready to make his final decision. I was scared that tough kid and I would have to bunk together. Then a kid by the name of Andy showed up.

Unlike the other kid, I took to Andy right off. He reminded me of Fish. Maybe it was 'cause he was small and wiry like Fish, or maybe it was that they'd both lost their father, and their mothers had a hard time making ends meet. Andy's father had died a year ago, and he felt it was time to leave school and help take care of his mother. She took in sewing, but the money coming in weren't enough. She wanted Andy to stay in school and make something of himself, but they couldn't afford it. Her only demand was that whatever job Andy took, he come home every night.

Perfect.

Eb changed his mind after talking with Andy and hired him instead of the tough kid. I felt pure relief once I knew I wouldn't have to share my room, or fight to remain Eb's right hand.

Each morning Andy came to work that first week, a shadow of a girl by the name of Sarah Jean came with him. The first day, she waited by the side of the road while Andy worked. She lived with her mother next door to Andy and his mother. The worm in that apple, he said, was the man who kept her mother. The bastard beat them both, not while drunk mind you, but out of pure meanness.

The best of friends, Sarah Jean and Andy were four years apart in age, and opposites in most every way: Andy being the younger of the two, and Sara Jean being the taller. Where Andy was friendly and talkative, Sarah Jean was quiet and standoffish, and closer to me in age. Her right eye held the fading hues of a beating and a dark frayed braid hung past her waist. Her unkempt appearance and fading injuries aside, I thought her pretty. If she lived through the mistreatment meted out at home, she would grow to look like the widder that fed me on the road after I left the orphanage three years before. A real looker.

The first day she showed up, Eb frowned at her and told her to go home to her mother. From then on, she slid out of sight whenever Eb was around. And when he weren't, I drew her along with Andy and me as we did our work. I felt sorry for her, but I think the way she looked at me with worshipful eyes probably had something to do with my defying Eb's decree and allowing her to tag along.

Sarah Jean loved horses. Like me, she saw them as critters with likes and dislikes, not just working beasts. Her timid ways had me feeling lucky to have escaped from the orphanage and found a place with the Balchs. I taught her how to approach a horse while humming, I let her pet the horses, and allowed her to brush old Chester. But the day came when Eb caught her in the stable with Andy and me.

"Girlie Girl," he said, grabbing her by the upper arm and pulling her through the door. "I told you to go home, and I meant it. Go back to your doodads and geegaws where you females belong. Don't come back. You hear?"

She didn't blubber like the girls at the orphanage did. In fact, she didn't say a word as we followed them to the door, but I noticed tears rolling down her cheeks. To this day, I remember the empty look in her eyes as she turned away to walk down the road alone, head bowed, arms wrapped around her waist. I felt as though I'd betrayed her somehow, given her a hope she had no right to have being a girl.

Eb turned on us and swore to fire us both if we allowed her in the barn again. Andy and I nodded, and went back to work. But the way Eb had booted Sarah Jean out of the barn had me worrying what he'd do to me if he ever found out I was a girl and had lied to him. Would he throw me out? Yes. He might regret it later, but I would be out. Didn't want that.

Andy worked out well, but it was about five years before I saw Sarah Jean again.

Now that we had help, Eb took the time to teach me to drive a span of Cleveland Bays. Mares they were, plain-looking, about sixteen-hands, with long bodies, broad chests and large hindquarters. Their legs were short compared to their bodies and their hooves large. We kept their black manes cropped so's to keep them from becoming a tangled mess damn near impossible to comb out. Mostly they were nice, but being mares, there were times they weren't.

Course, while I'd been with Eb, I'd helped him harness a two or four-horse team many times, and showed Andy, explaining how the Y-shaped reins crossed through a ring between the team of horses, so that the rein in the driver's right hand would pull both horses on the right side of the bit to make them turn. How the traces were attached to the hames on the collar at the horse's neck and were connected to the whiffletree and how two whiffletrees were attached to a doubletree at the front of the wagon, so the team could pull a load evenly. Andy was quick to remember things I taught him, and easy to get along with.

One fine morning found me and Eb sitting in the driver's box of a wagon heading out the back of the barn down the road for a practice drive with the mares. At Eb's command, I clucked them up to a trot and held them in hand.

Now I had to deal with two beasts that thought differently from each other and me, and, at the start, none of us seemed to agree with any of the others.

"Charley," Eb said. "You got to be the brains of this team. It's up to you to make them work together. Always remember, you are the boss."

"Molly's not listening, and Meg's getting annoyed."

"Don't go girlie on me now and start whining. Flick the whip so it whistles behind Molly's head. Make sure you don't hit her," Eb warned. "Meg will hear it, too. Every once in a while, you got to make them step up and take notice when they don't listen, and the snap of a whip will usually do it."

Sure enough, they took notice of my voice again after they realized I meant business.

As before, the circles I made with the team had to be perfectly round and my figure eight circles had to be the same size. Again, all I heard from Eb was, "If you're going to do a job, do it right, and do it the best you can."

Although many a time Eb set my teeth on edge with his nit-picking perfection, I knew he was doing his best to make me a good horseman like he knew I wanted.

So, when I got my circles and figure eights precisely as Eb wanted them done in the field, as I had during my lessons with Chester, Eb took me out on the road again. We drove up and down hills so's I could learn how and when to slow the wagon with the brake, so the horses wouldn't spook, or get pushed into a run.

Seein's how the wagon weren't loaded during our beginning lessons, all I had to do was be prepared with my foot on the brake handle on the lesser grades. That changed when we took on the steeper hills of Worcester, of which the whole town is made, and practiced with a loaded wagon. I had to hold the wagon back so that the breeching wouldn't push the team down the hill. If the load were too heavy and forced the team to break stride, Eb said, chances were they'd run away, a situation, he warned, I would not likely live through.

11

Females

B efore Eb let me drive a team on my own, I had to pass three driving tests to his satisfaction: rolling both wheels of a wagon over a silver dollar at a trot, pulling the wagon up to a dead stop aligning the front wheel hub with whatever mark Eb decided upon, and turning the team around on a narrow road, which meant backing them off the road and having them sidestep to one side, so they could move out in the opposite direction. The day I completed them all to Eb's satisfaction, I had permission to drive that team wherever necessary.

A year or more after I'd passed my tests with Molly and Meg, we were heading home after hauling a delivery over Paxton way. The mares were tired, just plodding along when I thought to cut through a field, striking about a half a mile off our return trip. Another wagon had crossed the field and was rejoining the road on the other side. It looked to me like others had done the same thing before us. In fact, it was beginning to take on the look of a new road.

As I said, the mares were plodding along when Molly give a squeal and the team started off at a trot. My reflexes had me holding them back, and trying to quiet them when I felt the reason behind their upset.

Yellow jackets.

We must've upset a whole nest of them 'cause they stung us all to beat hell. There I was, swatting angry bees and trying to slow the horses who were getting stung as bad I was. I swatted and hollered for the pain when the mares took it into their heads to run. They broke into a canter, then flattened their ears and extended their noses. The wagon rumbled and clattered behind them. They lengthened their strides into a dead run while I bounced around like a piece of popcorn in the driver's box.

The run-away mares and careening wagon had left the road and were headed toward a big oak tree that loomed closer with every heartbeat. I braced myself as best I could and shortened the right rein. I pulled that rein with all my might. At first, it didn't seem I was getting through to them, then I remembered to use my voice.

"Gee." I yelled the word for right turn again and again before they took notice and started to turn. I pulled them into a tighter circle and kept pulling until they slowed to a trot, then down to a walk, all our sides heaving from fear and hard use. I brought them to a standstill and looked for bees that would scare them up again. Squashed a dazed one under my foot and decided we were far enough away from the nest that we'd lost the swarm. I wanted to get down to look the mares over, but was afraid they'd spook at the mere sound of a bee and take off without me in the box, so I sweet-talked them on home and took stock there.

Ten minutes later the mares entered the yard in a high step- ping trot, lathered and blowing. Eb glared at me as I passed. Before I had a chance to explain what happened, he tore into me for running his horses into the ground. Figured he was too riled to listen to a word I had to say, so I kept my mouth shut and hurriedly unhitched the team while he fussed. He fired me, again. Told me to get packing, yet I kept tearing the harness off the team faster than I'd ever done before, hanging the harness on the sides of the nearest stall instead of trucking it to the tack room like usual. I pulled the mares out to the water trough and started throwing buckets of water on their sting-welted bodies. Eb got pissed and promised to beat the shit out of me if I didn't face him front and center while he was talking to me. It turned quiet as I continued to refill the bucket and throw it over the mares instead of facing up to him.

"What the hell happened to you?" Eb asked.

"Bees." I said, scooping mud up and slapping it on the mare's welts to draw the stinger and cool the skin. Next thing I knew, I had a face full of mud myself.

"Get to the house, I'll take care of these two," Eb said, pulling me away from the mares. "Have Tilly tend your stings."

Course, telling the story straight out over supper that evening calmed the upset between us. Eb figured the first wagon probably stirred the bees up, and my coming through right after gave them a slow moving target on which to focus their agitation.

I ended up not being able to work for two days on account of my eyes swelling shut with the three fiery stings I took in my cheeks and neck. Other stings swelled on various parts of my body and hurt like fire, then began to itch after a few days.

Not long after, Eb got it in his head that it was time I settled down to raise a family. I was about twenty then.

Damn! No matter what I said, he kept at it.

"Not interested," I said for at least the hundredth time.

"What's the matter with you? Aren't you normal? You're not one of them that likes men now are you?"

Course, I couldn't come right out and say yes, I would prefer a man, if I were interested. I almost smiled. "No, just don't want to get tied down is all." I felt my voice raising.

"Damn glad I did." Eb said.

"Well, you got Tilly. There's only one of her."

"Got that right."

"If I could marry Tilly, I would consider it."

"Why am I hearing my name bandied about at the top of your voices," Tilly asked, walking into the barn. "I heard you all the way out to the clothesline."

"Trying to get the boy married is all."

"I was telling Eb, I would marry you if you were free," I said with a grin.

"You talk some sense into him," Eb said, turning away.

Tilly rolled her eyes and shook her head at me before walking back to the house.

I'd had a number of these discussions with Eb and thought nothing of it. I figured, knowing Eb as I did, that I would be having them regularly from now till doomsday.

Over the next few days, I caught Andy looking at me with a thoughtful expression a couple of times, but he'd look away without saying anything. I thought maybe he was thinking to ask for a raise in pay or something, so I didn't question him about it, figuring he'd get around to saying what was on his mind when he was good and ready.

Then one morning a few days later, Andy was late coming to work, and, since he was rarely late, I gave him a long look to let him know that I'd noticed, and turned back to harnessing Chester for a fare. A few moments later, I felt a soft tap on my shoulder. I spun around so fast I knocked a woman on her bustle. I found a hand amongst the flurry of petticoats and flailing legs, and helped her to her feet.

"Sorry, Miss," I said. "Didn't know anyone was behind me." She didn't regain her balance right off, but leaned on me, the top of her head tucked under my chin. I wiggled my hand out of her trembling fingers and stepped back, only to bump into the side of a horse stall.

"Charley, don't you remember me?" she said, looking up at me with a small smile. The large brown eyes that gazed into mine held a trace of fear that increased my own unease. She stepped closer.

I stepped back. Sweat broke out on my upper lip.

The woman's long dark hair framed a delicate heart-shaped face that was beginning to seem familiar.

"Charley," she said with reddening cheeks. "You don't, do you?"

"Don't what?" My well-rehearsed male voice broke, ending in what could only be called a squeak. Somehow, she had inched closer again. I caught a movement at the barn door. Relief started to flood through me as Eb walked in. I figured he'd chew this woman out as he had with Sarah Jean back when she followed Andy to work. Then my belly churned and my mind spun, leaving me reeling in surprise. Eb walked into the livery office with a smirk on his face as I realized who stood before me.

"Know me," she said.

I drew a deep breath. "Course I do, Sarah Jean." By now, a trickle of sweat had formed between my shoulder blades and had started sliding down my backbone.

"You guessed."

I'd had little enough experience being a woman, much less studying their ways of snaring men, but I had the feeling I was on the receiving end, which only made the sweat trickle faster. I slid my shirtsleeve along my upper lip, wiping away beads of sweat. It never pays to show anyone you're running scared. And I was passed scared. I was riding on terror-stricken.

"Well, nice to see you again," I said, not wanting to hurt her feelings. I looked around for help. Andy stood in the shadows watching us, but as soon as he saw me glance his way, he hurried out of the barn. Now I understood his recent actions, those long looks I thought he was giving me while getting up the courage to ask for something had meant he was considering matching me up with Sarah Jean. I wiggled my fingers from her sweaty clasp again. "How've you been," I asked, trying to be polite. I needed to get rid of her and didn't know how. Damn Eb, why didn't he throw her out again?

"I been doing fine," she said, but her eyes flickered away. "Missed you, Charley." Her voice sounded desperate, but before I knew what was what, she threw her arms around my neck and planted her puckered lips on mine.

My eyes popped wide open and the hair on the back of my neck rose like hackles on a dog. I pursed my lips tight and grabbed her forearms to pull them from around my neck.

The sound of throat clearing broke Sarah Jean's vice-like grip. I straightened and stepped away from her. Two voices tst-tsted behind me. I knew who they were before I turned and saw them. The prim and proper Eisley sisters. Worcester's gossip queens.

"Charley," they said in unison while the elder continued, "Shame on you for taking advantage of a young woman in such a manner. We shall make it a point of telling Mr. Balch about this. Such behavior is not acceptable. We thought better of you. You're getting wild ways like the rest of the young hooligans in this town."

My cheeks must have turned from ashes to ripe apple red in under thirty seconds 'cause I could feel them burn in shame. At that moment, Eb came out of the office, where I'm sure he'd been watching everything that went on. His lips had the puckered look of trying not to smile. Though he didn't glance my way, I knew Eb would've burst out laughing had he laid eyes on me.

"Miss Jane, Miss Julia," he said. "How are you lovely ladies today?" Although he was looking at them, I knew the grin that finally split his face was at my expense. "Chester is almost ready. I'll have him hitched in a minute."

Sarah Jean stepped closer and rose on her toes to whisper in my ear, "See you tomorrow."

"No," I almost roared. I had to put a stop to this before things went from ridiculous to rotten. I turned on my heel and walked out of the stable, figuring she'd follow. Sure enough, she tucked her hand around my elbow and floated along beside me. I glanced at the traffic on the road, wishing it were empty. Acquaintances passed by, waving and helloing. I knew I would have some explaining to do what with the Eisley sisters and now those passing by. Word would get around. It always did with something you wanted kept quiet.

"Sarah Jean," I said, wondering what I was going to say. "It's nice to see you again. You're all grown up. It was nice of you to stop in, but you know that Eb doesn't like girls in the barn. You mustn't come here again."

"But I'm in…"

"No, no," I said. My intuition told me she was going to declare her love for me. "I'm not the marrying type. I will never marry. Ever. I don't like girls." I blurted. Oh, shit, what have I said. "I mean, I mean—"

"You mean to tell me you like men?" she said at the top of her voice, releasing my hands as though I were a dead cat. She, Eb, and the Eisley sisters all turned wide-eyed stares on me.

"No, I didn't mean that. I don't want to get involved. I'm not ready." I looked at each of them in turn. "All I ever wanted to be was a coachman," I said with a small shake of my head, willing them to understand. "I don't want to get married. I want to drive a coach and six."

Eb's lips pulled to one side with a look of disappointment. The Eisley sisters appeared relieved. Sarah Jean's shoulders drooped and the color drained from her cheeks as she turned away.

"I'm sorry," I called after her. I figured to kill Andy, he was the one responsible for all of this. I went in search of the son of a bitch I thought was my friend. "What the hell did you think you were doing?"

"Just trying to help," he said, looking sheepish.

"Well, don't."

"Both of you are my friends, and I wanted you both to be happy," he said.

"Whatever made you think I would be happy to get married? You've heard my arguments with Eb. I don't want to get married."

"Well, she's my friend, too."

"What the hell does that mean?"

"Oh, never mind, what the hell would you care anyway?"

"I care. Just don't want to marry is all."

"Well, she needs to get married."

"Needs to get married?" At this point, I was yelling so loud the whole town could hear me.

"The man who keeps her mama took her and now she's pregnant," he said in a low voice so that only I could hear. "She didn't want it to happen. She kept running from him, but he trapped her...he made her..."

I took a deep breath and tried to calm down. "I'm sorry to hear that, but why did you try to foist her off on me? It's a big decision to take on a wife, much less starting a family right off. Friends don't do that to each other."

"But you're both my friends, and you both need to get married. I was only trying to help."

"Why the hell don't you marry her then?"

"Can't afford to, got my Ma to care for."

"Get this straight. I don't need to get married. Remember that in the future." I turned on my heel and strode away. "And don't try to fix me up again." I added over my shoulder.

The only good thing that came out of that sad, embarrassing mess was that Andy never tried matching me up again, and Eb didn't pester me about marrying for quite a while, though it didn't stop him completely.

12
Rose

We had no stallions at the livery and never bred our mares because, as Eb said, "I want my stock concentrating on work, not other things. Too dangerous."

But as luck would have it, Eb bought a scrawny mare one time and named her Rose. We fed her up, and rented her out hitched to a large wheeled, single seat gig. She worked out fine. But about six months later she got quite a hay belly on her, leastways that's what I thought, until Eb examined her and said she was pregnant and would drop soon.

Eb didn't hold with breeding livery mares, said having foals around was too distracting. The little ones took mares out of service for months, then had them so distracted during weaning when they were put back to work that accidents happened and more valuable time and money were lost. He also figured that a foal weren't worth anything until it grew up and had some training, but meanwhile a body had to feed it. Eb put the word out right away that he had a pregnant mare for sale, and we moved her into a box stall in case she dropped her foal before we found a new home for her. Sure enough, we weren't fast enough.

I'd never known a mare to foal and didn't know what to expect, but before bedding down for the night, I checked to see that she was all right. She looked alert, munching hay and standing with her right hind leg cocked as if to say, can we please get this over with?

I fell asleep while reading that night as I often did, but woke hours later to the rustle of straw and low nickers from some of the horses. I yanked on my britches and padded down the aisle barefoot. The light of the full moon showed the mare lying on her right side and straining. I hurried back to my room and threw on my boots and coat, then ran for Eb. Soon as he was awake, I ran back to peer through the bars of the box stall. I didn't want to miss a thing. She lay quiet for the moment, but the other horses were restless. Chester's stall lay alongside Rose's box, and he watched her as I did. I walked over to him and stroked his neck as we both stared through the bars at the mare awaiting her next contraction.

"See any legs or a nose yet?" Eb asked upon entering the barn. He hung his lantern outside the stall door, its soft yellow light splashing through the bars onto the sweating mare.

"No. Just her pushing."

"She's soaked. Must've been at it a while."

"Didn't hear her till just before I came and got you."

Eb entered her stall crooning soft words of comfort and encouragement. He walked around her to stand at her back and lifted her tail to look at her progress. "She doesn't look to be ready yet. Needs to stretch more. I think the young'un decided to come before the mare's body was ready. We have to get her up and walk her around some to slow down the labor. Her body needs a chance to catch up with what it's trying to do."

Chester brushed his muzzle past my ear, flaring his nostrils to catch the scent of the mare in the next stall.

"Get a move on, Charley. I need your help."

I gave Chester's neck a pat before rounding the corner of the box and entering the stall. Eb had eased his way to the head of the mare where she lay stretched out in the straw.

"Bring in her halter and a lead," Eb said. "What's the matter with you boy? Wake up, you're not thinking.

He was right. I was fascinated, but scared for the mare. Both my mother and my aunt had died in childbirth, and I wondered if that could happen to Rose, too. I'd come to like the mare's plucky attitude since she came. I would hate to see her die. Eb lifted her head, and she rolled onto her chest. I slipped the halter over her nose and poll, and buckled the head-strap beneath her near ear. Eb pulled her nose in and to the off side. Rose stretched her forelegs out in front of her and leaned back on her haunch to lurch forward onto all fours.

"Put a rug on her and walk her out."

I drew her out of the stall and swung a heavy blanket over her back, and we began walking.

"Eb? Is she going to make it?" I asked before stepping out into the yard.

"Only time'll tell, but we'll give her the best shot at it we can."

Through the night, Rose and I walked in slow circles for about an hour, then would stop so's Eb could examine her. As the rim of the world turned from black to a deep blue and the stars disappeared one by one, Eb told me to take Rose to the trough for a few gulps of water, then return her to her stall. I removed the blanket and halter, and stepped out. We watched her circle a good fifteen minutes before she sank to her knees and rolled to her side.

In silence, we stood at the door of the box and watched her begin to strain. From the other side, Chester waited and watched along with us. A gush of discolored water issued forth, but no small hoof appeared.

"Water broke," Eb observed. "Hopefully it will be soon now."

Bird chatter bespoke the arrival of another day, and still we waited and watched poor Rose strain to give birth.

"Go wake Tilly, and ask her to bring warm water and soap."

As I turned to leave the barn, Rose got to her feet and began to circle the stall again.

"Hold it, Charley. Let's walk her some more since she's up. It'll give Tilly time to wake and prepare."

This time Eb covered her with the blanket, and I put her halter on.

"Walk her slow while I get my wife."

The birds sang as we circled the yard. Rose started to buckle at the knee intending to lie down, but I urged her on. I felt mean doing so, yet knew she'd be more comfortable in her stall. Eb and Tilly didn't take long to return. Tilly said she'd already been up and had water heating on the stove.

Eb waved me to bring Rose in again. I offered her water, which she refused. We walked into her stall, and I removed the blanket and halter as I had an hour ago. Again, Rose paced circles before lying flat in the straw to take up the matter of birthing once more. But before Rose began to strain, Eb was at her head, and Tilly approached her tail, bucket of warm water in hand. Tilly wet and soaped her hands all the way up to her elbows. I watched in fascination as she inserted her hand into the mare, her eyebrows pinching in pain each time the mare strained.

"Feel anything yet?" Ed asked.

Tilly only shook her head no.

Chester and I watched.

"Feel something now," Tilly grunted. "I think the foal's fetlock is bent down. Oh, for pity's sake horse, stop straining for a minute, will you."

I could see Tilly give a mighty push.

"Think I did it," she said, extracting her arm.

With Rose's next push, we saw a small rounded hoof and fetlock. The next time she strained, the second front hoof followed the first. Two more contractions brought a small nose covered with a film, which Tilly rolled away from the foal's nose. Not more'n a dozen pushes later delivered the entire foal. Tilly inserted her fingers into the baby's nose to make sure the passages were open. She rummaged in her apron pocket, removed two short pieces of string, tied one around the birthing cord near the foal's belly, and the other a few inches away from the first. Then she took her sewing scissors and separated mare and foal. Tilly slowly got to her feet and moved away from the newborn.

The mare lurched to her feet and turned around to sniff her new baby. Rose started licking the foal dry, and the baby raised its head, shaking it like a dog, its long ears flopping. Mother kept licking, and within minutes, her daughter scrambled to her balled feet. The filly's first unbalanced step caused her to ram into her mother and bounce back a step. She stretched her nose between her mother's front legs and made sucking sounds with her tongue and toothless upper gum. Rose licked the foal's coat with such force she sent the little one back into the straw, but the filly scrambled up for another go at finding food. Rose stepped past her baby's searching nose so the foal could nuzzle under the barrel of her belly for the nearest teat. The filly's tail gave a quick little wiggle as she started sucking down her first meal.

Eb and Tilly moved out of the stall to join me at the door. We were all grinning. Even Chester looked pleased now that it was all over. Eb put his arm around his wife and gave her a squeeze.

"Thanks for you help, honey." Patting me on the shoulder, he said, "Good job, son."

I gave Tilly a what-can-I-do look. Eb still didn't know my secret, and I weren't about to tell him. I was damned if I would chance losing this job, or the closeness of almost family we shared.

"Time to feed," Eb said, giving his wife another hug before letting her go.

"Guess you boys would like some breakfast, too, wouldn't you?"

"Sure would," we both answered.

"I'll give Charley a hand here to feed, and we'll be up in a couple of tail swishes."

"Now don't you wish you had a wife, so you could start some little ones of your own?" Eb asked me.

"Don't start, Eb. Don't start," I said, shaking my head.

13
Moving On

S ome years later, Eb put me in charge of the livery for about a week, saying he had business in Providence, Rhode Island. He took Tilly with him, leaving me with no one to dish up my meals or wash my clothes. Had to eat down the road at the Hatfield House and pay for my meals. That cook weren't as good as our Tilly for sure. It's a terrible day when you got to pay for food not as tasty as what you're used to. Course, I've had much worse since then and been damn glad to get it. Guess I was a mite spoiled back then.

All I remember of that week was feeling like I was the center of a taffy pull. Andy had moved on by then, but we had two stableboys to do the pitch and shovel work while I ran the schedule. Other than a green driver having an accident with the buckboard, all went well as I remember. The boys did most of the saddling and hitching, and, so's I would be on hand, I didn't hire out my driving services.

Felt like a Bantam rooster ready to crow, I was so damn proud of myself that week.

Course, when Eb and Tilly returned at noon on Monday, I had the wind kicked out of me. The pair of them arrived looking pleased as a span of just fed horses.

Tilly put her arm around my shoulders and gave me a hug and a quick peck on the temple before heading into the house.

"Anything go wrong while I been gone?" Eb asked.

"Over all, things went pretty well," I said.

"What happened?"

"Green driver caught the rear wheel of the buckboard and broke two spokes," I said with a grimace, knowing one of his rants was coming on. I mouthed every word Eb spoke as we entered the barn.

"How many times have I got to tell you to put Plodding Bob in the shafts when you got a green driver?" Eb said, speaking of the nursemaid horse that had replaced old Chester after he'd passed on.

"The ancients had Plodding Bob out and this guy came in after they were gone," I said, referring to the Eisley sisters who were both nearing the hundred-year mark by then. "Charged the man for damages. Took the wheel down to the wheelwright, got it fixed. Nobody was hurt and everything's fine. I handled it."

Eb grunted. "Did good. Was that all?"

"Yup."

"Tilly and I bought an inn and livery whilst in Providence."

"You what?!"

"The Franklin House Inn and What Cheer Stables behind. Nice setup."

"Why? You got a good business going here."

"Time to expand. There's big money to be made down in that town," Eb said, turning away to inspect the condition of the horses and barn.

Well, what about me? Son of a bitch. Were they going to up and leave me here without a job? All this time I been working for Eb, helping him build this business, and he's going to leave me here high and dry. I had always looked down my nose at the other liveries hereabouts. Was I now going to have to go hat in hand to them asking for a job, or was I to be a leftover for the new owner?

A rental returned, and instead of calling for the boys, I took care of unhitching the horse myself while Eb talked with the customer. I almost rolled the buckboard over the driver's kid who didn't have the sense God gave a jackass to get the hell out of the way. Then I ripped the harness off the gelding, upsetting him to the point he was prancing in the crossties.

"Damn it, Charley, what the hell is the matter with you?" Eb said. "Get your head on straight, boy. You're worse than a fractious colt." Then he stomped out, mumbling to himself and wagging his head.

Boy? Though I was now well past 25-years old, he still called me boy. Who the hell did he think I was? Didn't he realize how much work I did? I walked the gelding till he calmed, then I dusted down the buckboard. All the while arguments warred within me. Since I hadn't been sure when Eb and Tilly would return that day, I hadn't scheduled myself for any driving work. To keep busy, I did work the stableboys were paid to do.

True, I had worked hard for Eb. Helped him build up this livery and all. But on the other hand, he'd spent many a morning teaching me to drive and ride, so that I would become a capable whip. Maybe he figured we were even. I guess I allowed myself to imagine I was one of the Balch family since I never had a family of my own till they took me in. Felt as though I'd found my place. I'd gotten comfortable.

Shouldn't have.

At dinner that night, Eb had on that purse-lipped, trying-not-to-smile look.

Tilly stood at the stove, fist on hip, braid swishing across her back, stirring chicken and dumplings, my favorite. The smell of that woman's cooking could make my mouth water a mile away. And she always made plenty, never skimped.

"Damn glad to have you home Tilly," I said. "That Hatfield House cook don't come close to your cooking."

"That's mighty nice of you to say," she said over her shoulder. "I guess you missed me then, did you?"

"Sure did. Course, I didn't miss your husband none," I said as a way of seeming all right with what was happening. Not that I felt that way exactly, but during the afternoon I'd come to grips with the fact that Eb had always been fair with me. Figured he wouldn't start cutting me out now.

"Huh." Eb snorted. "I think we ought to leave this smart-mouthed barn rat behind when we go Tilly. What do you think?"

"Now, Eb," Tilly said, turning from the stove with her lopsided teasing smile. "Who's going to do justice to my chicken and dumplings if we don't take him?"

"You mean you want me to go along?"

"Unless you'd rather stay and try to find work at one of them other stables they got in this town." Eb chuckled at his own joke. I weren't the only one who thought we were better than the others by a dozen horse lengths.

Since Worcester was growing, Eb was able to quickly sell the house and barn, and some of the horses of lesser quality, keeping the best for our new livery in Providence. While Eb made a couple of trips with Tilly to move their household items and as many of our best stock as practical for each trip, I kept things running in Worcester. I moved with the last of our equipment and animals.

224 Benefit Street, when I finally rode in, was to my liking.

Course, Tilly had already taken over the Franklin House and had started drawing patrons on the strength of her cooking alone, though when she showed me through the place, the rest of the Inn was neat and clean and welcoming—just like Tilly.

The What Cheer Stables was one of the oldest established businesses of Providence. Eb was lucky to buy it. Got the inn and livery at a good price, too, from what he told me. The past owner had gotten old, his wife had died, and he didn't have any sons to take over, so he had to let the place go. The barn could hold seventy-five horses and our full line of carriages, hacks, landaus and the like. The stable was well lit and ventilated, a must when horses are to be kept healthy and happy, but not as clean as Eb and I made it in short order.

The stableman's room weren't any bigger than the one I had back in Worcester, but it was done up a little nicer. Instead of plank walls like the horse stalls, my room was plastered and painted, keeping most of the multi-legged crawlers from bunking in with me.

As for the three stableboys that had worked there, we had to weed out two layabouts, train the remaining one into shape, and hire another. I missed Andy. He'd always been eager to learn and would put his hand to anything Eb or I asked of him. Not these boys though, they had to be instructed every step of the way, but they came along and life took up a day-to-day rhythm that had the business humming along. Business got so good Eb invested over a thousand dollars in a brand new Concord coach from Abbot Downing over in New Hampshire. It was a beauty.

The Concord coach was the finest ever made. Coach bodies solidly built and reinforced with iron bands rested upon five-hundred pound, multiple-layered, oxen-hide straps called thoroughbraces. 'Braces make it easier on the horses when starting or stopping, not so much weight to stop dead as with springs. Course, some of the ladies and gents got a little seasick from the swinging and swaying that the thoroughbraces allowed, but it was good for our horses, and when you're in the horse business, you got to keep the stock healthy and happy. A driver don't want to deal with a cranky span of wheelers 'cause they ain't comfortable stopping three, maybe four thousand pounds of coach, passengers and baggage, let me tell you.

They say that the Concord Coaches didn't break down, they wore out, and I would have to say that's true. I helped wear out more'n a few in my time and never had anything need repairing whilst on the road.

Eb and I pulled together a beautiful team of six matching blood-bays, buying them a span at a time here and there. It weren't easy to match teams of horses in work temperament much less in the more unusual blood-bay color we wanted, but we did.

The first span we got were the twelve-hundred-pound wheelers, which we bought off a breeder north of town. This, the largest team of the six-horse hitch, were harnessed closest to the driver and had the work of holding back the weight of the coach as it stopped and so had to be large and well muscled.

Within two weeks, we found a swing team weighing in at about eleven-hundred a piece at an auction, and the thousand-pound leaders trotted into our stables pulling a light carriage and a frazzled driver who wanted nothing more'n to be rid of them. Fractious, he called them, but Eb and I knew better. The driver was greener than grass and didn't know how to handle a team. We got a bargain on those two.

On a fine summer's day, the copper-bright coats of our six-horse hitch would glisten in the sun, their black manes and tails waving in the breeze as they trotted down the pike, their black legs covering the ground with pride, their black-tipped ears erect. I loved riding up in the driver's box above them. Felt like a king up there guiding that team on one of them tallyho parties people would schedule for a community dance or the like. We made quite a show, my team and me.

While I'd been working for Eb, he'd give me a raise in pay each time I learned to drive an additional span of horses, or took on more responsibility with the business. Most I saved but for buying clothes and books, and a snort or two down at the pub once in a while. Though early on, I got me a pair of fancy beaded gloves for driving that I wore all the time no matter the chore I was working. They hid my small hands and kept them warm much of the time, but more importantly, the leather gave me a better grip on the ribbons. And when handling six of them, each pair with a team on the other end, a driver can't have a mouth slip away from his contact, or all hell could break loose.

Over the years, Eb's exacting lessons always stood me in good stead, helping me to establish a reputation for safety and reliability. When old folks needed a driver, they asked for me. When a body needed hauling done of a fragile nature, they often asked for me. When groups of people my age planned a tallyho party, they scheduled me, some of them changing the date of their party if I was already booked. Eb rented me out a time or two to drive for the rich when their coachman was sick and they'd come to ask for my services.

I was damn proud of myself.

And as always happens, to me at least, when I get that cocky feeling, shortly after, I find myself kissing the ground.

One bitter January night, I'd been hired to drive four couples to a dance in Pawtucket. Though the sun had tried to burn off the oncoming haze, the sky had grown a thicker ceiling of gray clouds all afternoon and the temperature kept pulling down the mercury. I figured the snow would hold off until early the next morning, so I picked up my party at the door of Tilly's Inn, as I called the Franklin House. They had already enjoyed dinner, and were in a jolly mood as we headed out of town. They weren't going far, only about five miles is all, though some of it was hilly.

As we left town, I clucked my six-up into a ground-covering trot. I could tell from the frequent laughter behind me that the celebration had already started. About halfway to their stop they started singing popular tunes. Old Rosin the Beau was their first and my favorite. I figured they had brought a little something to nip along with them, 'cause it's been my experience that women'll burst into song with little encouragement, but men generally keep their mouths shut. Not this time though, and that was fine with me. I enjoyed listening to them, hummed along to the ones I knew between sweet-talking my team. The singing kept me company.

We pulled up to the door of the dance in under an hour. I climbed down to swing the coach door open for my passengers.

"When you expect to leave, sir?" I asked.

"Give us three hours, Charley," came the reply.

I moved my team down the street past the fire barrel and the other waiting drivers, and brought them to a standstill off to the side. Now, not every livery blanketed their horses for a layover on a cold winter's night, but Eb and I always did. Ignoring the warmth and camaraderie of the fire, and the possibility of being asked too many questions about myself that I wouldn't answer, I climbed back into the driver's box to wait. A breeze picked up, ruffling the long hairs on my team. I shrugged deeper into my greatcoat thinking on the nice tip I'd most likely get for this night's work. Shards of icy snow danced and swirled on the wind. My hands began to ache with the cold, but I held my reins and talked to my team keeping them company, reassuring them and myself that it wouldn't be too long till we could trot on home.

Though the smell of the fire barrel and the sting of the icy snow tempted me to give up my usual safety measure of standoffishness for the evening, I ignored the urge as best I could. Didn't want no truck with nosey questioners and prying eyes.

Two and a half hours later, I uncovered my team, shook the snow off, folded and stowed the horse blankets in the front boot. Once more, I climbed to the box to drive around the block and pick up my party. I brought the team to a standstill, the coach door opposite the community hall door just as Eb had taught me.

"Make a show of it, Charley," he'd say to me. "People want a safe ride, but they love a good show. Makes them look and feel important."

I know I was on time and not too early, but no one came out. I waited, stiff as an icicle.

"Hey, move on up there," another driver yelled from behind me. "This is my fare."

I glanced at the group coming out the door and tried to see whether my group was behind them. Couldn't see a thing, so I got my team in hand and headed around the block at a walk figuring to give the coach behind me enough time to load up and move out. When I pulled up as I had before, there was still no sign of my party. I pulled out my pocket watch; it'd been four hours since I dropped them off. Though I didn't generally go asking for my fares, it was late, and I began to wonder whether they'd checked for me while the other coach was loading. I clambered down from the box and knocked on the door, inquiring as to whether my fare was ready to depart. The warm air that breathed past me when the door opened felt so wonderful my eyes teared with yearning. The man closed the door with a stately deliberate motion after telling me he would inquire. He came back ten minutes later with the news that my fare would depart shortly. My team stamped their hooves at the cold.

I waited.

By the time my fare stepped out the door, I couldn't stop shivering. I didn't even try to get off the box to open the door as I usually did, though I could hear Eb's voice in my head: "You want people to tell their friends how good a ride you gave them? Be nice. You want a fat tip? Be nice." Their three hours had turned into five. No, I weren't feeling the least bit kindly, and I weren't going to be nice toward them inconsiderate sons of bitches.

I no longer had any feeling in my fingers or feet. I couldn't feel the reins. I couldn't open my hands. I realized I would have to ask for help to drive my team. My hands, stiff as they were, made it impossible to drive safely. I couldn't move my index fingers. They were past aching. I couldn't feel the reins of the leaders my dead hands clutched.

Another coach pulled up behind me as my fare was loading up. "Hey, that you, Charley?" a voice called over.

"Yeah, that you Liberty?" I called back with a glance over my shoulder at the struttingest damn peacock that ever sat a box, Liberty Childs. He climbed from the off side of the coach to open the door and assist the ladies in boarding. "What? You out for a joy ride this evening?" I asked after he'd closed his coach door, jutting my chin at the driver still in the box. "Or have you finally been taken down a notch or two and put in your proper place as a footman?"

Damn it all. Why did it have to be him of all the drivers in Providence? I shook my head.

"Never happen," he called back. Liberty climbed into the box before I swallowed my pride enough to call him over.

"Hey, Liberty. Got a minute?" I jerked my head that he should come to me.

"You going to move this sorry excuse for a coach, or do I have to move it for you?" Liberty said, standing on the hub of my coach.

"I need your help. My hands froze. Can't drive."

He gave me a long searching look. "Yeah, sure Charley," he said without his usual arrogance. "Just give me a minute to speak to Sam."

When Liberty climbed aboard a minute later, I handed off the lead span, but held onto the swing and wheeler teams.

"Geez, Charley, you take up most of the bench," Liberty said, wiggling his butt. "You're built like a block of ice, don't ya know."

"Ain't no need to get insulting. Get up my beauties." I shouted. The team stepped out taking Liberty unawares. "You going to drive them leaders or not?"

Liberty grabbed up the slack in the reins. I could tell he weren't going to have them in hand in time to start the turn.

"Gee," I yelled, starting the team into a right turn down the next intersection.

"Damn, you in a hurry to get back to that stable of yours or what?"

"Course I am. I'm cold, you jackass. Been sitting out here five hours waiting for my fare."

"Well, why didn't you get on down off your fat ass and stand at the fire barrel? That's what they're there for, don't ya know."

Shit! Just what I didn't want to get into. "My leaders were feeling a might fractious, so I figured to stay—"

"So you do a dumb fool thing like going and freezing those damn small hands of yours. You could loose fingers doing that, don't ya know. Then where would you be?"

"Oh, for the love of god, give it up, Liberty."

"Those hands of yours look pretty damn small even when you're wearing those boss gloves of yours. If you wasn't so ugly a body might think you was a girl or something."

I gave him one of my you-stupid-or-something looks, my heart thumping to beat hell. "You're one damn insulting son of a bitch tonight. It ain't right to kick a man when he's down."

"S'pose not," he said, turning his attention back to the lead team to guide them through the last turn out of Pawtucket.

The drive back to town was torture. Though we took the five mile drive back to town at a swinging trot, it seemed like a hundred miles having to listen to Liberty and his "don't ya knows" every step of the way. The only relief being that my stature weren't mentioned again.

I don't know which hurt more, the pain in my fists, or the pain in my heart at having Liberty help me drive. But I do know the fear of getting found out got me to sweating. My pride was rumpled to beat hell, having to listen to him crow about helping me out of a spot of trouble, and knowing he'd repeat the story to every living person in Providence whether they wanted to hear it or not.

To top off the most miserable night of my life, the generous tip the party offered as an apology for being late in coming out of the dance, I felt had to go to Liberty for helping me out. Damn. Insult to injury.

I made sure that it never happened again. Thereafter, I sided up to any handy fire barrel to warm myself regardless of who huddled next to me, or any questions asked. I thought out answers to questions that I imagined might catch me off guard and had them ready in mind each time I stepped up to a group of men. From that night on my coach was driven by me and only me. I learned the hard way that bringing trouble on myself could come from any quarter. This time it'd been my damn small hands and my aloof habits, what would it be next time?

As it turned out, it was my hands again.

But years passed before they drew attention I couldn't get rid of.

14
Matchmaking Men

B eing female in the world of men weren't easy. The bloody time of the month being one, and taking a piss without an outhouse at hand was another. I had a story ready to explain why I was squatting if anyone found me peeing. Figured I would tell them someone had cut me when I was a kid, chopped everything off and left me for dead. Luckily, that never needed explaining.

It was the blood that gave me away, though I didn't know it right off.

As a general rule, I only relieved myself in the outhouse at home. Felt it safer that way. But as with all rules, general or otherwise, they get broke. Seemed when I was in the female way, I always had to piss more'n usual, and sometimes I would have to relieve myself elsewhere. It was one of those times that brought about my downfall.

Drivers size up one another more thoroughly than any other profession I know or ever heard of. A driver had to earn his reputation every day. Driving while neighing at the wind, as some of us called being drunk, was frowned upon, as was driving too fast in town, not being on time, cutting a fellow driver off, wheel locks, poor treatment of horses, too much whip, discourtesy to clients and the like. Each of us sized up every other driver, and as is human nature, spread the word about the abilities of those who called themselves whips.

Thus, I'd heard about Dom Ramirez before I saw him.

"He's a little fast on the road."

"Sees himself a charmer."

"Sweet-talks the ladies."

"Generally runs a little late."

All in all, not too bad, I thought. Probably driving a little fast and running a little late 'cause he doesn't know where he's going yet. I generally slacken the rein till I've had an opportunity to size them up myself.

Ran into him the first time coming out the outhouse behind the Peddler's Rest over Cranston way and didn't have time to exchange pleasantries.

"Domingos Ramirez," he said, sticking his hand out for a shake. My gloved response was brief but firm. "You are Parkey, yes? I hear about you."

"Yup," I replied and drew away. The man's black eyes had dropped to our brief handclasp before flying up to my eyes again. I don't know what it was that put me on edge, but those black eyes seemed to bore right through me. Didn't like that I couldn't see their black centers. "Got a fare heading out," I said, and walked past him back to my rig.

Saw him a few times here and there, but avoided looking at him. Didn't want to draw him on. Only gave him a polite salute with my whip when he'd cry out, "Howdy, Parkey," in passing.

Almost ran into him coming out of Pierce's General Store one day. Before I stepped out the door, I looked into those black eyes of his, and felt my heart start to thump like I'd been scared sudden-like. I noticed we were at eye level before I stepped out the door. He stood about three inches taller than me, making him five foot ten or so. I could feel my cheeks start to redden and moved on with a curt nod. I was known around for not being much of a talker, so I hoped he'd size me up as unfriendly as most did. By the time my heart slowed, I was about a block away and disgusted with myself for reacting like some brainless damn female.

Next time I saw Ramirez, his wave drew my eyes to him. He stood on the walk smiling up at me as I drove by. Damned if my heart didn't start slamming in my chest and my cheeks redden again.

The more I wanted to stay away from the son of a bitch the more it seemed I saw him everywhere. Got on my nerves.

Generally, Sunday was mine, and I liked to ride out with a packed lunch and a good book. I had a few places I liked to go where I could sit back and enjoy a peaceful spot, read a while, maybe take a snooze. There was one spot I liked to go swimming through the heat of the summer, a quiet place beside a small lake surrounded by a natural stand of pitch pine and sugar maple with a scarlet oak here and there. Lots of brush, some with thorns and fruit, the rest grew leaves and hid birds. Had a special spot where I could keep an eye on everything without being seen. Course, the only thing that had ever come near was a pair of red fox that were chasing each other. Just the same though, I liked my privacy and didn't want to be seen, especially when swimming, which I did buck-naked.

It had been a warm summer that year, and what with the bindings hugging my chest, it seemed twice as hot. I visited my cooling off spot every Sunday it weren't raining. This one particular Sunday the sun hung in a still sky. Humid air made clothes and spirits wilt without a breath of air to turn a leaf or a blade of grass and give a body relief. The perfect day for a long swim.

Tilly wrapped me up a chicken leg and small loaf of bread while I picked up a jar of beer from the inn's wet room. I threw a saddle on old Plodding Bob and headed out. It was a matter of about four miles, and I took it easy. After all, this was the gelding's day off, too.

I unsaddled and hobbled the horse in a small clearing sur-rounded with tall sugar maple and oak where he could graze and get to water. As soon as I saw him settled, I hurried to my special spot, a copse of young trees with a dense thicket that grew right up to the waterline. Over the time I had spent there, I'd worked a narrow path through the thicket to the water's edge, with a small area cleared out in the middle where I could lie in the sun to dry without being seen. And, generally, by the time I reached the water's edge, I had shed all my clothes, draped them on the bushes, and was ready to jump in.

To say I dove in wouldn't ring true. I ain't a good swimmer, never learned how. But from experience I knew the water was not deep near the shore and out a little ways, so I would throw myself in and float around a bit, bobbing under the water with the fish to cool my head. As long as I could touch bottom, I was happy.

First time I got in over my head, I bucked and plunged like a scared weanling. Went under a time or two, got water down my nose and mouth, but with all the thrashing I managed to get my feet under me and wade to shore. I'd seen dogs paddle in water and decided to give their way a try. Practiced over firm footing till I got the knack of it; thereafter, when I wandered out of my depth, I would paddle like a dog back to safety slick as you please.

That day, I had cooled off and was headed back to my thicket. As I rose from the water, a pair of boots faced me at water's edge.

They weren't my boots.

My eyes flew upward and locked with a pair of black eyes crinkling over an ear-to-ear grin. I let out a squawk and ducked back into the water, covering by breasts with my arms. I could feel the heat of a blush redden my cheeks.

"These yours?" Dom Ramirez asked, holding up my clothes in one fist just out of reach and extending his other hand. "I help you, signorina? You slip?"

"Get the fuck out of here."

"Not nice for signorina to use this word."

"Give me my damn clothes."

"Come get them," he said, wiggling his black brows. Straight white teeth peeked out from under a thick black mustache in need of trimming.

The teasing look on his face had turned downright lusty, causing an aching, longing sensation that I'd only felt upon waking from one of my strange dreams. It weren't unpleasant, but it made my knees feel weak.

I stared him down. I had a way of looking at men that generally brought them up short real fast.

"You win," he said. "Come out, we talk." He dropped my clothes in a heap and walked out of the thicket without looking back.

I crept out of the water and peered through the brush to see where he had gone. He stood outside the copse facing away from me. I tried dressing quickly, but it didn't seem to work. My arms and legs refused to work together. My clothes dragged along my wet skin, catching and making me loose my balance. I crashed around in the brush as though I were a wild horse trying to break free. When I finally got my clothes on, I bent over to rake fingers through my hair to get rid of the bits of twig and leaves caught in it during my fight with the bushes.

"So what the hell do you want?" I asked, walking out of the thicket behind him.

"Be friends."

"Bullshit."

"I figured you for a female. I wanted to see. The others, they going to laugh when I tell them the signor Charley be a signorina. They not believe."

"You tell a single soul, I'll kill you." I looked him straight in the eye, giving him my special look. No blush flooded my cheeks now. We were talking my life and livelihood here, and I'd worked too damn long and hard to have him foul it up for me.

Ramirez stared back.

"You understand?" I continued to scowl at him through slitted eyes.

He nodded agreement.

"How'd you know?" I needed to know how I'd given myself away. My life as it was depended on my ability to talk, act, and think like a man.

"Fresh blood on the outhouse bench," he said, "and your small hands.

"Outhouse?"

"In Cranston, remember? You were coming out. We shook hands."

"Damn."

"I watch you. I see you stay away from the other drivers. I see how you look at me. You timido. You get red in face, you hurry away."

I couldn't look at him, I was too embarrassed. He lifted my chin with the tip of his finger.

"Why you wear men's clothes? Why you not married with babies?"

"Like being able to do what I want, when I want. And I don't much like the way men treat women."

Ramirez nodded as though he understood, yet I doubted he did.

"I love horses, and I'm one of the best whips hereabouts. A woman can't do what I've done without acting like a man."

"But a driver? Hell, you need be strong, much muscle and grit," Ramirez said, flexing the muscles in his arms and shoulders. "You need strong hands."

"No, it takes brains, a little horse sense, and respect for your team."

"What your familia say?"

"Got no family. Don't need none."

Ramirez sat there looking at me through eyes so black they made me feel he could see right into my mind. I couldn't gauge what he was thinking as I could with others that had lighter colored eyes.

"What about you? Got family?" I asked, hoping to head the conversation off in another direction. Didn't want to give too much of myself away, or give him ammunition if he decided to tell others my little secret.

"My wife, she die. She no give me children. I come to America with my many brothers and sisters," he said, holding up first five, than six fingers. "Cinco sisters and seis brothers. I first child in my familia."

"Sounds crowded. What's this lingo you speak?"

"Lingo?"

"How you talk, familia, cinco, seis. What's that from?"

"Portuguese."

I nodded at his answer, but I guess my face showed my confusion, for he explained further.

"Me familia come from Portugal. We come to America to be free."

Maybe he did understand better than I thought.

"You good driver," he said. "Many say you best."

"Aim to be."

"You no talk much signorina?"

"Get too chatty, and I could give myself away. Can't afford to do that."

"Ever try being a woman?"

"Nope."

"Could be fun," he said, wiggling those dark brows again.

"Doubt it." Wished the hell my heart wouldn't go bouncing around in my chest when he did that. I could feel my cheeks redden.

"You no wonder when you take a fare to dance? You no want to be in coach?"

My quick glance and reddening cheeks gave him the answer he was obviously looking for.

"Ah ha, you do," he said with a grin. "We try it, you and me."

I shook my head no.

"Sure, we go where no one know us."

My next look lingered on his eyes.

"I get buckboard take us to dance. We have fun."

His eyes spoke mischief while his rich, lilting voice wheedled its way under my defenses.

"We go to dinner like other folks."

"When?" I said, wishing in the next thought that I hadn't asked, but had just said no.

"I keep my ears open. I let you know," he said with a winning grin. "We have good time you will see." With that, he stood to leave. "I be in touch, Charley."

"Remember what I said about keeping my secret under your hat. Say one word, and you're a dead man. I promise you."

A few minutes later, I heard him ride away. I moseyed back to the edge of the lake and stared at my reflection. My large gray eyes asked why he would want to go someplace with me? My big ears still stuck out, peeking through my shoulder-length hair at odd times. My wide jaw reminded me of that fighter I saw back in Cumberton when I was a kid. His head had been shaved, which made his jaw look wider than the top of his head. I sure weren't pretty like some of them girls I saw. I gazed at the water in a dazed state when it hit me.

I didn't know how to dance.

What was I going to wear?

It took three weeks, and a short squabble with Ramirez who figured I was backing out of our agreement, before the plan, as I thought of it, started taking shape.

"They have dance on Saturday," Ramirez said in a rough but hushed voice after pulling me out behind our livery late one evening. He stood so close, I could smell the garlic and beer he had had for supper.

"Well, it'll look pretty damn stupid if we both show up wearing pants," I said. "Can't just go trotting off on a shopping trip. I work six days a week like you do, and every shop is closed on the day I have off. "

"You tell me when you get dress. We go then." Pointing a finger at my nose, he said, "You make me fool, I make you fool."

"You make a fool of me, I kill you," I replied, pointing my finger at his nose as though it were a gun.

A week later, I got a fare to Tipton, which luckily had a dress shop. I had a bit of a layover while my fare completed her business, so I stood down the street a ways from the shop, leaning against the wall of the general store watching the goings on in town to make sure no one knew me. When I felt it was safe to make my move, I returned to the carriage and took off my hat, vest, and gloves, hoping to look less like who and what I was before making my way to Miss Sally's Emporium for Ladies.

"Can I help you, sir," a bright-eyed young woman said. She hurried toward me with a startled look and an outstretched arm, as though she was about to herd me out the door.

"You Miss Sally?" I asked.

She nodded her assent while blocking me from entering further.

"I wish to purchase a dress and such that goes with it," I said, hoping I didn't sound as stupid as I thought I did.

"Excuse me?" Her eyes widened.

We both had to move out of the way when two old biddies insisted on leaving. I say insisted 'cause they scooted toward the door like a couple of hens tst-tsting, and eyeing me up and down as though the proprietor had allowed vermin in the door.

"Oh, Mrs. Riddle, Mrs. Watson, won't you please wait a moment."

The lips of the two women pursed tighter than their reticule strings.

"Mrs. Riddle, the corset you ordered came with today's post."

Mrs. Watson gave Miss Sally a look that would've stopped a runaway team cold. I assumed it was for the mention of a corset in what they thought to be mixed company. I damn near burst out laughing at the old hen. Miss Sally wilted as the door snapped shut, cutting my laughter to an inner groan. I had probably lost her a valuable customer by walking into her shop. Why the hell did I ever agree to this tomfoolery in the first place?

"It's for my twin sister," I said.

"What?" Miss Sally appeared to be trying to pull her attention back to me, but was not meeting with much success. Her brow remained wrinkled with worry over Mrs. Watson leaving.

"It's for my twin sister's birthday. We're built the same."

Miss Sally's eyes slid up and down my frame, pausing at my chest and hips.

"Yes, of course," she said with a small shake of her head. "This way please."

She showed me what she had available ready-made.

I pointed to the one that caught my eye. "I think she'd like that one."

"I think that should fit," she said, holding the dress to my shoulders and eyeing my chest and hips again.

"She has more up here than I do," I said, patting my chest with both hands.

"I thought as much," she said matter-of-factly.

"Got shoes?"

I tried the shoes on, but their higher heels convinced me that I didn't want them. I would end up breaking my fool neck right in the middle of the whole damn show. Figured I would shine up my regular boots and since the dress would mostly cover them, I would get by. I didn't expect to ever do such a fool thing but once in this life, and weren't about to waste a pile of money on a pair of shoes I would never wear again.

"Wrap up that dress and whatever under things that go with it." I paid Miss Sally and left her emporium taking a roundabout way back to my horse and buggy, careful not to draw attention to myself.

With this dress, I was corralled and heading for the chute. That or moving to the other side of the world. Hadn't decided yet.

15
Decisions

W here?!"
"Tipton," Ramirez repeated when I told him that I had bought a dress. "Saturday night."

"Shit!"

"It been near a month now. No more. You got dress, we go."

On Wednesday, I asked Eb for Saturday night off. He gave me a long hard look before his eyes lit with understanding and a grin spread across his mouth.

"Never you mind," I said, forestalling the questions that were sure to fly fast and furious once started.

"Help yourself to a buggy, if you like, so you can pick up your lady friend," he said. "I'll take the fare I scheduled for you."

"No, no, I'll take the fare. I didn't realize you scheduled a run for me." Relief flooded though me. Now I had a reason not to go. Surely, Ramirez would understand. Business comes first.

"No, Charley, I insist. You go. I'll drive the fare." Eb had that bullish look on his face that told me no argument would change matters.

"Thanks," I said. The dry tone of my voice must have confused Eb 'cause he gave me a questioning look.

I took my Saturday night bath early and snuck out the back of the stable, skirting the main street of town until I reached the nearly tumbled-down barn where I'd told Ramirez to pick me up. I got there about a half an hour early so's I could put on the dress and petticoats I'd brought with me. Didn't want anyone to see me dressed as a female. I was already wearing the chemise and stockings under my usual box-pleated shirt and belted trousers. I'd polished my boots for the occasion, and Ramirez would have to help me button up what I couldn't reach on the dress. Another reason not to wear woman's clothes; buttons down the back. What sense did that make?

Although nervousness had eaten a hole in my belly all week, there was a part of me that was excited about the evening. Deep down, I hoped Ramirez would think me pretty in my new dress.

I combed my hair and pulled it back with a black ribbon. Tilly had been so excited when I told her I was going to attend a dance that she insisted on seeing me in my dress. We arranged to meet in my room late Thursday night. She helped me into the dress and did up all the buttons. She pulled a mirror and a ribbon from her apron pocket, and showed me how to tie my hair back and arrange a few hairs in front of my ears to soften my wide jaw. When all done up, I looked more feminine than I thought possible.

With the exception of a few buttons that needed doing, I was ready for Ramirez. I looked in the hand-held mirror I'd brought along and pulled a few hairs loose from my ribbon. My gray eyes looked as pensive as I felt, and my cheeks appeared bloodless. I chewed my lips and pinched my cheeks till they reddened like Tilly had suggested.

I began to pace and found my strides shortened by the mere fact that I wore a dress. The full skirts and whispering petticoats made me feel pretty. That was a first.

I heard a horse approaching at a brisk trot and threw my everyday clothes and the mirror into the dress box. The door creaked on its rusty hinges. I turned to see Ramirez enter.

"Well, look at you," he said. Admiration brightened his eyes as they slid up and down my body. I felt like a horse being appraised at auction.

"Like it?"

"You look pretty, Charley," he said, looking at me for a long moment. "This name no work for tonight."

"Charlotte is my given name." It sounded strange on my tongue. I hadn't been called by my true name in so long. It brought back memories of Aunt Martha and my life before the orphanage. "Could you do these few buttons for me? I can't reach," I said, turning my back to him to hide the sudden watering of my eyes that came with the thought of Aunt Martha, and the wish that she were here to see me off to my first dance.

"I like Charlotte. It sound pretty," he said. He pushed my hair to the side and did up my buttons. His warm breath on my exposed neck gave me a shiver. With a smile and a sweeping gesture toward the door, he said, "We go."

I climbed to the driver's seat and picked up the reins.

"No tonight, Charlotte."

"Sorry," I mumbled. The blood rushed to my cheeks as I slid over to the passenger side. "I'm used—"

"I know," he said with a smile. "Tonight not be easy for you. Watch the others. Do what they do. I help you."

I smiled my gratitude for his understanding.

"A little nip—to relax?" he said, pulling a small flask out of his pocket and passing it to me.

Though not one to drink regular-like, I took a long swallow and felt the liquid warmth spread through me, loosening some of the knots of worry and tension that had been gnawing at me for most of the week. Ramirez took a swig and pocketed the flask.

On the way, we compared recent work schedules and a tale or two of our best and worst fares. Though we didn't name names in the telling, we each picked out who the other was talking about. The silence that cropped up now and then felt comfortable.

We stopped to eat at a small place before we got to Tipton and had a delicious steak dinner with mashed potatoes, honeyed carrots, bread and butter, and finished it off with a wedge of apple pie and coffee. Not too bad in comparison to Tilly's cooking.

Over coffee, we fought about who was going to pay for dinner. I lost. But only 'cause I'd left my money in my pants pocket back at the barn where I had dressed. Ramirez soothed my ruffled spirits by telling me that the man always pays the bill.

By the time we arrived in Tipton, I had lost the huge knot in my belly, but wouldn't you know, the first people I laid eyes on as we walked into the dance were the old biddies that skedaddled out of Miss Sally's Emporium the day I bought my dress.

Mrs. Riddle and Mrs. Watson had their heads together, no doubt jawing about some poor soul they didn't like. Leastways that's what I took their sour expressions to mean. When their eyes widened at the sight of me, my heart sank. It weren't recognition that spread across their pinched faces at the sight of me but self-righteousness. It took me a minute to reason why.

"You the brightest flower here," Ramirez whispered in my ear.

He was right. The men and matrons were dressed in black and white; the young ladies wore soft colors. And there I stood, decked out in red. Shit.

Ramirez moved me to the side as another group entered the room behind us. I wanted like hell to skedaddle out the door and head for home. He must have sensed my mind 'cause he whispered in my ear, "No, no, no. We stay."

"I ain't no coward," I said, straightening my shoulders.

"Good. We sit." With his hand on my back, he guided me to a table in a dark corner where another couple was already seated. My boots scuffed the floor, weighted down with embarrassment. Though someone had blown out the candle on the table, I recognized the man, but not the woman with him. He hauled freight out of Providence. We'd never spoken. I'd seen him around and heard that he was of a surly nature, heavy on the whip.

"I get us something to drink," Ramirez said as soon as my bottom hit the chair. He placed his hand on my shoulder to keep me seated and gave it a firm squeeze. "I be back. You folks need something?" he asked the others at the table.

"Naw, we're good, thanks."

I felt the eyes of the other couple upon me as we sat there. My gaze floated all over the room looking for other people I might know, or worse, who might know me. A film of sweat broke out on my upper lip.

"Hey, do I know you?" the man at my table asked.

I clamped my teeth together and swung my gaze to meet his. "Don't think so," I lied.

"Can't recall where I seed ya, but I never forgit a face."

"Name's Charlotte," I said. A trickle of sweat slid down between my breasts as I shook my head.

"Sam," he replied. "And this here is Ann."

I nodded at both, wishing myself back in my room at the What Cheer.

"Hey, Sam," Ramirez said, taking the seat beside me. "Not know you in the dark. You hiding?" He pulled the flask from the pocket of his coat and added a liberal dollop to the glasses of punch he'd brought to the table.

"Relaxing," Sam said.

Ramirez placed a glass before me. I downed the punch, barely noticing its sweetness, but eagerly embracing the numbing warmth of the whiskey.

"Another?"

I nodded. He pushed the chair back that he'd scooped under himself. I put my hand on his arm. "Skip the punch, just pour," I said.

"Drinking your courage?" he said, spilling a double shot into the party glass with a smirk. "Have all you want. Got more in the buggy."

I gave him a wry smile and sipped from my glass. While Ramirez talked with Sam and Ann, I watched the dancing. Everyone looked to be having a good time. A few of the young men would turn the wrong way during a reel and bump into a woman and apologize as their partner drew them back into the dance. Though the interruption caused the couples to lose step, no one showed the slightest anger. In fact, as the evening wore on, everyone good-naturedly pushed the confused dancers into step.

"Where do I know her from?" Sam asked Ramirez as though I weren't there. "I seed her before, but can't remember where."

"Charlotte is visiting from Worcester. You haul there often?" Ramirez asked. I could have kissed him for that.

The Monongahela whiskey he'd brought numbed my belly and spread through my arms and legs, making me feel as relaxed and supple as well-oiled leather. Ramirez caught me smiling to myself.

"Why you smile?"

"I got no bones." I started to giggle like a schoolgirl.

"Time to dance."

"No!"

"Come, it no hurt." He rose from his chair, holding his hand out to me. "Follow what I do."

Before I knew it, the tunes had me a-stepping and a-swaying. Ramirez took good care that I stepped in the right direction. I surprised myself at the fun I had. When the band took a break, we went back to the table and sipped some more. First time back, he started rubbing his thumb across the back of my hand.

I let him.

Next, he draped his arm across my shoulders.

I let him.

But when he started rubbing my back, I got the shivers and told him to stop.

Don't know what time it was, but the party started breaking up, so we headed out to the buggy along with the others, waving and calling goodbye. All said and done, I was damn proud of myself.

As we left Tipton and the few swashes of lantern light left in windows to guide late-night stragglers home, the glow of the full moon slipped between maple and oak leaves to imprint the night with beauty and a sense of magic that would live long in my mind's eye. I slipped the flask out of Ramirez's pocket to chase away a chill but found it empty. He reached under the seat and pulled a bottle out and passed it to me. I took a long swig and offered it to him. He tilted back his head for a long draught and handed it back.

"I'm damn glad Sam didn't place me as Charley," I said. "Thanks for covering for me."

"He not know you."

"Shit, I can't have anyone spreading rumors about me."

"Pull hat down when he go past."

"Ramirez, I'll always remember this night and the fun we had, but I can't—"

"You say we no do this again?"

I nodded my head, saddened by the prospect of never being with him again. Sure, I'd see him around Providence. It was impossible not to run into each other being in the same business. But not on a man and woman basis.

"I change your mind?"

"It's made up."

"We see," he said, giving me a sideways look that started the blood pounding in my ears. "We not home yet."

We each took another swig of the Monongahela. I was about to plug the half-full bottle when he grabbed the cork out of my hand and threw it into the bushes. "We finish it."

I studied his profile in the moonlight. In fact, I couldn't take my eyes off his handsome face. He slung his arm around me and snugged me in close beside him.

"Why you look?" Strong white teeth flashed under his thick mustache, sending a wave of shivers down my arms.

"Remembering you and this night. Burning it on my mind."

His eyes bore into mine. I couldn't look away. I wanted the kiss I knew was coming. I wanted it more'n the air I couldn't seem to breathe. His arm drew me closer with an insistence I could not deny. My lips parted as his touched mine. They were soft and gentle and made me melt into his side. His lips became more firm and insistent. I was unsure of myself and pulled back. Was I doing it right? I had no idea. I looked into black eyes that laughed back at me. His lips were pulled to one side in a smug little smile. I tried to pull away, but he would not allow it.

"Have more whiskey."

I took a long pull then held the bottle to his lips. By the time we reached the outskirts of Providence, we had finished the bottle, and my kissing had become a little more experienced. He no longer breathed evenly, nor was he smirking at me. There was a light of fire in his eyes that sent shivers through my body and left me aching for something I had only an inkling of. I sensed what I wanted, but my only experience with sex was the coupling of animals.

When we arrived back at the barn where he had picked me up earlier, he tied off the reins and climbed down from the rig then handed me down. The moment my feet touched the ground he scooped me up into his arms and carried me into the barn.

With the early morning birdsong came a wave of embarrassment and a sense of guilt for what I had done. Waves of regret and agony pounded my head and belly making me want to heave. My first morning after and my first hangover. While Dom slept, I pulled on my trousers, shirt and boots, shoved the red dress in the box and left the barn. Sometime during the night he must have come out and unhitched the mare and hobbled her so she could graze, for she stood knee deep in timothy a hundred yards or so from the barn. I hurried back to the What Cheer and took up my life as though nothing had happened.

But that didn't last.

Now that I'd experienced sex, I'd go mushy inside when Dom came around. One lopsided smile from him had my blood rushing, He always brought along a bottle of Monongahela that made all good sense skedaddle. I just couldn't seem to say no.

16
Even Bigger Decisions

Though breakfast had made me queasy a few times, it weren't till my pants were a little tight one morning that the realization hit me like a Concord coach at full tilt.

I was pregnant.

At thirty-five years old, I was going to give birth. I didn't think it was possible. All the other women I saw with babies were a lot younger than me. I felt stupid for not knowing the trouble I was in sooner, but didn't miss not having my flow until it didn't come a second time.

Panic had me all skittered inside.

I wanted to be rid of it.

I didn't know how to get rid of it.

And, I was afraid to get rid of it.

There was a part of me that thought that getting rid of it was a killing act. The guilt I felt came from the church-going required of us orphans 'cause the Presbytery paid our living.

The results of one such out of wedlock pregnancy kept running through my head. Sarah Jean. Back in Worcester when it became known that Sarah Jean was pregnant, people talked behind her back, but refused to talk to her, wouldn't even see her as she walked through town, unless of course, she was in a store buying something. Then, I guess, they had to see her. Least ways, they saw her just enough to take her money. All that and it weren't even her fault. People turn on you right quick, and I didn't want that to happen to me.

Didn't want people staring at me. Didn't want people talking and quit soon's I walked in. Even supposing Dom would marry me, I'd be stuck for the rest of my life doing woman things. Keeping house. Sewing and cleaning. Taking care of children. Cooking three squares a day with no thank you to it all. No pride, no respect, no—I couldn't bring myself to face that kind of life. I weren't built for it. Society had unwritten rules for womenfolk that I wanted no part of. I weren't no humble Hannah. I wanted to be working at what I did best—driving a six-up, getting well paid, and being admired for what I did.

Fear and shame kept me thrashing in my bed of a night as I tried to find a comfortable spot in my mind so's I could get some sleep.

I couldn't think of giving up the respect of my position. I had worked too long and hard to throw it all away. I weren't no mother. Horses were my life, not kids. I hadn't a blessed notion of how to raise a kid. What was I to do?

I finally went to an herbalist. But couldn't seem to bring myself to open the door and walk in. I'd reach for the knob, change my mind and walk on, then I'd walk back and reach for the knob again. I dripped with worry sweat. Did I want to be trapped or free?

Free.

I turned the doorknob and walked in. The tinkling of a small bell at the top of the door announced my arrival. Herbs hung from the ceiling of the shop and smelled like summer in heaven. Glass jars of tinctures lined shelves along three walls. A mortar and pestle lay upon the counter with a dusting of what smelled like crushed thyme. As I waited at the counter, a merry looking matron entered the shop from the back, soothing her white apron with both hands.

"What can I do for you, sir?" she said with a smile.

"A friend of mine got herself in the family way, and she don't want it."

The sunny smile faded from the woman's lips as she shook her head, "How far along is she?"

"She didn't get her flow for the second time almost two weeks ago," I told her. I didn't know how long it took a woman to grow a baby. Horses took eleven months. People I guessed took less time, being smaller. I'd never paid attention, and it weren't something talked about. Most women disappeared until they were done giving birth, then reappeared carrying a cloth-wrapped, squirming bundle.

"You're sure she wants to do this?"

"She don't want it," I said again, wiping beads of sweat from my upper lip with the cuff of my driving glove. When she poised to ask another question, I pulled her up short with my special look.

She pursed her lips and shook her head with disapproval.

"You got something she can take, or not?"

She nodded and told me to come back later to pick it up.

The brew she contrived and told me to take all at once tasted worse than a winter cow shed and twice as strong. It had me shitting and shivering a whole damn night in the outhouse, wondering if I was going to die. The second longest night in my life. But it didn't work the way it was supposed to. My bowels were as slick as new pipe, but no blood issued from my wretched body.

Maybe this child was meant to be born after all. An unexpected sense of relief washed over me that I hadn't succeeded in killing it. But what was I to do now?

I ran into Liberty Childs in town early one morning near the beginning of December.

"Hey, Charley, did ya hear the news?

"What news?"

"Call's come up from Georgia, don't ya know. They need drivers and are willing to pay top dollar."

"Being warm in Georgia while you freeze your ass up here this winter sounds mighty good to me," I said.

"Yeah, keep those little hands of yours from freezing like they did when I had to help you drive your team home that night. Remember?"

"Liberty, you're a pain in my ass. How the hell could I forget when you remind me every year come winter?"

"Speaking of your ass, anybody ever tell you you're built like a brick shit house, Charley?" he said with a grin. "Straight up and down, as wide on the bottom as you are on the top, don't ya know."

"You're jealous 'cause you can't brace your butt in the box like I can, snakeyhips. Whereabouts in Georgia? You hear?"

"Word's got it, Atlanta. You'll have to ask around."

"Anybody we know going?"

"Can't say," he said. "I ain't a going though. Got me some good customers I don't want to lose. Got my family to think of, too, don't ya know."

Family to think of. The words kept running through my head. Georgia could be just the thing. I could disappear, give birth, and come back, with no one the wiser. I would find a nice couple and give it up for adoption. No orphanage for this kid, not after what I went through back in Cumberton. But I would have to pack up and head out soon. The cold had already set in hereabouts, baring the trees and hardening the ground.

That thought gave me an awful sickish feeling. I would miss Eb and Tilly terribly. Over the past twenty-three years, they'd become family to me, not that they knew that in so many words, but I felt it deep down and figured they did, too. That was a good part of the reason I never left to go work for some rich feller. I couldn't bring myself to leave. Eb's hard to please fussiness, and toe-the-line work ethic aside, more than made up for all I learned. I figured I learned more from him than from a score of mean-spirited hoity-toity coachmen worried that I'd take their place. I got experience all right. The best. And now I was giving it all up; Eb's expert knowledge, his you-can-do-it attitude, and his pride in my abilities. And losing Tilly, my mother, sister, friend. Leaving them ripped a gaping hole in my chest the size of Massachusetts.

"I'll be back," I said at dinner that evening. "But I've got to give this a try." Tilly's eyes filled with tears, but she took pains not to spill them at the table. With a quick wipe of her apron and a small sniff, she held herself in check. Eb, on the other hand, looked like he was about to bite my head off.

"Might not have room for you. If I have to find somebody else to do your work, you can't expect me to give them the boot because you've decided to return now, can I?" Eb said, scraping his chair away from the table and jutting to his feet.

All I could do was look up at him, his response tearing through my heart like a stallion's striking hoof.

"No." My heart sunk into my boots. "I guess that wouldn't be fair."

Eb turned on his heel, leaving the inn without touching his dinner. I looked at Tilly, but she had returned to the stove, her plate untouched, and was wiping her face with the hem of her apron. I'd hurt the two people I loved most in the world and found that I couldn't eat either. Making the move sound as though it was a short adventure hadn't set up the idea well in their minds.

I went back to my room in the stable and sank onto the cot, holding my head between trembling hands. Time to pay the piper, I thought. There's no turning back now. If I'd only—what? If I'd only been born male? If I'd only kept my pants on? If I'd only not gotten with child? A huge sigh escaped my lips. Tomorrow I would buy a carpetbag for my clothes and few personals, and crate up the books I owned. They were the only thing I spent money on, seein's how I didn't spend a lot of time at the pub like the other drivers. I would take one or two with me to reread as I went, and would ask Tilly to send the rest to me when I got to wherever the hell I was going. I ran my fingers through my hair. I didn't feel the excitement I had after I left the orphanage and was looking forward to being out on my own, excited to be working with horses and learning my trade. I'd never felt so lonely or frightened as I did then.

A tap at the door brought me back to the present.

"Come in."

Tilly entered, nose and eyes bright red. She sat beside me on the cot.

"There's something behind all this, isn't there?"

I could only nod. Words could not have escaped my throat at that moment without pulling tears along with them.

"You in trouble?"

I nodded again.

"You got gambling debts? I can help you out this once to get you back on your feet."

"It's not that kind of trouble. I got myself in the family way."

Her sudden intake of breath drew my eyes to her face. She wore a look of surprise and wonder. "How on earth did that happen?"

"Remember that dance back in August?"

She nodded.

"Well it all started there, and I couldn't seem to bring the fun to an end." I couldn't quite look her in the eye, her being like a mother to me and all. "Plan to adopt it out, so I can get back to doing what I do best." My plan sounded hardhearted and crass even to my own ears.

Tilly pleated her skirt, running her nail along the crease. We didn't say anything for a long time. "You'll let me know how you are from time to time?"

I nodded.

"I wish I could take the baby. But Eb and me, well, we're getting on, and with running two businesses, I don't see how I could raise a child and do it justice." She patted the back of my hand and rose to leave. "I got an old carpetbag you can have for your travels. I'll dig it out and bring it down tomorrow."

I smiled my thanks and watched the door close behind her. About an hour later, Dom arrived.

"So when you going tell me?" He leaned against the wall shoving his hands deep in the pockets of his coat.

"Tell you what?" I hedged, afraid that somehow he'd found out about me being in the family way.

"About leaving?"

"Damn, I just decided over supper. Geez, how did you—"

"Liberty. He said—"

"I said it'd be nice to be warm through the winter. That's all."

"Yes, it be nice," he said, wiggling his brows. "When it not warm outside, we keep warm inside."

"You want to come with me?"

"I drive, I get job, too."

I had to laugh, relieved not to be facing the journey to Georgia alone. I wondered what he'd say if he knew I was carrying his child. He often spoke of his large family and regaled me with stories of his brothers and sisters, nieces and nephews, but my gut feeling was he'd disappear in a wink if I told him we had already started one. Figured he'd find out soon enough.

I bought a bay gelding from Eb at a give-away price, and for the first time in my life, I owned something more'n the clothes on my back and a few books. The horse had been a recent addition to our stable and a disappointment. Every horse in the livery had to be both rideable and drivable in order to keep our renting schedule flexible.

The gelding moved nicely under saddle, but refused to wear harness blinders. We'd fitted him out when we first got him, but as soon as we put the driving headstall on him, he went berserk. We tried those eye flaps every which way, but he'd have nothing to do with it. Under saddle, he was a nice ride. I bought him figuring I could work with him to overcome the blinder problem somewhere down the road.

Chester, Eb's reliable old clod that had taught me not to cut my corners way back when, had died years back, so I named this one in memory of him for the good times and the bad we'd shared. Just like the time I was facing now.

Eb didn't talk much after I bought the horse. Work went on as usual, but more quiet than we'd ever been before. I think my buying the horse and naming it as I did made my leaving a sure thing in his mind. I could tell by the way he looked at me as though he was missing me already, that it was sadness keeping him quiet, not anger.

Tears filled Tilly's eyes every time she looked at me. She made sure every stitch of clothes I owned was clean and mended before she packed them into the carpetbag. Soap, needle and thread, toweling, and herbs and spices for cooking were tucked in between my clothes, and an old coffee pot and a cast-iron fry pan showed up on my cot for the journey. Each kindness Tilly showed stabbed my heart with sadness.

17
Heading South

O ur goodbyes, four days after my decision to leave, were short and quiet. Me and Tilly, and even Eb had tears dripping down our cheeks after we hugged. Dom sat his horse looking ill at ease until I mounted up. We headed down Benefit stopping at the first cross street to look back. Eb had his arm around Tilly, who waved goodbye with a white hanky.

We traveled much of the time in companionable silence; sometimes single file, sometimes side-by-side. But at night, we shared the same bedroll and enjoyed each other's bodies. Not much talking there either, but I didn't mind. I'm not big on talk. I liked having someone beside me; someone to share the trail and the day-to-day chores with. Seein's how we worked well together, I began thinking we'd settled into a nice bond that might have some life to it beyond the mutual enjoyment of sex.

We were nearing Philadelphia when Dom startled my wandering thoughts. "You shoot a gun?"

"Sure," I said. Eb had taught me how to fire a rifle, crack a twenty-foot blacksnake whip, and whistle sharply through my front teeth, them being manly things he thought I should know how to do.

"Handgun?"

"Rifle."

"Should have handgun. More useful."

"Don't care for 'em much."

"You good with the long gun?"

"Not bad." As with all I did, I did my best and practiced till I became good, though I didn't care for the noise. I kilt a few varmints sure, but as to killing a body, I didn't believe I could.

"Why are you going on about guns?"

"You never know. Good to have when someone come at you in-close and fast."

We rode on in silence for a while, and I thought on what he said.

"We near big town. You should get a gun," Dom said, patting the holster he wore on his right thigh. "I show you how to shoot."

I figured maybe he had a point. Needed more time and room to fire my rifle. A handgun can be kept close and used fast if need be, always handy.

I bought a second-hand, single action Colt revolver with a five-chamber cylinder when we reached Philadelphia. He told me firing a rifle weren't the same as shooting a handgun, and he was right. That night he taught me how to load it—no readymade bullets, had to load each chamber with powder and shot—fire it, and clean it after he explained all the parts and how they worked.

We practiced every night from then on. No fancy stuff, mind you, but a slow point and shoot while keeping both eyes open and fixed on the target. And like learning to shoot Eb's rifle, I knew it would take lots of practice for me to hit what I was aiming at.

While in Philadelphia, I had stopped in a dry goods store without Dom and bought three yards of soft white flannel. I hadn't figured on sewing till I got where I was going, but wanted to be prepared with the cloth for when the time came, and we'd settled in down in Georgia. I would have to start making things; some diapers and a bunting or two. Didn't figure to be much good at it, but wanted to try to stitch a few things together. Didn't want the kid I was carrying to go bare-bottomed to its new parents. The pregnancy had me thinking strange things. My mind even played on me and Dom staying together.

We were a week out of Philadelphia when all hell broke loose. Dom came across the flannel while preparing to camp for the night. "What you got here?" he said, pulling the flannel from its brown paper wrapping.

"It's just some cloth," I said with a shrug of my shoulders, not looking him in the eye.

"I know this cloth. My mama, she use this to make small clothes for my little brothers and sisters. I watch her." His dark brows drew together over accusing black eyes.

"I wouldn't know about that. I was raised in an orphanage."

"You keeping something from me?"

"What is it to you?"

"You have my baby in your belly?"

My eyes slid away from his.

"Yes!" He spun away, then whipped back to face me. "Why you not tell me?"

"I figured it was my problem."

"When you going to tell me, the papa?"

I shrugged and shook my head. "I've decided to give it up for adoption."

"Why didn't you just get rid of it?"

"I tried. The potion didn't work."

Dom threw the flannel to the ground and strode away. I picked it up and dusted it off best I could. It would need to be washed.

I set up camp by myself that evening. Fed the horses, put together a stew, and ate alone. I set the pot near the embers to keep the food warm and wrapped up in my bedroll. Tears rolled down my cheeks, but I refused to sob though I longed to release the heavy weight in the center of my chest. I wanted control over my life, but everything seemed to be turning to shit before my eyes.

The spoon scraping the stew pot brought me awake enough to realize he was back. I figured we'd discuss the matter further in the morning, so I didn't say anything, just relaxed back to sleep. My sleep must have been deep 'cause I didn't hear the snake slither out of my life. I woke in the morning to one horse, one-half our stores and one package of flannel.

I kept asking myself as I rode on that day why it is that a woman's got to be ready for responsibility even if she ain't, but a man doesn't ever have to be ready if he don't want to? He can ride away, free as a spring wind pretty much any time he has a mind to.

Problem was, I couldn't play the role of being a man this time around. And I weren't happy about it. I wanted to ride free of this, too, but couldn't, not only 'cause of the kid growing in my belly, but something deeper still.

Dom had thought nothing of suggesting I kill our unborn child, though I had tried, there was more to it than just making the decision. There had been the doing, which had been even harder. But more than that, there had been something deep inside of me that hated the idea of killing it. I had tried and was relieved it hadn't work. Would Dom have had the same qualms? I didn't think so. Men and women are made different at their core. Men protect and women preserve what's important to them. Wished I could have turned this one around—leave Dom alone and pregnant.

I wondered how many women wished the same for the man that had planted them with a child.

With all my thinking on the matter of men and women, I never quite figured out why I got soft in the head thinking we might make a go of it either. Must have been some deep down pregnant woman thing, 'cause once I pushed it from my mind, and cried it out of my heart, I ain't allowed such foolishness about a man into my life since.

Well, good riddance. What the hell did I need with a man that had no backbone? Once the child got born, I figured never to have sex again. My life was more to my liking without anyone attached to it anyhow.

Christmas and the beginning of 1848 passed without much notice on my part while I rode through North Carolina.

In South Carolina, I arrived at a smallish town to pick up supplies like I done other towns on other days.

It looked to be market day as I neared the village, joining a stream of people, some on horseback, some in wagons, some walking. Nobody looked happy. Though it was early, the bright morning sun gave no quarter. I figured the sun and the dust had everyone feeling travel worn, but somehow I could feel that weren't quite right. Chester sidestepped, flicking up dust with his nervous fidgeting. I began to read the faces of the dark-skinned people. There were fresh tears on some faces, and streaks of past tears on the cheeks of others. Some were angry, some fearful. And some wore chains.

Chains on people.

I'd seen slaves before up north, but nothing like this. Northern slaveholders appeared to treat their slaves with some humanity. Most times, I didn't know whether the dark people I saw were slaves or free, I hadn't thought about them much one way or another.

Chester wanted to take the bit and leave the fear that streamed down the road with us. I reined him in, but couldn't blame him, I felt the same way when I heard them singing in a low moan that made my skin pucker like I was scared.

The human funnel poured into the market place where the mass of people and horse-drawn traffic trickled to a stop in one hopeless logjam. A high platform sat about two-thirds of the way into a dusty lot and was backed by a long, low shed that faced away from the block. Looked like a horse auction except it had no paddock.

People milled in the street. Many of the dark people were herded toward the platform. I kneed Chester into openings that ebbed and flowed between small groups of people trying my damnedest to get through, so I could buy my supplies and head out. I made little headway through the crowd before an auctioneer's chant drew everybody's attention, and I knew for sure it was to be an auction of people, not animals. I was trapped dead center to the goings on. I didn't want to be there, I had no choice. From the bottom of my heart, I wish I could have looked the other way, but I couldn't. Curiosity took hold.

Near the end of the auction, a pregnant mother and her daughters were put on the block. The sneering auctioneer told the crowd she produced only females.

A mare, having foaled as regular and produced only fillies, would've received more dignity and interest than that poor woman got.

She was bloated with child, had one on her hip, another hugging her opposite knee, while two more clutched her skirts as though they would never let go. Each child looked like her sister. I overheard that the father of the children—the owner of a considerable plantation—had married and his new wife refused to have his offspring around.

The slave woman shifted her weight and rubbed the side of her distended belly throughout the slow bidding process. I found myself rubbing a circle on my belly, too, and quickly put my hand on my thigh, looking around to see whether anyone noticed. All eyes were on the unfortunate woman and her children. She seemed drained of emotion, but was more than likely in shock. When the bidding for the lot did not please the owner—or bastard father, as I have always thought of him—he ordered the three eldest children auctioned separately. The mother came alive, screeching her fury. Her wailing blended with the higher-pitched screams of terror the girls let out as they realized they were to be torn from her. The owner strode up the platform stairs and slapped the woman's face telling her to be quiet. Then he stood there for all to see, his face frozen like a marble statue.

I wondered whether he felt their agony, whether he felt any regret, any responsibility for this hell of his making. I cursed him under my breath, hoping he would never be able to sire a son with his new wife. I hoped they would experience years of unhappiness for what they had done to that poor woman.

The two hours it took to auction off the people for sale seemed to me an eternity in hell. Maybe it was 'cause I was pregnant that what I saw sickened me to the core, yet there were others around further along in pregnancy than me that showed less compassion than if a barn cat had gotten kilt under the misstep of a horse.

As the crowd thinned, and I was able to rein Chester out of the press of people, I realized how lucky I was to have had Dom cut out on me like he did. And I realized, too, that I was far luckier than that poor black woman. I could make a life of my own. I had choices.

She did not.

18

A Place to Stay

I had been thinking on finding a quiet place to settle down where I could start-up a business training and doctoring horses while I got the pregnancy and adoption over with. And about a week after the slave auction, I came upon the sleepy little town of Pineywood, Georgia. It weren't much different from many of the towns I'd passed through on my way down, but I took a liking to it soon as I rode in.

I dismounted in front of Beck's General Store. I pulled my hat down over my eyes, walked up the few steps to the store, and stepped inside. Place was quiet. A little black boy sat on a stool inside the door half asleep. In each hand, he held a cord that was tied to a large fringed tapestry hanging from a bar that swung from the ceiling. The boy pulled first one cord than the other, stirring the thick, humid air above. I later learned he got a ha'penny a day for the job seein's how the storekeeper couldn't abide slavery, a rarity in those parts.

"Afternoon there, stranger," a kindly looking man said from the counter straight ahead of me. The proprietor was about my size, but portly. A circlet of strawberry-blonde hair crowned his bald head with a dash of the same covering his upper lip. The sleeves of the white shirt he wore were rolled to the elbow, a spotless bibbed apron covered his belly, wrapping around his sides with the strings tied in a bow at the front. He drawled as though he preferred not to say the tail-end of his words. I had to slap some hard endings on them before I understood what he said.

"Afternoon. I'm here for supplies," I said, telling him what I wanted and how much. "But I'm also looking to rent or buy a small piece of land fit for horses. Know anybody I should talk to about that?"

"For the time being, I can he'p you with both. I own this here sto' and I can tell"—sounded like "tail" to me—"you where you might find a few acres to your liking, and, if you be interested in buying the place, y'all come back, and I'll notify Luis Montoya, the owner. He's down Atlanta way now, but he put me in charge of the place, and I know he wants to sell. Y'all can probably get the place at a good price."

"Sounds good. Name's Charley Parkhurst," I said, sticking my hand out for a shake. "I got me a wife's going to give birth come spring, and she's nagging to nest."

"I'm Avery Beck. Pleased to meet you," he said, shaking my hand. "Me and my wife own this place. Congratulations on the one that's coming. Lacey and me, we don't have any children blessing our family."

Avery said it with such regret, it set my heart to thumping. Maybe Avery and Lacey Beck would consider adoption. He gave me directions to a place off the beaten track about five miles south of town.

"See if ya'll like it," he said, handing me the supplies I'd ordered. "The cabin will keep the rain off'n you while y'all take stock. Let me know if it'll suit your needs, and we can go from there."

From the road, Cozy Hill didn't look like much. Weren't on much of a hill neither, more like a small bump in the land. Course, the rain that had soaked me over the past hour had made the road slick and the cabin's yard, a pond. The cabin, if the damn roof didn't leak, looked to be the haven Avery Beck said it would be.

The water rose over Chester's fetlocks but no higher as we crossed the pond that was the cabin's front yard. We walked around back. The cabin looked stronger than it had at a distance. There was a swale in the cedar shake roof, but all the shingles were in place.

A one-horse shed some fifty yards from the house looked solid. A lean-to sloped from the barn into a small paddock area, perfect for what I had in mind. I would need to widen the paddock, but it would hold a couple of horses. I pulled Chester in, unsaddled and rubbed him down, and fed him. I climbed the rungs built into the barn wall that led to a mow near the peaked roof. I smelled the musty hay before I saw it in the shadows. I kicked half of it down to Chester to chaw on and made a memory to buy some first chance I got.

I meandered around a series of shallow puddles to get to the cabin and had to put my shoulder to the door to get in. I hesitated at the door, peering into the dark room before walking in. As my eyes adjusted, I made out two cobwebbed windows that let in a small amount of gray light, and a wide hearth for cooking. Dust blanketed the room. A bunk lay along the back wall of the cabin to the right of the door. A folded blanket lay at the foot of its tick, the dust making both a blend of gray. Across from the bunk, next to the front door, stood a small table with an oil lamp and two stools. A neat stack of split wood leaned against the side of the clean stone hearth. My eyes searched the corners of the room, looking for any critters that might take exception to my moving in. Nothing squirmed or scurried, so, leaving the back door ajar, I crossed to the hearth and started a warming fire.

Looking the cabin over again by firelight, I saw that all was dry and decided to stay. I sat on the bunk. My body seemed to tire short of day's end, and my mind tended to wander into the dark corners of my own youth now that I was carrying the child. The way the cabin was situated, with the fire barely lighting the room, reminded me of my father's house. I could almost hear Papa's gravelly voice, his hacking cough.

"Where the hell are you?"

I huddled in the shadows under the bed trying to stay warm and out of sight. Sleeted wind knifed me in the back as it blew through the cracked walls of the one room cabin. Fear of my father outweighed the pain of frozen fingers and toes, and the constant shivering of my belly.

"Least you coulda done was been born a boy." Papa bumped the jug into the side of the plank table in his attempt to set it down. "Damned mother killer," he mumbled.

I clutched a threadbare blanket close and made no sound.

A man had knocked at the door hours ago. Papa'd been sober then, and was scrambling two eggs the hens had laid that morning. Hadn't been any talk between us, rarely was, but at least we'd shared a quiet peace.

"All you are is a damn millstone 'round my neck."

He knew I was still in the cabin hearing every word he said. The oak door-brace was too heavy for me to lift from its bracket without making noise. He'd made sure it was in place when he shut the door behind the man who brought the jug. I'd scraped the eggs onto two plates, giving him more'n me, but instead of pitching into the food, he pulled the cork, slung the jug over his crooked arm and guzzled the smelly stuff without taking a breath—just kept swallowing. When he came up for air, he ran his mouth along his left sleeve while still holding the jug on his bent right arm ready for the next swig. I gulped my portion of the eggs, switched plates, and downed the rest knowing it would be a long, cold night, and he wouldn't even notice the eggs were gone. At least, he hadn't ever missed food before when a jug was at hand.

Though I'd only been with him a year, I knew sour mash did nasty things to my Papa, a quiet man when sober. His long silences and gruff looks froze talk between us. We only spoke when necessary. I learned to keep quiet.

I had also learned to let my mind drift back to good times when Papa was not talking, or when he was drunk like this. Since I was cold and lonely, my mind drifted to warm summer days with Aunt Martha. Days of hugs and ring-around the rosie, and buttercup picnics while Uncle Zach was out in the fields.

Aunt Martha was my mother's sister, older than my Mama by two years. She had no children of her own but treated me like I was her daughter. She told me about my Mama, said she was full of fun and laughter, so different from my Papa. I knew he blamed me for Mama dying. Course, Aunt Martha told me that my Mama was small and fine boned and my Papa was built like a workhorse, and, if you mate two like that, there's bound to be trouble with the birthing. So, it weren't my fault at all. Aunt Martha said, "A dairy farmer should've knowed better."

Papa's deep-chested cough startled me. Sleet ticked the window and the fire glowed low in the embers. I tucked my feet up under my dress, my only dress, my only clothes in fact. I pulled the blanket tighter around my legs, trying hard not to make a sound. I hoped that soon his head would hit the table, and he'd start to snore. Soon, I kept telling myself, clutching the old horsehair blanket closer. Soon.

"Damn, gotta piss." Papa staggered to his feet and braced himself against the table for a moment before shuffling to the door. He lifted the brace and stumbled out, letting in a biting rush of wind that sought me out under the bed.

I scooted out as quick as numbed limbs allowed, and limped to the hearth. I scooped the warm embers together, tossed in a handful of kindling, then placed the last three wood splits on top. I took a burning splinter to the table to light the remains of a candle and threw the firebrand back into the hearth. I thought about heading out to the barn and climbing on the back of Zephyr, one of Papa's team of workhorses. I would be warm and a lot more comfy than I was under that bed. I went to the door to let myself out, but heard Papa cough on his way up the path and scooted back under the bed to avoid a beating. It was his way when he'd been hugging the jug. I wrapped the dusty old blanket around me as best I could. I weren't quite as far under as I had been before. I wanted to be able to see him, so that when his head finally hit the table, and he began blubbering through his slack mouth, I could climb out. The fact that he'd made a trip to the outhouse was a relief; he'd sleep without waking till well after dawn, allowing me to rest and warm up by the fire.

He coughed his way to the table, lifted the jug and took another long pull before half-stumbling, half-falling into the only chair in the house.

"Who told you to put more wood on the fire? Who the hell do ya think ya are—a damn princess or somethin'? You're not the one chopping or lugging the wood for this fire ya know—I am! And I'll say when more wood is needed. Ya hear me?"

I inched back under the bed. It would be quite a while before he'd fall asleep now that he'd riled himself. I heard him hitch the jug and swallow.

"Damn kid," he mumbled after the jug thumped on the table, then shouted, "six long years ago today you killed your mother!" Deep chest-wrenching coughs filled the small cabin, drawing me to the light again. Red spattered the hand that tried to stifle the coughs. He stared at the blood for a long moment, then wiped it on his pants and reached for the jug, taking long swallows. When the bottom of the jug hit the table again, Papa rested his forehead on his crossed arms and soon made the blubbering sounds I'd been waiting for. It weren't like the snoring he did every night when he slept on his back. No, this was more like the sound a horse makes when she blows dust from her nose, only Papa did it with his cheeks.

I could see the light of the fire, hear it crackling, and yearned for its warmth, yet I waited before creeping out. My entire body shivered as I waited. The cramping of my muscles drove me from under the bed. I couldn't wait a moment longer. With caution, I slipped out, making little noise, only the soft scuff of the blanket along the rough floorboards. I kept my eyes on Papa, and sidled my way past him to the hearth. I stepped up to the fire and spread the blanket wide like a bat to trap the heat of the blaze. After a while, my belly and leg muscles stopped quivering, and began to relax as the heat baked my body.

A loud crack behind me threw my body into a sudden crouch. I spun to face the sound. It took a moment for my eyes to adjust to the dark room after gazing into the flames, but my ears translated the soft crackle of the cornhusk tick and groaning of the rope webbing beneath it. Papa had gone to bed, knocking the chair over as he got up.

With a long sigh of relief, I turned back to the fire and extended my blanket to harbor the warmth until I was baked through to my backbone. When sleep threatened to overtake me and pitch me into the fire, I rolled up in the blanket like a cocoon with my nose sticking out and curled around the mouth of the hearth for the remainder of that long, cold March night.

Our bellowing cows woke me well after dawn. They wanted to be fed and milked. Milking should have been done two hours ago. Looking over at Papa, I noticed that he still lay sprawled across the bed facing the wall, and figured he probably wouldn't move for a while yet.

I got up and folded the blanket crosswise to form a misshapen shawl, which I draped over my shoulders. I tilted the chair onto its hind legs and pulled it to the door. Papa didn't even twitch at the sound of the chair scraping the rough floorboards. Climbing up, I managed to lift one end of the heavy wooden brace, but in doing so, jabbed a splinter into my knuckle and let go, the brace crashed to the floor. Eyes wide, I stared at Papa's still form. When he didn't budge, I jumped down with a big sigh, and dragged the chair back to the table.

At the door, I crammed on an old pair of too-small shoes that crunched my toes. Grimacing as corns on my little toes pressed against the cold-stiffened shoe leather, I left the warmth of the cabin and made sure to latch the door shut. The night's sleet had put an icy crust over the yard. Twice my bottom hit the cold crust before I knew I was falling. I had to roll onto my hands and knees to get up, and once up, had to stamp my heels into the crust every step of the way to the barn.

I fed all the animals then climbed on the gentlest one of Papa's team of beautiful Clydesdale mares by hopping to her back from the side of her stall. Papa would yell if he found me, but I knew I would hear him coming, and have time to get down before he got to the barn. Zephyr was my favorite, though I loved Sonnet, too. Both lived in straight stalls side by side. I spoke quietly to them and listened as they chewed their hay. I hugged Zephyr's great neck and lay my cheek on her mane. Though my dress had ridden up to above my knees, the mare's natural warmth felt wonderful. I held off going back to the cabin for as long as I could, but the cows began lowing to be milked, and I had to go wake Papa.

When I got back to the house, I put three eggs I'd found in the haymow into a bowl and set it on the table before going outside to bring in more firewood. I visited the outhouse, brought three splits in from the cord stacked along the back path before prying off my shoes inside the door and wiggling my numb toes. The rough wood floor felt warm. I scraped the embers of last night's fire into a pile, added kindling to excite some flames, then laid the splits on top. Soon the warmth of the leaping flames felt so good that moving to wake Papa was out of the question, at least till I stopped shivering.

The wind was picking up. It howled around the corner of the cabin and roared as it rushed over the top of the chimney, snatching the smoke and heat, drawing the cold air past my bare ankles to feed the fire. I put some coffee to boil then turned to roast my back, careful not to step too close and catch fire.

Papa still lay as he had before I left for the barn. He slept solid when drunk, though he made animal noises through his nose and mouth most times. Waking him would be next to impossible. But the one thing that helped to wake him, and prevented his cuffing me when he came to, was the smell of fresh brewed coffee.

Bossy's loud bellow reminded me that I could no longer delay waking Papa. The cows had to be milked, or they would get sick. I poured a cup of coffee and went to the bed. Papa still lay as he had the night before, on his belly with his face to the wall.

Outside, the wind howled like a pack of wolves and Bossy bawled like she was about to die. But inside, it was much too quiet.

I set the coffee on the table and pulled the blanket shawl closer about me. I stared at his back. I didn't see no rise and fall, no sound of breathing in or out. I tugged the blanket closer with trembling hands. I no longer felt my wet dress or cold feet as I stared at the still body on the bed.

"Papa?" I nudged his shoulder. He didn't move. I prodded him again, only harder. Still nothing.

"Papa?" I shouted, pushing him with both hands and putting all of my weight behind the shaking.

He was cold and stiff.

Papa was dead.

I ran out of the house and stood in the wind trying to take it all in. I got to shivering so bad, my feet kept slipping out from under me in the still-slick yard. After I fell the third time, I decided to ask our nearest neighbor for help. The Biddles kindly took me in and sorted things out for me. Unfortunately, they sorted me back into the hands of Uncle Zach who dumped me off at the orphanage.

Heavy rain pounding the roof snapped me back to the present.

I didn't want no kid of mine in no orphanage.

I got up from the bunk and pulled both cabin doors wide open. The rain fell straight down. Evening had set in while I'd been lollygagging. After adding some splits to the fire, I took up the corn broom that leaned in a corner, and began sweeping the ceiling, walls, and floor, sending the dust, spiders and stale air out the nearest open door. Saw the cornhusk tick needed to be replaced, so I shook the blanket outside, flipped the tick and covered it with the blanket. Inside an hour, the place was livable. I started up a pot of coffee and put an open can of beans in the coals to warm for my dinner.

If the god-awful rain stopped, or slowed, I figured to go back to town the following day to speak to Avery Beck about renting the place before buying it from that Luis Montoya feller. I also hoped to look over the horse population and get the word out that I was looking to buy horses that needed training or doctoring. I would let it be known I was willing to work on difficult horses other people owned, if they had a mind not to sell.

While in town, I wanted to meet Lacey Beck. After the memories of my childhood, I wanted to make sure the child I was carrying found a good home, one without drunkenness or beatings. I wouldn't be there to give it love, but after what I had lived through, I wanted to make sure it got a leg up in life by having a good family. It was too soon to make mention of adoption to the Becks, but I wanted to look Lacey over, maybe get a feel for her notions on children.

Though the rain hadn't let up much the next morning, I went to town anyway. I got the feeling that morning in the outhouse that time was galloping by, I almost couldn't button my pants closed. I would have to change into Charlotte soon, or the whole parish would know my marriage story was a lie.

19
A Home of My Own

Any chance I can rent?" I asked Avery when all but his wife and one customer remained in the store. Lacey Beck turned out to be a little slip of a woman with sad eyes. Though she didn't smile much, she seemed agreeable with the customers. I shifted my gaze back to Avery. "I got to be a little sparing with my money these days, what with the child coming and all. I want to buy some horses my wife can tend while I'm away, so's we can turn a profit. She's good at doctoring and training them up for resale."

"She Indian?"

"Naw, fact is, she's my second-cousin. We been sweet on each other since we were kids, but she can be one cussed bitch, let me tell you. Knows horses though," I said with an approving shake of my head.

"Ya going to leave your wife whilst she's expecting?"

"She's got plenty of time, I'll be back before she's ready to drop."

"How long ya'll be wanting to rent?" Avery asked with a frown.

"Couple of months. If things work out, I'll buy in six months. If it don't, we move on leaving the place as we found it. What do you say?"

"Don't think the owner will go for that idea. He's wanting to sell."

"Well, if I got to buy right off, maybe I better find another place. What's he asking?"

"Six hundred."

"Whew. How much land comes with it?"

"Ten acres."

"That'd do to begin with, but there ain't no room to grow."

"Maybe he'll go for less. Make an offer, I'll send it down to him. See what he says."

Knowing horsemen as I did, I knew they wouldn't want to do any horse-trading with a pregnant woman, especially one they didn't know. I didn't have a whole lot of time to get settled in before the child was to come.

"Four hundred."

Avery's brows shot up.

"It's the best I can do," I said. "I got to buy horses to get my business going before the wife gets too big to be of any help."

"I'll send him a letter with your offer. If he don't go for your price, ya'll still got time to look around, see whether it'll work out for ya and the missus."

"I'll give you some money in advance on good faith," I said, handing him fifty dollars. "It'll probably take at least a month to get an answer from Montoya."

"Sounds about right. Let me give ya'll a receipt," Avery said, reaching under the counter for some paper and a pencil. He scribbled in silence for a minute, then turned the paper for me to read. "Can you make it out, or should I read it for ya?"

"I can read," I said. Avery signed his name and handed me the paper. I folded it up and stuck it in my coat pocket.

I handed him a list of staples that I'd need now that I was going to be setting up house for a while, and told him I would be back to pick them up in a couple of hours. I walked about town, taking notice of the four-legged population. At the livery, I introduced myself and put the word out that I was in the market for horses that needed special attention and where to find "my wife" and me. Figured I weren't going to get much help from the stableman, but thought maybe he'd send something my way if it was on its last legs, just to prove I didn't have what it took. I think he figured we were in competition, but I didn't see it that way.

Before I left the livery, I dickered with a farmer for a load of hay, which he promised to deliver to the farm the following day. I asked directions to the nearest stage way-stations, figuring I would head out to them to check their stock and offer my horse doctoring services the next day.

I had a stroke of good luck as I neared the general store to pick up my supplies. I spied a gray mare limping toward me carrying a man that should've been driving a carriage instead of sitting a horse.

I watched him dismount in front of the general store. "Hey mister, got a minute?"

"New in town are you?" he said.

"Yup, got in yesterday." I walked over to the hitching post. "See your horse is limping. Let me take a look for you, maybe I can help."

"She isn't used to carrying me. I usually drive, but I broke a wheel yesterday and had to get out to the Lupin place to deliver a baby this morning. Hate riding. Wasn't built for it."

"You the doc?" I said.

"Yes, I've tended this town now for nigh on twenty years. Good people here."

"Might need your services down the road, my wife is in the family way."

"Tell her to come see me the next time you're both in town. I like to get to know my patients before they need me, and it helps to have the husband to talk to, too."

"Let me take a look at your mare," I said, squatting to run my hands down the mare's foreleg. I gently pinched her flexor tendon to get her to lift her hoof. I tucked it between my thighs above the knee, leaving my hands free to poke around the frog. She tried to withdraw her hoof when I hit the sore spot. "What's her name?"

"Suzie, after my late wife."

"Looks to be a stone bruise and a bit of thrush. It'll need some attention. Suzie should have her frog tended to, and rest a few days." I let go the mare's leg and straightened.

"Thank you, young man," he said. "I'm Doc Schmidt. Who are you?"

"Charley Parkhurst."

"Well met. You seem to know your horses."

"Need to. Drive stage when I can get the work."

"Come down for the warmer weather?"

"Yup. You?"

"Hate snow. After my wife died, I came down from near Ogdensburg, New York, where the St. Lawrence meets the Oswegatchie." Doc half a smiled. "Not only damn cold, but damp cold up there. I'd better be heading along. Have to speak to the Becks, and I probably have patients waiting for me at the office. Don't forget to tell your wife to drop in to see me."

Avery Beck, carrying a sack of goods, followed an older woman from the store. He placed the bundle in the woman's buckboard, said his goodbyes, and walked over to join us. The Doc and Avery exchanged nods of greeting.

"Say Doc, this mare should be looked after. Me and Charlotte are staying at Cozy Hill south of town. Hope to buy the place. Avery'll bear me out. Let me take your mare on home, I'll bring her back good as new in a few days."

Doc gave me a long considering look then glanced at Avery, who nodded. "I guess Jack over at the livery will lend me a horse if I have to go out of town on a call. I've been doctoring his family since I got here. Don't see why he wouldn't help me out. Go ahead and take her."

"Thanks, Doc."

"Got your order ready, Charley," Avery said.

The three of us walked into the general store. I paid for my supplies, loaded them on Chester, and grabbed Suzie's reins. After dropping off the Doc's saddle at the livery, I headed out of town, my first job in hand.

I delivered the mare to Doc as promised a few days later and asked him to let it be known what I was about. When he offered to pay I declined, figuring word of mouth from him would get me some customers. It did. But I'd picked a poor parish to live in. Instead of making money, I made friends and earned chickens and such. Though it weren't what I had in mind, it worked.

My belly got bigger and the child got livelier as time passed. The day came when I had to shed my manly trappings and try living as a female. That took concentration just like it had to become a man. Had to remember not to lower my voice when I talked, though by now it had become naturally raspy. I took off my fancy driving gloves and began wearing skirts. Now there's a reason not to be a woman. Damn things would wrap around my legs, hobbling me at the damnedest times. Found myself tripping over them and ended up kissing the dust a time or two. Tied my hair back and let it grow past my shoulders. Bought a different broad-brimmed hat so's I wouldn't look like my other self. All in all, I felt bare-naked and cranky.

Finally got my nerve up to visit the doctor in town early in April, but by that time, I was pretty well along. Far as I could figure, I only had another month or so to go, but I was wrong.

I sat in his waiting room thinking of all the work I had to do that day, and that week, and all that needed to be done before the child came. I waited and waited and waited. Seemed like the day was pretty near shot before Doc ambled in. Said he'd come back from setting Jeb Miller's busted leg. The others started murmuring among themselves. From the stir, I made out he was a young farmer with a small family and would need help. Doc called in the first patient, but it only seemed a minute or two before he called me in.

"Mrs. Parkhurst I presume?" Doc said as I walked into his exam room. "Where's your husband?"

"Gone."

"Gone? You mean for good? He's left you?"

"Don't think so," I said. "Just for now. Off driving stage."

"Oh. I had hoped that he would be with you during the examination." Doc walked to the door and spoke to someone in the waiting room. One of the waiting patients followed him back into the examining room. "You two know each other?"

"No," we said in unison with a nod to each other.

"This is Mrs. Winifred MacFerran. She's a widow and your closest neighbor."

"Folks around call me Freddie."

"Howdy, Freddie," I said, reaching for a shake. "name's Charl—otte." Her clasp was firm and brief, her eyes direct as I tripped over my name. She looked to be used to work and close to me in age.

"I'm not widowed, Doc's putting a nice face on it," she said. "My man sired three sons in about as many years then up and left me."

"Bastard," I said without thinking.

Freddie laughed. "You got that right. You the one living at the Montoya place that doctors horses?"

"Yup."

"I live west of you. Got a nice spread, but have always had my eye on adding Montoya's place. Just can't seem to scrape the money together—"

"Ladies, this is all well and good, but we must get on," Doc said. "Now lay back Mrs. Parkhurst. I've invited Mrs. MacFerran in for propriety's sake, but I must get on with your examination. I have several patients waiting."

Doc pushed and prodded me like he was kneading a loaf of bread, and asked questions about my doings with "my husband" and my monthly flow, which I answered the best I could considering much of that happened months ago.

"Far as I can tell, you still have until about mid-June before we deliver this baby," Doc said. "Everything seems normal. Continue to eat well, do as much work as you can without working yourself into the ground. Tell your husband for me that come the first of June, he should stick closer to home until you deliver."

"Almost three more months of this?" I said. "I'm ready to get this over now. I'm sick of being tired all the time."

"Patience, woman," Doc said. "It'll come when the time is right. Come see me next month. I want to keep an eye on how you're doing since you're older than most having a first child. Bring your husband when you come."

"Yes, sir," I said, wondering how I was going to manage that one.

The doctor and I both thanked Freddie for attending my exam. She and I walked out into the waiting room together, followed by Doc who paused by the door to call his next patient.

"Stop by," I said in parting. "Pot's always on."

"Will do," she said. "Next chance I get."

I decided next time I was in town, I would let it slip that my husband had left me. That way I wouldn't have to make excuses to Doc and could ask him whether he knew of anyone who would like to adopt a child, and take good care of it. Once the child was born and adopted out, I would be on my way back to Providence.

20
Adoption Plans

A few weeks later, I was out in the corral sacking a skittish horse with a piece of burlap to calm him, when Freddie MacFerran drove up, squinting at me.

"What were you doing with that horse? I can't see too good at a distance anymore."

"Sacking him. You rub a sack all over a skittish horse, then slap him softly under his belly and around his legs until he stands still and almost goes to sleep. It gets a flighty horse used to you. After they realize you ain't doing them any harm, they calm down and learn to trust you.

"Step on down and come inside for a cup of coffee."

She climbed from the wagon. Freddie stood a half-head shorter than me, with gray streaked chestnut hair, freckles dotted her cheeks and arms. Her clear blue eyes had a direct look I knew right off I could trust.

"Avery sent along a letter addressed to you from Montoya and a small crate from Providence. Since neither of us have seen you recently, I thought to check on you on my way home and brought them with me. You look to be fine. How are you feeling?"

"Ain't comfortable any which way. Got another five weeks to go, and feel like its going to put a foot through my belly 'fore it's over."

"Know what you mean. I've been in the family way three times, and each time I wanted to get it over with at least a month beforehand," she said, rubbing a circle on her own belly. "So, where's that husband of yours?"

I looked Freddie in the eye and said, "There ain't a husband, never was."

"Thought as much."

"Whattya mean?"

"I'd seen a new man around town with an unnatural wide behind, and he looked like you. After I saw you in skirts, I put two and two together."

"Appreciate if you'd keep it under your hat."

"I'll not hold it against you as some would. Here's that letter, the crate's in the back."

"My books from Tilly," I said, dropping the tailgate. "Glad she got my letter. Thanks a lot for going out of your way, Freddie. It's got so's I pace the floor nights with nothing to read while the kid dances on my innards."

"Glad I brought them along. Hope you let me borrow one now and then."

"Sure. Come on in. I'll put the pot to warm."

We sat and jawed much longer than either of us had planned. I told her about the orphanage, Eb and Tilly, and Dom. She told me about her Fergus running off, and how she raised three sons with next to no money.

"We're doing better now that the boys are grown and have taken over much of the running of the farm, but I see the day coming when they are going to want to leave."

"Then you'll be on your own again I take it. And men call us the weaker sex."

"My two youngest want to head out on their own. One wants adventure at sea, and the other talks of Atlanta. But the eldest is the one that'll stay on the farm and make a go of it. I love all three and wish I could keep them close, but they're men now. I've got to let go, much as I hate the idea."

"Well, at least you got one staying."

"He's nineteen and will be wanting to take a wife soon. But I can't say I cotton to the idea of having another woman in my house. All said, a woman's got to do what she's got to do."

"Maybe she'll be a help to you."

Freddie wrinkled her nose in distaste. "Not too happy about the one he's got his eye on just now. Seems to be a lazy sort. But enough about me. What are your plans for the new one coming?"

"I came down here to birth the child and give it up." There, I'd said it. Freddie gave me a long look, then nodded her head once. "I drive coach for a living. Good at it, too. There just ain't any room in my life to raise a child proper-like."

"Got anyone ready to take on the responsibility?"

"Was thinking of the Becks. Avery sounds like he'd love to have children. But Lacey, I'm not so sure about. I've never spoken with her, but she has a bit of a sour look around her mouth, like she's angry or something. I know what it's like living with people that think you're a bother and little else. It don't make a kid feel cared about."

"Lacey is a good woman, quiet, but does no one harm, not even much of a gossip. That sour look she wears is disappointment. She can't seem to carry full-term and has had three or four miscarriages. I think they've given up hope of having a child of their own." Freddie set aside her cup and rose from the table. "I have to be going, but I think you're on the right track in considering the Becks. They're good people. Now don't let on I told you their troubles, they'd not thank me for it."

"Never. I just want to find a good home for it," I said, rubbing circles on my rounded belly. Sounded poor to my ears, kind of like I was trying to get rid of a pup.

I saw her off and went back to the house. I ripped open the letter from Montoya and read that he had accepted my offer to rent then to buy Cozy Hill. Buying seemed an unnecessary thing to do considering that I was heading out right after the child was born, but my gut feeling was to purchase it. I figured I could always sell it to Freddie before I left Pineywood.

So, next morning, I headed for town with most of my remaining life-savings to pay Avery Beck the money for Montoya's land. Figured while I was there, I would make it known that my husband had abandoned me, then approach the Becks about adopting the next time I went to town. The news, I felt sure, would spread through town like wildfire and set up the reason behind my putting the kid up for adoption.

And it did.

Two weeks later, the first set of would-be parents arrived at Cozy Hill before I had a chance to speak to the Becks.

They drove in on a splintered wagon behind a swaybacked mare. The man climbed down, leaving his worn-looking wife on the wagon seat, and approached me in the paddock where I was working Chester.

He wore a faded shirt rolled past the elbow and canvas pants. Both were clean, yet he didn't smell clean. He thumbed back his sweat-stained straw hat and rested his left foot on the bottom rail of the fence. A web of small red lines covered his nose and stubbled cheeks. I didn't need to smell his breath to know he had a taste for whiskey.

"Heard tell your man left you," he said. "I been figgerin' you might be wanting to get rid of that kid you're carrying."

I was flabbergasted by his crudeness. When I didn't say anything, he continued.

"I do my woman regular-like, but she ain't given me no children yet. I want a boy to help run my farm. You could do worse. If he worked out, I would leave the place to the boy when I'm gone. That's if the missus don't give me one of my own."

Rage set me to breathing heavy. I walked past him and on out of the paddock without ripping his throat out. He strode beside me, talking away real confident-like. I stopped at his wagon and looked his wife over. The woman's dress looked to be her Sunday-go-to-meeting best, spotless except for the dust from the road. Her left eye was mottled with purple and yellow bruises. She looked down at me without saying a word. A chill ran through me at the defeat I saw in her eyes.

The man kept talking all the while. About what, I don't know, I'd stopped listening. It was either that, or I'd have beat the shit out of the stupid ass. I never had a name to go with the couple, but they had as much chance of adopting my child as Chester had of growing his testicles back.

"The child won't be born for weeks yet," I said with an edge on my voice that the bastard could have shaved with. "And I have not decided to give the child away." Till that day, I'd always thought adoption was good; that an adopted child became a member of a family. After all, the parents wanted the child. They came and picked the one they wanted. It weren't like a girl being born into a family that only had room for a son; like I'd been to my papa. But I'd been wrong. I never thought of the possibility of my child becoming little more than a slave until this bastard showed up at my door.

"We can wait," he said with a t'bacca-stained grin. "Say it's ourn, and we'll be back soon as he pops out."

"My husband may return," I said.

"Don't lie to yourself, he won't be back. Remember we're first come. We get the boy."

That did it. "Get off my land," I yelled.

He raised his fist, but I looked him full in the face, "You hit me mister and you're a dead man, make no mistake." My slit-eyed look brought him up short. "Head on out of here, before I load your ass with shot. And don't come back."

I watched them drive away. He backhanded his wife as they left, whether to punish her for what she may have said, or for what I did, I don't know, but I felt sorry for that woman. Thought about her off and on over the years, wondering whether she lived through his beatings, or died from them. I doubt she had it in her to make a break for freedom.

I must have stood there for some time 'cause when I snapped out of my wandering thoughts the couple was gone and another rig driven by a single person was trotting toward me. A smile spread across my face as I recognized my friend Freddie.

"What the hell happened?" Freddie asked. "Saw a couple turn out of your road; the woman held a bloody handkerchief to her nose, and the man was shouting at her and laying the whip to their sorry-looking horse."

"Bastard wanted my child," I said.

"What did you do to him?"

"Nothing, told the piece of shit to get off. Come on in, I'll tell you all about it."

A cup of coffee later, I had finished my story and got up to refill our cups. "I guess I'd better get up to town soon and speak to the Becks and see Doc Schmidt while I'm at it."

"Good idea. Best to have it settled."

"Been putting it off. Don't want anyone hanging around, or giving me orders 'cause the child'll be theirs."

Freddie nodded. "They will probably want to be near when the baby is born."

"I guess they got that right."

"You going into town to deliver?"

"Guess I'll have to. Been worried about how I was going to get there and where I was going to stay through it all. Riding is getting damn uncomfortable lately."

"I'll drive you in," Freddie offered. "The Becks would probably put you up if they take the child. It's the least they could do."

I nodded my agreement, feeling out of sorts in my mind.

"Well, I've got to get on home, got a list of chores long as my arm," Freddie said, getting up from the table. "When your time is close, I'll stop in to check on you regular-like. Doc said mid-June, didn't he?"

"Yup."

"I'll see you before then and we'll plan it out." Freddie gave me a warm smile and an unexpected hug. "You'll do fine."

I hoped she was right.

21
Remembering Mama

I rubbed circles on my swollen belly as Freddie left. It took me back to the short time I spent with the Biddles after my father died.

I remember pounding on the thick plank door of the Biddle's house with my fists the day I couldn't rouse my father. It felt as though my hands would shatter like dropped icicles before anyone heard me. Mr. Biddle flung the door wide and caught me as I fell into the room.

"What is it girl?" he asked, holding me at arm's length.

"My Papa is dead. You got to milk our cows."

"Good Heavens, child, what are you going on about?" Mrs. Biddle asked from across the room. "Close the door, Clive. You're letting all the cold in."

"Papa is dead. The cows are going to die, too."

"Surely you're mistaken," Mr. Biddle said.

"Come in by the fire so's you can warm up and tell it all from the beginning." Mrs. Biddle set aside her knitting and crossed to enfold me in a warm welcoming hug.

I told them about Papa not waking up when the cows bellowed to be milked. How he didn't budge when I shook him and called out. Mr. Biddle went to our farm to check and found things as I said.

The next morning, I stood in the middle of the warm kitchen breathing in the smell of coffee, lamp oil, and wet dog while Mrs. Biddle bustled around the wood stove, heating water. Mr. Biddle had gone to bring Papa's cows and horses back to their farm after reporting my father's death in town and sending word to Uncle Zach.

"I know you've had it rough, child, what with losing your Ma," Mrs. Biddle said. "Then your aunt, and now your Pa, but much as it hurts Mr. Biddle and me, we can't take you in by way of doing the good Christian act. Times are hard, and money scarce. Do you have any other family that you know of?"

I shook my head no, never taking my eyes from her face.

"Then it's only right that your uncle take you in, since he's the only family you have." Mrs. Biddle's eyes slid to the surface she was wiping. Her plump hands idly brushed a few crumbs onto a plate held just under the edge of the table. "It ain't as though you're going empty-handed. Your Pa's farm must be worth something, and the cows, and that fine team of Clydesdales of your Pa's should bring a pretty price. That should sweeten your uncle's temper, I'd say."

At the mention of Zephyr and Sonnet—my dearest horse friends—being sold, I crumpled in on myself and started crying. Life seemed to drain right out of me.

"Now, don't fret. Things'll work out, you wait and see," Mrs. Biddle said with a kind but tired smile. "What say you have a nice hot bath here in front of the fire?"

After the bath, the first I'd had in weeks, Mrs. Biddle combed my hair straight down my back.

"Your hair is such a lovely light brown shade, child, the firelight dances along the strands."

"My hair is pretty?"

"It looks so like your mother's. Has gold glints in it."

"You knew my mama?" I turned to face her, my eyes wide with surprise.

"Yes, child. We were friends." Mrs. Biddle smiled and drew me into a warm hug. "Your eyes are the same lovely shade of gray as hers were."

"What was my mama like?" My eyes hungrily latched onto Mrs. Biddle's face, searching out the story.

"Turn around, and I'll tell you while I braid your hair." She combed the strands straight down the center of my back.

I tried to stand still, but the silence was too much. My chest felt as though it would burst for want of air.

"Please," I whispered above the crackling fire.

"I'm trying to gather my thoughts," Mrs. Biddle said, turning me to face her. "You're all aquiver. Be still a moment and let me get the part straight then I'll start."

Mrs. Biddle drew the corner of the comb across the crown of my head, separating the hair in a straight line, then turned me around and did the same down the back of my head. I shivered.

"Your Mama was a small woman. A couple of inches shorter than I am," Mrs. Biddle began, putting half of my long hair over my left shoulder and starting to braid the other half. "She was full of fun and laughter, and was the light in your Papa's soul. I could see it in his eyes every time he looked at her. He treated her like a princess, he did. Your Papa smiled a lot back then. Didn't drink much, enough to be sociable at the town's Fourth of July picnic and maybe a little during the holiday season. He was a good dairyman, respected by folks around these parts. He's the one who told my Clive how to increase our herd's butter fat."

"You was going to tell me about my Mama. I already know my Papa." I wiggled in anticipation.

"Don't be too hard on the memory of your father, Charlotte. I think he was a good man whose whole world shattered the day your Mama died. Maybe when you're older you'll understand." Mrs. Biddle tied off the first braid with blue thread, then wrapped a ribbon around it and tied a neat bow.

"Anyway, your Mama was fun-loving as I said, and she was kind, too. She loved children and was so looking forward to having you. She sewed and crocheted beautifully, made a number of beautiful buntings while waiting for you to arrive. Embroidered flowers down the front of them as I remember. The second Christmas she was here, she crocheted me a shawl that I wear only for special. Fine work she did." Mrs. Biddle tied off the second braid and created a matching bow. With a pat on my shoulder, she said, "Come with me, I'll show you."

We went into Mr. and Mrs. Biddle's bedroom where she lifted the lid of an old trunk and drew out a creamy white shawl with long fringe. The pattern was delicate and lacy, its beauty just melted my heart with awe. My mother had made that shawl.

"You can touch it if you want Charlotte."

My eyes flashed to her's for an instant to make sure I heard right. I petted the shawl, as one would pet a horse's nose. And I remember thinking, my mother made this. My, oh, my.

Mrs. Biddle slipped the shawl around my shoulders and crossed it in front. She gave me a hug. "Looking pretty, girl, just like your Mama."

I felt so proud when she said that. The pretty weren't important to me, but being like my Mama meant the world.

We looked straight into each other's eyes for a moment before she continued. "Charlotte, it is important for you to know that your Mama's death was not your fault and that she loved you very much." Mrs. Biddle smiled into my eyes.

"I stopped to visit on my way home from town one day not long before you were born to see how she was faring. I came up behind her standing before the fire, lost in thought and rubbing big round circles on her tummy. I asked her what she was doing. She smiled and said, "I'm loving my baby." It was you she was loving. I remember doing the same myself before my two were born." Mrs. Biddle took the corner of her apron and brushed it across her eyes. "Now that's a good memory for you to take with you."

I stopped rubbing my belly and dropped my hand to my side; I didn't want to love this child I carried. She would belong to someone else. She would be a member of a family, around people who would love her. People like the Biddles. The Becks, I hoped, would love her as their own.

If she lived.

Aunt Martha's child died with her.

I'd tried not to think about that. Tried not to think about dying while giving birth.

Tried to forget, but kept remembering.

Kept wondering whether I should speak to the Becks before I gave birth, or wait till after, in case we didn't make it. Seemed cruel to have them say yes when both of us might die. Then I would worry about what would happen if I died and the child didn't, like my Mama and me. What would happen to her then? I spent another two weeks trying to decide the right thing to do.

I woke up at first birdsong one morning, swilled a cup of coffee, fed the stock, and headed into town to speak with the Becks, my belly rubbing the pommel of the saddle like an old fart's beer gut. Disgusting.

Got into town before the general store opened, so I stopped in at the eatery and had myself a couple of fried eggs, half a dozen rashers of bacon, fried potatoes, toast with butter and jam, and a couple of cups of well-brewed coffee. Felt like a stuffed turkey when I was done, but I sure enjoyed it going down.

When I got to Becks, I found Avery opening up for the day.

"Can we talk private-like for a few minutes?" I asked, stepping past him into the store.

He gave me a long look, shrugged, and flipped the sign on the door back to 'Closed.' "Surely, what's on your mind?"

"I would like to talk to you and Lacey about adopting the child I'm carrying."

Avery's eyes popped wide.

"If you don't want to talk on the subject, that's fine," I said. "I don't want to offend you none. I remembered that you looked kind of regretful when I—what I mean is—Oh, hell." I raked my fingers through my hair trying to figure how to talk my way out of the corner I'd talked myself into. When Avery had looked regretful about not having children, I was Charley, not Charlotte.

"Let me get my wife, and ya can start over." Avery passed between the heavy blue and white striped curtains that separated their living area from the store and called to his wife.

Both Becks entered the store a few moments later. I could tell Avery had told his wife why I was there 'cause her expression was one of rapt attention mixed with curiosity and a little excitement.

"I'm both Charley and Charlotte," I started out.

They both nodded.

"You knew?"

"Guessed," Avery said.

"I'll be plain honest with you. I'm a coachman from Providence, Rhode Island. Got myself in the family way some months back. The father left me on the way down here, but I came on ahead hoping to give the child up for adoption, so's I could return to doing what I do best, if I live through the birthing."

"Why do you say that?" Lacey asked. "Women have babies all the time."

"Both my Mama and her sister died in childbirth."

Lacey lowered her eyes, "Oh, I see. I'm sorry."

"I don't want to give it up for adoption through an orphanage. I was raised in one. Wouldn't wish that on any kid."

"When ya expecting to give birth?" Lacey asked.

"Three weeks."

Lacey looked at her husband with such hope in her eyes.

"We'll take it," Avery said.

"Either way, boy or girl?" I asked.

"Either way," Avery said in a firm voice. At her husband's words, Lacey's face split into a grin a moment before she burst into tears and threw herself into her husband's arms. It was the most lively I'd ever seen the woman, and cleared away the small doubt that had lingered in my mind about her raising a child.

We agreed that I would stay with them to deliver, and they would find a wet nurse. Unfortunately, that was not to be.

22
New Life

That first week of June, my belly felt like it was fitting to burst with every move the child made, and believe me, it made plenty. Felt like a damn circus going on inside sometimes, complete with acrobats tumbling off the trapeze and landing on my bladder. Yup, I was ready to get the birthing over.

Figured I would stay at Cozy Hill as long as I could manage. Didn't want to spend days in someone else's house with nothing to do and them staring at me. Freddie was keeping an eye on me, stopping over every other day or so to see how I was faring. She'd been in the day before and said she'd be back again the next day. Said I looked near but hadn't dropped yet. Whatever the hell that meant.

I woke up to dark clouds and heavy rain, feeling like a fractious mare. Wanted to kick and stomp and bite. My belly felt different this morning, and though I seemed to need more trips to the outhouse, I could breathe easier.

Went out and fed Chester, then groomed him till his coat gleamed, but that didn't take long. I was still restless. I'd made sure the horses I'd been working on were returned to their owners the previous week. Didn't want unfinished business hanging over my head, but now I wished I had another half-dozen to groom so's I had something to do. Generally, being around horses soothed me and that's exactly what I needed that day.

Deep down I was scared the child within me was dead. I hadn't felt it move all morning.

Went back to the house and cleaned the cabin for want of something to do. That done, I paced the floor till my belly hurt, then sat and read till my back hurt. No position felt comfortable for long.

I kept an eye on the lane hoping to catch sight of Freddie coming so's I could put the coffee into the pot I had steaming by the fire. But the more I looked out, the more I doubted she would make the trip over. Rain beat the ground. Wind raged through the trees, lashing them one against the other. Rain-speckled waves whipped across the pond-like puddles surrounding the cabin. Small branches and leaves flew through the air while larger limbs spun and cracked like the clap of thunder.

I felt fidgety as a cat trapped in a root cellar clawing to get out. I paced and sat, and sat and paced, until I thought I could hang from the rafters by my fingernails. Until, that is, a pain grabbed my whole belly and squeezed, leaving me terrified and panting.

The pain subsided and I sat down. I buried my clenched fists in what little lap I had and waited. Kept telling myself many women safely bore healthy babies, but the echo of my thoughts said that my mother and aunt hadn't been so lucky.

At the time, God and I were not on speaking terms, but I panted out a short prayer hoping He was listening.

Last trip into town to see Doc Schmidt, I'd asked about birthing. Didn't get too much that was helpful as I recall. He said it's best to let my body do the work and not get myself tied in knots of fear. Some women, he said, found it helpful to concentrate on a flame, or a picture of their mother, or some such when the pain was at its worst. He also said the pain would get stronger and occur more often as time went on, but that each pain wouldn't last more'n a minute. He assured me he'd be there to help me through it all.

When I spoke to Freddie about it later, she told me deep breaths calm the body during and after each wave of pain.

With that first contraction, I'd already learned that bilking fear and remaining calm was easier said than done.

Knowing I'd be better off working than sitting and thinking, I got up and started to prepare as best I could, which weren't much, considering I didn't know what the hell I was doing. Brought in firewood, filled a large pot with water and hung it over the fire, got a bucket of fresh water to have on hand for drinking and keeping cool, put my bedroll canvas over the bed tick and put a fresh sheet over top.

Every moment I expected another pain and steeled myself to take it bravely. Horses gave birth as though they weren't in great pain. I figured I could do as much.

When my second spasm came, I happened to be sitting at the table where I had laid my freshly wound pocket watch shortly after my first contraction. I figured I would keep track of the time in between to see if the pains were getting closer together. Forty minutes. I took a deep breath. How long would this go on?

The night Eb and Tilly and me delivered Rose's foal floated across my mind, and I remembered Tilly tying off the foal's cord. Struggling to my feet, I poked around until I found a length of cord and cut two pieces off about six inches long. I dragged the table close to the bed, making sure the cord and jackknife were within easy reach. I brought out a few fresh candles and laid them on the table, and placed a cup of water nearby. I didn't know what else to do, so I sat and waited for the next wave of pain.

Morning dragged into afternoon and afternoon into evening without the pains getting much closer together. I lit a candle and stared at it while the pain clenched my belly. I walked. I sat. I laid on my side for awhile. Around what would normally be suppertime, my waves of pain started to come every fifteen minutes, and lasted about a minute. Each one hurt more'n the last.

I learned how to ease the pain some. I would feel each contraction begin and take a deep breath or two, then pant like a dog through the harshest part, ending with a couple more deep breaths as the pain subsided. It seemed to help me through the worst of the hell, that, and rubbing my belly.

No matter how hard I tried to push during the pain, there seemed no end in sight. I could feel pressure in my crotch, but no baby's head. By eight o'clock that evening, my fear began to build again. Trusting my body like the Doc said weren't working. I seemed to be at cross-purposes, my belly and I pushed while the bottom didn't open. The waves of pain came every ten minutes and hurt like hell. I'd removed all my clothes but my shirt, and now that was soggy with sweat. I felt as though I'd been ridden hard and put away wet.

Around ten o'clock that night a rush of fluid burst forth while I stood at the window looking at my reflection and listening to the rain slap the glass and the wind moan around the corners of the cabin. I burst into tears. What the hell was going on? Was this a good thing? Was it normal? Doc didn't mention anything like this during our brief talk. I cleaned up the mess best I could and lay on the bed. I had never felt so tired and scared before in my life.

As I lay there, I thought back to the night we delivered Rose of her foal and remembered that she too had water gush out of her. Then I figured my body was working same as hers and some of my panic eased off.

The pain got so bad and came so often that I screamed. I couldn't stand it any longer. I didn't have any more bravery left in me. I wanted the child out. I didn't care whether I lived or died, just so's the baby lived. Course, being of a practical bent of nature, I realized that I would have to live, too, at least until Freddie came.

In my mind, the child was a girl, always had been, so I talked to her as such. In my exhaustion, I told her to be strong for me and kept telling her we'd make it together. Told her I loved her. The words surprised me but echoed true in my mind and heart. I loved my baby sight unseen. We were in this together. If one of us weren't going to make it, I wanted it to be me.

I think I passed out a time or two for brief moments between contractions before they came fast and furious and my baby girl was finally born at two-ten in the morning.

"We made it baby girl," I said, holding her in my arms, and wiping her eyes and nose free of mucus. Her father's dark hair covered her egg-shaped head. I watched her open deep dark eyes so like her father's and look at me as if to say "we made it Mama."

Such welcome flooded my heart. I was filled with feelings I'd been yearning for my entire life without realizing. Silent tears ran down my face and dripped off my chin.

"Yes, we did Sweetie," I said, wiping my tears and the birthing mucus from the baby. I was tired as hell, but feeling prouder than I had ever felt before. Closest thing to that feeling was driving a coach and six-up to the door of an inn with a precision and flourish that made the customers look at me in awe. Now I had done a truly awesome thing, and I realized in that moment that I would never be able to give my baby away. I loved her with such fierceness that I knew I would kill to protect her. She was mine, and, strange to my mind, I was hers. Her mama.

We looked into each other's eyes and suddenly I knew her name.

Mattie.

"You'll never be a millstone around my neck little one, not like I was to my elders. I been hoping you were a girl. Girls are better. Stronger, I think."

When Freddie walked in the next morning, I dropped my baby.

The night before I'd cleaned up the bed and wiped us both down a bit. I dumped the wood-box and lined it with a fresh sheet and my pillow. I placed my sleeping daughter in the kindling box after diapering and wrapping her in a poorly sewn, too-large bunting I'd made, then tucked the box between me and the wall. Granted it weren't comfortable, but neither of us seemed to care; sleep and safety being my prime concern.

Small unfamiliar animal-like sounds woke me with a start. I propped myself on my elbow and peered at the new person I'd brought into the world. She was trying out her new body, fluttering her arms and fingers, jerking her knees. Tiny fingers with the tiniest wax-like fingernails scratched the air. I reached down to stroke her hand. She grabbed my finger.

I found myself cooing. Me cooing; something I never figured I would be doing. Like one of them woman folk I'd see in town and thought them silly for all their soft talk and proud smile. Though I felt embarrassed at first, I kept on. I guess it was the pride. The way I saw it, we were beginning to get to know each other. We were strengthening the bond that had sprung between us during the birthing.

Mattie's happy bouncings turned into a prune-faced squall. Breakfast, I guessed. That was a whole new one on me. I put her to my breast. Her nuzzling caused my nipple to pucker, and she latched on. It felt pinchy at first, but I got used to it. When she had her fill, I noticed she'd peed the diaper and that we both smelled worse than winter cow muck.

I was giving my squirming little girl her first bath in the dishpan with about a cup of warm water for fear I would drown her in anything more, when in walks Freddie. In that flash of surprise, Mattie squirted out of my wet grasp to splash in the pan. I slid my hand up her back, cradling her head and scooped her close to my heart. We both burst into tears.

Freddie bit her lips together in an attempt not to laugh. "My, my, my, what have we here?"

I sheepishly wiped my tears on the sleeve of my sweat-stained shirt. "My baby's come."

"So I see. Do you want me to take her to the Becks?"

"No. She's mine." I clutched my daughter close, too close, for she let out another wail.

A knowing smile crossed Freddie's lips. "What's her name?"

"Matilda Winifred Parkhurst. Mattie. For my friend, Tilly Balch, and you."

"I am honored, Charley. Truly honored." Tears glistened in Freddie's eyes. "Let me hold my godchild." She wrapped a towel around Mattie and eased her from me. She sat on the edge of my cot and unwrapped my now silent daughter. "She's perfect."

"Promise me you'll take care of her if anything happens to me?"

"Wouldn't have it any other way."

"We worked at the birthing most of the night. I've never been so scared. I feared I would let her down."

"Birthing does that to a woman," she said, wrapping the towel around my baby.

"But once she came out, I knew we were meant to be together."

Freddie nodded with a knowing look.

"Yet, when you came in I dropped her. What the hell am I doing trying to be a mother, for god sakes. I don't know shit about mothering." I took my daughter back into my arms.

"I'll show you what needs be done. Some things'll come natural. Like the way you hold her."

"Suppose I do something wrong?"

"You won't be the first."

23
Life with Mattie

F reddie brought me a cradle from home, one her boys had outgrown years ago. "Want it back for my grandbabies though," she said.

I wondered most every day whether I'd made the right decision, but I would look into my baby's eyes and know in my heart I was doing the right thing. There was something between us, taffy-thick, sweet with love.

About two weeks after Mattie arrived, Freddie returned from town with a bundle of baby clothes and a note from Lacey Beck.

> Dear Charlotte,
>
> I cannot lie and tell you I don't mind your change of plans. I am deeply disappointed, but I think I understand. Had I given birth to your precious baby daughter, I would never part with her either. I am sincerely glad that both of you are well, and, from the bottom of my heart, I wish you the very best in raising your daughter.

I hope you will bring her to see me that I may wheedle my way into her heart with sweets.

May God Bless,
Lacey Beck

P.S. Thought you might like to have these clothes for the baby. Am keeping a few aside to embroider her initials on. Come see us when next you are in town.

I couldn't help but admire the woman's fine character and feel proud that I had made such a good initial decision in choosing her and Avery to be Mattie's adoptive parents. I hoped that I would do my daughter justice in raising her.

Mattie and I started a whole new life together. Freddie taught me how to take care of my daughter, how to give her baths, what to feed her, how to keep her warm and comfortable. Anytime I had a question, Freddie was there. If my baby got sick, Freddie was there. When I needed someone to watch over Mattie while I had business to attend to, Freddie was there. I could not have had a dearer, more trusted friend.

Much to my surprise, Freddie was right. Mothering came naturally. Though I hadn't much cuddling and attention throughout my life, I did remember what little I had from Aunt Martha and Mrs. Biddle. And some of what I did came from my heart. I'd been starved for attention most of my life, and I was determined that my daughter would never want for love or caring, so we did a whole lot of cuddling. I read to her from whatever I was reading at the time, be it The Farmer's Almanac, Mr. Cooper's The Last of the Mohicans, or Mr. Dickens' Pickwick Papers. When upset, she always seemed to calm at the sound of my voice, so reading made us both happy.

To keep food on the table and clothes on our backs, I took in horses as I had before Mattie was born. We trained or doctored them together, me and her. I would ask her opinion as she sat in a flour sack-lined bushel basket nailed to the side of the shed, then I would give her my take on the matter and set to work.

As she grew out of the basket into a wooden box, then out of that onto her own two feet, we continued to work together. I tied a leather tether around her waist and fastened the other end to a corral post to keep her from wandering off or getting under foot. We pretended she was a horse waiting to be trained.

I was proud of the fact that Mattie never spoke baby talk. Don't know whether it was that I never spoke it to her, or all that reading she heard, but she amazed her honorary aunts, Freddie and Lacey, and Uncle Avery.

When she was old enough not to put every damn thing into her mouth, I made her a doll out of a corncob and a few wisps of old rags. She held it in her fist wherever she went and called it Onna. Where she came up with the name, I don't know, but Onna was her best friend until her second birthday.

On that day, her Aunt Lacey gave her a real doll and her Aunt Freddie gave her a pair of shoes. After she tripped on the cabin's uneven floorboards and fell flat on her face a few times, she didn't want to wear the shoes anymore. In fact, she learned to untie them and pull them off when I weren't looking. We had our worst mother-daughter fight over those shoes when I double tied the laces and she couldn't get them off. Fine time that was! Screamed like to lift the roof.

The sun that summer baked the earth and fried the living. Every creature, whether man or beast, sweated while standing still and acted fractious when asked to move. Those were the times I wished I was back in Providence where hot, as I remembered it, was bearable.

Everything got so's it had a red cast to it thanks to the Georgia clay. After the nearby brook and marsh dried up, the only running water we had were the rivulets of sweat that trickled down our bodies, or dripped off the end of our noses, or seeped into our eyes. By the end of the day, I could hardly see, my eyes were so blurry and sore from rubbing the sweat out of them.

Mattie and I slept poorly most nights. There weren't a comfortable, dry spot on the tick within five minutes of lying down. Every day my daughter seemed to do the exact opposite of what I asked of her and disagreed with everything I said. Come bedtime, I prayed for her to behave, and she prayed that her mama would behave. Cheeky little chit.

Since my well hadn't run dry, I took to keeping the water trough full not only for Chester and whatever other horses I had on hand in the coral, but out of kindness for the wild birds and animals as well. By the looks of the animal sign, I had a lot of takers since they didn't have the brook to slake their thirst. Some of them I didn't want, the snakes especially, but they came, too. Them I would shoot. Got so's I could drill them through the head at ten yards when my eyes weren't stinging with sweat.

I kept my Colt loaded and lying in a small wooden box I'd nailed almost out of my reach near the rafters of the cabin. Didn't want my daughter getting at it. Though I needed it handy, I never took to wearing it as some did.

"Mattie, you stay away from the water trough now you hear?" I said every time she edged toward the cabin door. I repeated myself to the point that she no longer heard what I said. "Mama doesn't want you to fall in."

"Yes, Mama." And away she would go, and within minutes, she would be heading for the water. I explained why I didn't want her near the trough, I spanked her, I yelled at her, I sat her in a corner to think—Freddie's idea—but water seemed to draw her like food draws a starveling. She couldn't seem to help herself.

This particular day I watched her from the doorway of the cabin. We'd finished working the horses and returned to start dinner. She was playing near the backdoor, when I went in to set some potatoes to boil. Not an instant later, I heard a shrill scream. I raced to the door. Mattie weren't where she had been half a minute ago. She now lay in the dust beside the house clutching her arms to her chest. Her high-pitched screams continued in small quick blasts. I rushed to her side and scooped her into my arms. From the corner of my eye, I caught movement in the dust nearby.

A four-foot long pinch-crested black body with yellowish belly and mottled cross-bands constricted its body and opened its white mouth defying me to come closer.

A water moccasin.

I rushed into the cabin and placed Mattie on the bed.

"You're going to be all right, baby. Mama's going to take care of you." I kept saying over and over in a soft voice while running my hands over her body in search for sign. I ripped the dress off her upper body to see whether the blood I saw on it came from a bite to her chest. Her screams subsided to crying as I crooned to her.

"It hurts," she said. "I'm scared Mama."

"Show Mama where it hurts, sweetie."

She extended her arm toward me. One puncture wound and a scratch about an inch apart oozed watery blood half way between her right wrist and elbow. I grabbed my sharpest kitchen knife in my right hand and her wrist in my left. Her eyes widened and she started screaming again while pulling away from me with all her might. She kicked me a few times then wedged her feet against my belly and used the strength in her legs to force herself away from me. I lost my grip on her arm.

"Mattie, stop it," I yelled, trying to recapture the flailing arm. "Mama's trying to help."

"No," she screamed, trying to roll off the bed. "Don't cut my arm off."

"I'm not going to cut your damn arm off. I need to suck the poison out."

"No."

"Mattie stop. Lie still." Wedging her legs between my thighs, I grabbed her arm and slashed an ugly X between the two fang marks. The cuts went deeper than I had wanted, but I had no way to prevent her from swinging her right arm while I worked. I sucked her blood into my mouth and spat it on the floor. Again and again and again, I sucked and spat.

"Mama, my head hurts," she said. "My leg, too."

I released her legs from between my thighs and soothed the damp hair from her eyes while I sucked and spat.

"My leg hurts."

"It'll be ok in a minute, sweetie."

"Where the snake bit me, Mama."

"Oh my God!" I pushed the skirts of her dress up to her waist and there, red and swollen, was another bite on the calf of her right leg. There must have been two snakes. I grabbed the knife and cut an X between the two oozing punctures. My daughter had grown pale and did not cry at the added pain. I sucked and spat for all I was worth.

"Mama," she moaned, cupping her small hand over her mouth as she twisted to lean over the side of the bed to throw up. Again, I soothed her hair away from her face and started to hum as I did when she couldn't go to sleep as a baby. I sucked and spat and hummed in between. Her little face, with its soft smooth skin, looked so pale. I pressed my fingers under her chin to feel her heartbeat. It raced like a horse at a flat out gallop. After throwing up a second time, she began a restless rolling of her body. I didn't know whether it was a sign of the poisoning, or the fear she felt.

I needed to get her to Doc Schmidt.

"Mama's going to saddle Chester, and we're going for a ride," I told her as I slipped her arms through the sleeves of her dress. My daughter always jumped at the chance to ride, but today she just rocked her body while staring at me.

I left her lying on the cot and ran to the shed. I threw the tack on Chester so fast he got jumpy and wouldn't stand still. Kept pointing his nose at the roof, so's I couldn't put the bit in his mouth. Everything I did seemed drawn out and painfully slow to me. I wanted to move like lightening, but felt like molasses. I stilled myself and took a deep breath, then another, letting them out slowly. If I couldn't control the horse, my daughter would die. I stroked Chester and hummed as I did to soothe my daughter. In a matter of moments, Chester lowered his head and gave my shoulder a shove with his nose. I inserted the bit between his teeth, pulled the headstall over his ears and buckled the chinstrap. We trotted over to the house. There was no snake in sight. I dropped Chester's rein letting him know he was to stand still. I ran into the cabin and scooped my daughter into my arms. Her skin felt clammy, and her eyes looked dazed.

"Stick with Mama," I pleaded. "Don't die baby girl." I mounted Chester, settling Mattie across the saddlebow in front of me. Clutching my daughter to my chest, I kicked Chester into a gallop for town. I'd never pushed a horse as hard as I did Chester that day. Each time he slowed, I asked for speed and he gave his all. He ran five miles flat out putting us in town within twenty minutes. We slid to a stop in front of the doctor's office. I let the reins fall and stepped down with my daughter in my arms. Ran into the Doc's office. No one was there. I ran back outside. Knocked into Freddie.

"Saw you rush in," she said. "What's doing?"

"Water moccasins bit Mattie. Where's Doc?"

"On a house call," she said, guiding me back into the doctor's waiting room. "Where she been bit."

"Once in the leg and the other in the arm. I cut them open and sucked out the venom." We walked through to the doctor's exam room, and I laid Mattie on the table. My daughter stared at the light, then went into strong convulsions. Her whole body stiffened so that her back came off the table. She started choking. I lifted her head. Her teeth were clamped shut. Then she relaxed with a small sigh. Her dark eyes stared at the ceiling without blinking. I shoved my fingers under her chin, but felt no pulse. Put my head on her chest, but didn't hear the beat of her heart. I shook her. She didn't respond.

I crushed her to me and howled.

My baby was dead.

24
Life in the Bottle

We buried Mattie the next morning. I don't rightly remember much about my daughter's funeral except that when I close my eyes, I can still see the tiny casket in that deep red hole. My heart was buried in that box. Truth tell, I didn't give a damn about anything after that. I bought me a bottle of Monongahela, more'n one in fact, and every time I started coming out of my stupor, I yanked the cork and downed the whiskey till my thoughts were wrapped in cotton batting once again. Problem was, I couldn't ever get rid of the pain in the center of my chest. Felt like a rusty razor cut a hole clear through me and left shards of itself behind to keep the pain fresh. They say time heals all wounds. Well, I believe there are some that don't never heal, and a mother losing a child is one of the worst tortures for a body to bear.

I went back to wearing men's clothes. There was no need to pretend anymore. I no longer had a daughter to set an example for. No one seemed to notice. Either they didn't care, or already knew I'd been both Charley and Charlotte. Now it no longer mattered to me. Nothing did.

Owners of the horses I had on hand came and mumbled a few words at me, handed me some money, and led their animal away. I took their money and went to town, bought a fresh supply of Monongahela, and returned home to drink myself senseless.

I think Freddie stopped in a time or two and tried to get me to pull myself together, but it didn't take. She went home to her live children, and I crawled into the bottle with my dead one. We fit nice and snug in my bottle, my memories of Mattie, and me.

One morning, I woke up and had no idea where I was. Light streamed across my comforter-covered body. I lay like a log down the center of an honest to goodness feather bed. Hadn't ever slept in one of them before. Didn't have a stitch on underneath the covers. Wondered how the hell that happened. Tried looking around the room for my clothes, but my eyes hurt so that I resorted to turning my head, a move I regretted. Pain rushed through my noggin like a rampaging river rolling boulders out of its way. I closed my eyes, forcing the rising bile back with a swallow. I groped around hoping to find a bottle of whiskey at hand. Weren't none.

I must have fallen back to sleep after a while for when I opened my eyes again it was night and cool air streamed across the bed instead of sunlight. Since no blazing light cut into my eyes this time, I looked around the room best I could in soft moonlight, but didn't learn anything new. My clothes weren't anywhere close by, so unless I wanted to make a fine show of myself, I'd have to stay put till someone brought them back. Tried using my ears, since they were the only things that didn't hurt, but I couldn't learn anything from the buzz and chirp of the night critters. I couldn't think through the whiskey haze in my brain, so I gave up and fell back to sleep.

Next morning, I woke to the rattle of a doorknob. Bright sunlight met my eyes once again. Freddie walked in and set a tray of food across my lap. "Time you ate something."

My belly had mixed feelings on the matter. My mouth watered at the smell of toast and coddled egg, yet my belly twisted like it might spew bile if I took a bite.

"Here, lift up so I can stuff some pillows behind your back."
Much to my surprise, I was now wearing a nightgown.

"When…" There were so many questions floating about in my head, I didn't know where to start and none of the words that swam through the remaining numbness would take the form of a sentence.

"Everything in good time, Charley," she said. "You been through a lot. We'll talk it out over a cup of tea soon's you're done with your breakfast." Freddie forked the egg and toast into me, and, contrary to what I thought might happen, my belly accepted the food.

"My daughter?" I asked. As soon as the question was out of my mouth, my mind remembered. My face must have mirrored my thoughts, for Freddie leaned close and wrapped her arms around me. For the first time since the death of my daughter, I cried.

To say I cried sounds trivial compared to what flowed from my mind and heart that morning. I screamed. I raged. I sobbed. I kept asking why. Why did my daughter have to die? Why couldn't the snake have bitten me? Why didn't Dom see us through? Why? Why? Why? That day, I learned that asking "why" would put a person on the very edge of insanity.

I raged for hours. If it hadn't been for Freddie, I would've put an end to my life that day. When I calmed, she tucked me in for another nap, promising we would talk over a pot of tea when I awoke. Exhausted, I fell asleep again.

When I woke up, late afternoon sun baked Georgia's red earth and heated what little air there was to breathe. True to her word, Freddie returned with a fresh pot of tea.

My belly gave a deep rolling growl at the first sip of tea.

"Sorry," I said, rubbing my middle.

"No need to be. You probably haven't eaten in weeks. I'll bring you a bowl of the soup I got simmering on the back of the stove."

"What day is it?"

"Twenty-fifth of September. She's been gone six weeks, Charley, and you've been in the bottom of a bottle all that time. You must've spent all your money on whiskey."

"Most, not all—I think," I said, finding it difficult to look my friend in the eye. Always prided myself in being strong and there I was a cry-baby. A quitter. A drunk.

"It's important to mourn, Charley, and you haven't allowed yourself the grace to do it until today. It was long overdue."

"How'd I get here?"

"I was at Doc Schmidt's when Old Man Wainwright brought you in. Said he found you by the side of the road."

"I don't remember."

"Course you don't. Doc said you were unconscious. We didn't know if you were going to pull through."

"How long have I been here?"

"Three days."

"Did someone waylay me?"

"No, Wainwright said you looked like maybe you fell off your horse."

"Where's Chester?"

"Down in the barn. He's fine."

A long moment stretched between us.

"What's more to the point Charley, are you going to be all right?"

"Don't know." I couldn't answer any better than that. I needed time to think. Time to figure whether I could pick up the pieces of myself and go on, or whether I would be better off dead. There was no one on the face of this earth who needed me, why should I go on? But there I was asking why again.

"You're welcome to stay on as long as you need," Freddie said, patting my arm. "I know you'll figure it out and find a way to go on with your life. Somehow we women always manage to pull ourselves together."

In the two weeks that I stayed with the MacFerran's, I had plenty of time to think. When alone, I cried for my daughter many times, then brushed my tears away, determined that I would never allow myself to get close to another person as I had with Dom—and more especially, with my daughter.

Freddie was right, I could pull myself together and regain my self-respect by going back to doing what I did best, driving a six-up.

The day before I was about to leave for Providence, I went into Pineywood to take care of a legal matter, and say goodbye to the Becks and Doc Schmidt. I felt strong going in. Took care of business first then stopped in at the general store. Lacey Beck and I saw each other and hugged. Tears spilled down both our cheeks while Avery did some mighty fast blinking.

Hindsight, where death is concerned, is brutal. I looked at these fine people and guilt grabbed ahold of me, body and soul, knifing me once again in the heart and clouding my mind with thoughts of what might have been. Had I gone through with the adoption, Mattie would be alive. She would've grown up in a good family, and maybe had a family of her own one day.

I walked out of the general store and down the street where townsfolk mumbled words of sympathy. I didn't know what to say, and, for the most part, neither did they. I nodded and walked on, holding my breath so's not to break down and sob like a baby in the middle of town.

Doc was about to call in his next patient when I walked into his office. He told them to be seated for a few moments and waved me to come through to his exam room.

"Good to see you up and about," he said. "Wasn't sure you were going to make it through."

"I'm still not paid in full on that one myself yet."

"It's hard. Death is so final and in many cases too abrupt."

I nodded my agreement.

"I am sorry I wasn't here when you needed me. It comes with being a country doctor, I suppose. It still cuts deep when I lose a patient, believe me. It's not something you ever get used to either.

"I don't know why your daughter died so quick. Generally, something like that takes a couple of hours. I can only guess that it was her size and the fear she must have felt that sped the venom through her system. You did the best you could. Remember that, Charlotte. I probably couldn't have saved her had I been here."

"I didn't know there were two bites right off. I should've checked her all over. I..."

"You did the best you could," he said, laying a hand on my shoulder. "You were scared, too. Remember that." He gave my shoulder a gentle squeeze. "What are you going to do now?"

"Head back to Providence, I suppose. Too many memories for me here."

"You'll be missed. You gained yourself a fine reputation as a horseman and horse doctor. Many hereabout will be sorry to see you go." He patted my shoulder before guiding me to the door. "Take care of yourself, Charlotte. The pain will ease, given time."

"Thanks, Doc," I said, only half believing that last. In my head, I knew he was right, but my heart denied the truth as being impossible.

I headed for the tavern and ordered up a bottle of Mononga-hela. I made my way to the table furthest from the bar, hoping not to be disturbed. I remember pulling the cork and downing a few shots—the rest is a blessed blank.

I awoke the next morning back in Freddie's guest bed. Minutes later, she strode into the room to stand at the foot of the bed with fists on her hips.

"Charley, this is the last time I'm going to put up with this shit. You want to poison yourself to death with whiskey, you go right ahead somewheres where I don't know. You understand me?"

"Stop yellin'," I said with a groan, holding my head together with my hands.

"You understand me?"

"Yes," I bellowed back, curling into a tight ball of pain.

"You want something in that stomach of yours, you'll have to come downstairs and get it yourself!" She slammed the bedroom door behind her.

When the echo of the door slamming faded, and the pain in my head lessoned some, I sat on the edge of the bed. Not a wise move. I sank to my knees, groping for the chamber pot, and got it under my chin a second before what little I had in my belly spewed out my mouth. As I knelt by the bed wondering whether there'd be another heave, Freddie yelled up the stairs.

"Bring that pot down here and clean it out."

I didn't bother to reply.

After pulling on my clothes, I had to sit awhile to let my head clear and my belly settle again before going downstairs. I went out back to rinse the chamber pot before heading in to breakfast.

"Shame on you, Charley," Freddie said. "Going into town like that, telling me you were settling up, then coming back sodding drunk like you did. I thought better of you."

"Didn't plan it that way," I said.

"Well, what the hell happened then?"

"Everybody kept saying how sorry they were about Mattie. When I said goodbye to Lacey and Avery, I kept thinking that if I'd only let them have her, she'd still be alive. Then Doc said that maybe he wouldn't have done any better than I did. I don't know, it all came flooding back. I had a drink to make the pain go away.

"The pain is real, Freddie. My heart hurts so bad. My arms ache to hold my little girl. To hug her to me. To smell her. To kiss her till she laughs. To tell her bedtime stories. I'll never be able to do any of that again. I don't care if I live. In fact, I think I would be happier joining Mattie than living this hell all alone."

Freddie grabbed my arm. "You have to pull yourself together. Think those thoughts another time."

I nodded and hid behind my coffee cup a moment.

"It's a good thing you've decided to return to Providence," Freddie said, scraping her chair back and rising. "That place won't keep stirring up fresh thoughts of your daughter every time you turn around."

"I hope you're right," I said. "I'll pack and leave in the morning."

"No need to hurry," she said from the doorway.

The rest of our last day together was uneasy. Words did not come to either of us.

The next morning, I rose early as had been my custom, packed my few belongings, and saddled Chester. I knew Freddie was an early riser, too, but had to go in search of her when I was ready to leave. I found her weeding the kitchen herb garden.

"I'm ready to head out," I said, yanking on my wide-cuffed gloves and clenching my fists to work the stiff leather.

She nodded her head without looking up, her wide-brimmed hat shading her face so I couldn't read her thoughts.

"Thank you for all you done for me, Freddie. For me and for Mattie."

The hat bobbed again.

"Would you look at me once before I go?" I hoped I hadn't lost a friend.

Freddie got stiffly to her feet and came toward me. When she removed her hat, I saw the tears she'd been trying to hide.

"I'll be fine," I said.

"I sure hope so."

"Still friends?"

"Of course."

"I've signed it over to you, Freddie. I know how you've always wanted that piece of land, seein's how it takes a chunk out of your eastern border and all."

She threw her arms around me. "Oh my God, your farm? I'll pay you back somehow."

"No need. It's yours free and clear."

"Thank you." Freddie wiped away fresh tears with the back of her hand.

"We'll write."

"Where should I send a letter?"

"You can always reach me through Tilly Balch at the Franklin House Inn. She'll know where to find me." We drifted to where Chester stood waiting for me. "Thanks again for everything," I said. "Damn glad we're still friends."

We both got a little weepy-eyed at that, so we hugged each other goodbye, and I climbed on Chester and nudged him into a slow lope till I got to the end of the lane. I stopped for one last look around. Freddie stood in the front yard waving a white handkerchief in wide arcs over her head. I waved my hat high and wide so she would be sure to see me. Knowing I would probably never see her again, I reined Chester in the direction of town and loped away from one of the best friends I ever had and into an unknown future.

25
Moving On Again

Wish I could say I gave up drinking. Wanted to, but I couldn't.

That first night on the road back to Providence, I didn't get any sleep. All day I'd tried to think of something other than my daughter, like what I would say to Eb when I returned. Then I found myself wondering what I was going to say to Tilly about Mattie. Each time I tried to shed thoughts of my daughter, she seeped back into my mind.

I felt her little fingers clutch mine as we walked side by side. I smelled her baby scent as she rested her curly head against my chest during her bedtime story. I felt myself smile as I remembered her toddling run toward Aunt Lacey holding a fresh lolly, or Aunt Freddie holding out a just-baked sugar cookie. I heard the exaggerated grunts of the big hugs she shared with Uncle Avery. I heard her giggles and felt her soft little kisses. I heard her little voice wheedling me into a ride on Chester before going in for supper.

I would've gladly sold the rest of my life and my hope of heaven to have her alive and in the loving care of the Becks.

Truth tell, I was afraid to bed down at the end of the day. Was afraid of being alone with the unbridled thoughts that would darken the dreams I didn't want to have, afraid to face the dreams I knew would come.

Though it was a moonless night, and I couldn't see much further than the tip of Chester's nose, I kept riding. After a serious stumble that damn near sent my horse to his knees, I pulled him off the road to a spot under some black oak trees where we bedded down for the night. I poured half the water I had in my canteen into my hat and offered it to the gelding. He slurped it down and licked the hat dry. I took a swig from the canteen myself before stretching out on my bedroll.

As soon as I closed my eyes, Mattie's panic-stricken dark eyes met mine. Tears spilled over her lower lashes as she shrieked with fear and pain, seconds after the water moccasins bit her. My eyes snapped open, my heart hammering under my ribs like it did the day she died. I lay in my bedroll panting, staring at the stars trying not to ask why. I ground my teeth in rhythm to the word caterwauling in my mind and wished I had a drink. I squeezed my eyelids shut, determined to overcome my fear of sleep, the fear of watching my baby die again, and again, and again. As though engraved on my eyelids, I saw her small casket in the grave. I kept hearing the dull thud of the clods of red clay as they hit the small pine box. I smelled the moist red earth from the bottom of the pit.

I tossed and turned the night through. I watched the stars cross the heavens wishing Mattie were alive, wishing I could beat the tar out of Dom for leaving us, wishing I could go back and change everything. And I cried, asking myself what I would have changed? Ever knowing Dom? Never having Mattie? No. I couldn't do that. As bad as the pain was, I couldn't bring myself to wish I'd never had my precious daughter.

The next day, I bought a bottle of Monongahela, and, from then on, I made sure I had whiskey on hand for the long nights. I would watch the flames of my evening fire reach heavenward popping, hissing and whining. I drank until I couldn't feel the nose on my face. With my last shred of awareness, I pulled my blanket over me and went to sleep. By staring at the fire, I was able to postpone facing my baby's big teary eyes that came every night to haunt my heart. It was her voice in my dreams calling "Mama" and the small hand reaching from under the partially buried coffin that shocked me out of my stupor and got me moving before first light.

With the should'ves and the shouldn't'ves of the past three years putting their spurs to my heart and whipping my mind to the point of depriving me of most of my sanity, we finished the thousand-mile trip back to Providence in just over three weeks. Chester and I arrived gaunt and exhausted. Chester, 'cause I gave him so little time to rest or eat, poor horse, and me, 'cause my money was running out, and all I could afford to live on was Monongahela.

When I walked into the Franklin House Inn after stabling Chester in a spare stall with a good measure of oats and a forkful of hay, the first thing out of Tilly Balch's mouth was, "What the hell happened to you?"

Seeing the look of genuine concern in my friend's face, I passed out cold. I came to between fresh sheets the following morning. It took me some minutes to remember where I was, seein's how I hadn't been in a bed for weeks. Good God, I'd forgotten how good it felt. Not only the bed, but to sleep without dreams and to wake hungry.

By the looks of 'em, my clothes had been washed, and the coat and hat brushed. I threw them on and trotted downstairs.

"Where you been, boy? You look like hell," Eb shouted across the common room of the inn. "You look like you could use a cup of coffee. Bertha, bring coffee and a plate of breakfast for Charley."

"Coffee sounds good. Had a hard ride up from Georgia," I replied, shaking his over-sized, calloused hand. I pulled out a chair, and almost before my ass hit the seat, a cup of coffee arrived, followed by a plate of eggs, bacon, fried potatoes and Tilly's lighter-than-air biscuits slathered in butter. The aroma of the plate beneath my nose started my belly to growling like a wolf ready to attack. I looked up into Bertha's friendly blue eyes. She smiled and returned to the kitchen. "Business must be good. Had a hell of a time finding an empty stall when I rode in."

"Business is good. See you still got those damn small girlie hands."

"Left with them and came back with them. No place I know where a feller can trade body parts. Not that any man'd be interested in exchanging hands. More'n likely be more interested in what's hid below the belt."

Eb threw back his head and laughed, as I knew he would. "Still, it's a wonder you can handle the ribbons like you do. I'm sorry I couldn't hold a job open."

"I know, Eb. I just need a few days to take stock. Know of anyone looking for a driver?"

"I'll keep my ears open for you," he said, swallowing the last of his coffee. He pushed his chair from the table, his hands resting on the arms as though about to get up, then he relaxed back into the chair once more. "There's a couple of whips talking big about starting up a stage line out in California. There's been talk of gold for the taking out there. Some feller by the name of Marshall found a nub of gold big as my fist lying in the streambed where he was building a sawmill."

"Imagine that," I said. "When did this happen?"

"Back in January."

"Word's still circulating, is it?"

"Yep, could be something. Leastways, these two, Jim Birch and Frank Stevens, think it's only the beginning. They're young, younger than you, and they got big dreams. They stop in here now and then. Next I see them, I'll introduce you."

"Thanks, Eb." His chair didn't have a half a minute to get cold before Bertha removed his empty coffee cup, and Tilly planted herself.

"Well?" she asked. Her eyes bore into me. I forked eggs into my mouth and bit off a chunk of biscuit to give me time to figure out how I was going to tell her without breaking down and bawling in the middle of the common room. She must've read my face, 'cause she pushed back the chair, laid a hand on my shoulder and said, "I'll see you upstairs in ten minutes."

I nodded my head. For the first time since I knew Tilly, I couldn't finish a plate of her cooking. Couldn't get it down my gullet. Felt like I'd swallowed an apple the way my throat tightened. Part of me wanted to run, but I knew I couldn't do that to my friend. I walked over to the inn's tap room, ordered a shot, and downed it before mounting the stairs. The sound of my feet rasping on the stair treads sounded like sandpaper wearing away at the barriers I kept trying to build around my heart, only to have them ground down.

I closed the door of my room. Tilly turned from the window that overlooked the mews. Tears streamed down her lined face.

"What happened to my namesake?"

"How'd you know?"

"Woman's intuition, I guess. Knew something was wrong when you walked in yesterday. And this morning, soon as I sat down you turned three shades of ghost, and I knew."

I motioned for her to sit on the bed and sat down beside her.

"She died eleven weeks ago, on August 14, of snakebite."

Tilly sobbed, then wiped her eyes and the tip of her nose with the hem of her apron. "Wish I'd been there to hold her and spoil her some."

"Me, too," I said, putting my arm around Tilly's shoulders as much for my comfort as for hers. In the few letters I'd written to the Balchs over the three years I'd been gone, I'd always written an extra page especially for Tilly telling her about Mattie and our life together. "Mattie was the best thing that ever happened in my life. I feel lower than pond slime that I let her die. I keep going over and over it in my mind how I should've done things different. I'm like to go crazy."

"There's nothing you can do about it now. You did the best you could whilst you had the chance. But you are going to go crazy if you keep reliving it. You took to drinking didn't you?"

I looked down and nodded.

"I can smell it. I'm not setting myself to be your judge, but that's not good, and you know it, Charley. If you still consider yourself a whip, you have to stop. You know the danger not only to yourself and your horses, but to the passengers as well."

"You sound like Eb."

"He held off hiring a replacement after you left, figuring you would be back in a few weeks wanting your old job back. He sure was disappointed when you didn't come back."

I hung my head. Tilly patted my knee and rose.

"I guess you had to do what you done, but I'm damn glad you're back. You're welcome to stay at the Franklin as long as you like."

I looked up into Tilly's caring eyes and gave her a smile of thanks. "Don't know exactly what I'm going to do. Eb told me this morning he'd keep an ear open for me about a job."

"I hope you don't decide to do nothing foolish like going after that California gold like some of them witless men wanting to get rich quick. It's the ones who work hard at what they do best and save their money, they're the ones that get rich. The sober, honest ones." Tilly's eyes bore into mine as she stressed the part about being sober.

"Sounds about right." I said, nodding at her homey wisdom.

"You can put your money on it," she said from the doorway. "I'll see you at dinner."

"Right."

I saw Dom that first day back while I was out looking around my old stomping grounds. No soft feelings or memories of our time together plucked at my heart. We never spoke, him and me. Heard through Liberty that Dom had married, so there weren't anything to say between us especially since he'd already turned his back on me and our daughter.

That first night back, I already had big news to tell. Captain William Hayden, currently home from the sea and hearing of my reputation, and that I was back in town, hired me on the spot to drive for him. My dream of becoming a coachman for the well-to-do had finally come to pass.

I had dinner with Eb and Tilly that evening, and a time or two thereafter over the years I stayed in Providence. Often ate at the Franklin House to savor Tilly's cooking, but it weren't often that we got the chance to sit down together and talk like we used to.

I started out real happy. In fact, I was damn proud of myself. I'd done what few others had. I'd worked my way up, got what I was after; what I thought I'd wanted all my life. Don't get me wrong. I enjoyed being stableman and driver for a rich man. I had a few boys working for me. They did the feeding, pitching, shoveling, and grooming, just as I did when I was their age. The work was to my liking, but I weren't as busy as I'd been at Eb's. At the start, I liked the slower pace. Had time to work with the horses, give them the extra training I thought they needed, especially when we brought new stock into the stable.

Too, the newness and excitement of attaining the job I'd always wanted helped me corral my morbid thoughts of Mattie and control my need for large amounts of Monongahela in order to sleep. I kept a bottle in my bunkroom. Generally knocked back a shot or two before turning in, but I never wanted to be caught in a position where I was so far gone that I couldn't do my job anytime day or night. Freddie'd been right, Providence didn't remind me of Mattie at every turn of the corner.

Even so, after a while I quit and moved on to work for a wealthy business man, Charles H. Child. Mr. Child was one of the higher muckity mucks of Brown Brothers & Co. with millworks over on Dorrance and showrooms on Exchange Place.

There I had a six-up of beautifully matched grays. Each horse's light gray coat mottled with darker gray dapples throughout; their manes, tails, and legs a charcoal gray. Real eye-catchers. They were my babies; nobody took care of them or drove them but me. We looked mighty fine when we were out. A peacock couldn't have out-preened me when I was driving that team. Life was good.

But I was bored.

Working for the rich got to be too many of the same roads week after week. My schedule weren't busy most times. A lot of waiting mostly. Waiting to pick up. Waiting to drop off. Can't leave the drop off point unless told to return at a certain time. Can't over train horses, or they get sour. I had too much free time to myself. Time I generally spent in my bunkroom in the stable reading or sleeping. Got twitted about my solitary habits and told the fool I got along better with horses than humans and liked it that way.

Sure, I would go out now and then for a nip down at the pub where the drivers stopped in to wet their whistle. But I weren't one of the boys no more now that I worked for rich folks. So, for the most part, I kept to myself and saved my money like I'd always done.

I got to know those two whips Eb'd told me about that first day back, Jim Birch and Frank Stevens. Nice fellers. About ten years younger than me. They had an itching to go to California to startup a stagecoach company. It was all they would talk about. Tried to get me to go in with them and invest in their venture, but I liked my money safe in the bank. Too many things could go wrong, what with horses dying, coaches breaking down, and robbers. At the time, I was comfortable.

They finally headed out West and started their line. Did pretty well, too. We kept in touch. They kept telling me they needed good drivers, and would love to have me drive for them. I turned them down. But they said if I changed my mind, there'd be a job ready and waiting for me.

Hadn't seen or heard from Jim or Frank for quite a while, but as luck would have it, I ran into Jim just when I needed him most.

I was walking past Abernathy's Emporium on my way to the apothecary, when I saw my daughter coming right at me. My heart slammed in my chest, making the blood in my ears rush. There she was, clutching her dolly and tripping on the uneven walk boards in new shoes, her dark curls bouncing as she lurched forward. I reached for her, but the hand holding hers pulled her upright. My eyes traveled up the adult arm to meet Dom's black eyes as he scooped his daughter into his arms. With a quick uncomfortable glance in my direction, he opened the emporium's door and held it for a dark-haired woman carrying an infant. I took the much younger woman to be his wife. There was no doubt the little girl was his.

I don't know how long I stood there. It seemed like ages before I turned away. Without knowing where I was going, I made my way to my usual watering hole, slapped money on the bar, and grabbed the bottle of Monongahela and glass the keep slid my way. I found a dark corner, yanked the cork with my teeth and spat it to the floor. I guzzled straight from the bottle till the raw pain in my throat matched the stabbing pain in my heart, and I had to come up for air.

My mind's eye kept seeing the little girl's bouncing curls...her look of love as her father scooped her into his arms... the way she clutched her dolly to her small chest... the brief look of fear when she tripped and was about to fall. My memories of Mattie refused to remain tucked away. When I felt tears burn my eyes, I tilted the bottle and swallowed.

"Hope you're not driving tonight," a voice said. My eyes climbed the tall form standing across the table from me. I had a hard time focusing, but when I did, I couldn't believe who I thought I was seeing.

"Jim? Jim Birch? That you?"

"Sure is. Mind if I join you?"

"Sit right down," I invited, feeling relieved to have someone to take my mind off my sorrows.

Jim signaled a barmaid. "We'd like some dinner," he said. "Make it hot and plentiful." With a nod, she disappeared into the kitchen. Jim looked around without saying anything. The woman returned with two heaping plates of savory lamb stew, a fresh loaf of bread and a bowl of butter in the time it took for a foal at the teat to wiggle its tail.

We ate in silence, shoveling the stew in and biting off chunks of warm buttered bread. I felt a little panicky. I'd never let anyone in Providence see me drunk. I kept hoping the food would sober me enough not to make an ass out of myself in front of Jim. I glanced at the bottle, only half of it was gone. Thankfully, I still had my wits about me.

I pushed the bottle and unused glass toward him. "Help yourself."

"Thanks," he said, pouring a stiff shot and knocking it back. "You do this often?"

"What?" I asked past a mouthful of food.

"Get soused?"

Somehow, I managed to swallow the food past the lump in my throat. "Don't happen much. Had a shitty day."

"I've never seen you like this before."

"Never drink like this when I'm driving."

"Glad to hear it. You ready to get out of this town yet and go adventuring with Frank and me?"

That thought hit me just right, and I began to warm to the idea as Jim talked on. He'd come East to find some new investment money and hire good drivers if he could "wean them away from civilized town life," as he put it. California, he said, was young and raw in many ways, but ripe for the picking for those who had the gumption. Their new California Stage Company was going great guns. Frank was still out West managing the line.

"We're not losing money," he said. "We're expanding, and we've got to have working capital to do that."

"Is there a lot of gold out there?" I said.

"Some poor slobs manage to eke out a living. Some do pretty well, but spend it fast and free. Fewer become wildly rich. Charley, the money's not in the gold fields. It's to be made in the growth of the state. Cities are springing up like mushrooms. San Francisco's booming. Sure, there's a lot of men arriving expecting to make it big in the fields. But almost as many are buying up land, building homes, warehouses, shops, opening businesses. They, like us, are there to stay. There's plenty for everyone who wants to work."

I figured then and there that it was time for me to move on. I never wanted to run into Dom and his daughter again, that was for damn sure. Boredom ruled my life here in Providence. What did I have to lose?

"I think it's time I take you up on your offer."

He jutted his chin at the bottle. "You being truthful with me about the drinking, Charley?"

"I'm steady as ever, Jim," I said, looking him straight in the eye. "Just had a day from hell, is all."

A large grin spread across his face as he slapped me on the shoulder. "Yeah, we all get them from time to time don't we?" he said, shrugging off my lapse. "Welcome aboard. We're glad to have you. I expect to be here for a couple of months yet. Got to spend some time with my wife, and, like I said, I've got to drum up some investment capital. When you get to Sacramento, see Frank. He'll get you fixed up with a run before you have a place to bed down. We're glad to have a fine whip like you working with us, Charley. Damn glad."

It took me a couple of weeks to make arrangements, but I climbed aboard the R. B. Forbes and set sail for Panama, joining the rush West in search of a new life.

26

Expanding Horizons
1851

A s our steamer rounded the headland and entered San Francisco bay, at least a hundred naked trees jutted from the shoreline to our right. My first thought was that there'd been a recent forest fire to the south.

"Masts," John Morton observed, coming to stand beside me at the rail. "Look closer at the waterline." John was the president of Morton Draying and Warehouse Company. We'd spent most evenings aboard the Golden Gate playing cards since leaving Panama thirteen days before. "The gold rush has deckhands jumping ship as soon as they drop anchor. Everyone's got the fever. The captains can't keep their crews once they enter port. Many have tried standing guard with loaded guns to prevent their men from going overboard, but to no avail. Some swim for it, others pay the Chinks to smuggle them to land with the cargo."

"Chinks?"

"The Chinese. The town is crawling with them. They do a lot of the manual labor we need done. Enterprising fellows. Cheap, too. Here come a slew of them now," John said, jutting his chin in the direction of the wharf. Along the shoreline, dozens of small boats and canoes splashed into the bay. Dark-haired men jumped into them as they hit the water and started rowing, their bodies bobbing in rhythm as they paddled toward us. "Some enterprising captains sold their unmanned ships at the beginning of the rush. A couple of the more seaworthy vessels were made into restaurants, while others were turned into warehouses. Many of the ships entering port following the initial rush were simply moored, stripped and left to rot by their gold-crazed crews and captains."

The Golden Gate's anchor chain clattered through the hawsehole followed by a loud splash as the great hook hit the water.

"Seems the Captain is worried the crew will jump ship like the others."

"What about hiring on new crews?" I asked, wondering at the lack of common sense of a man giving up his livelihood for a pig in a poke.

John snorted and shook his head. "Can't be had."

"But I hear there are a lot of men about to starve. They ain't got the money to outfit proper-like. Why don't they go back to doing what they do best?"

"You heard wrong," John said, shaking his head. "Any one of them can make more money in town in a day than they'd make in a month aboard ship. Besides, the fever's got them. Some of the captains, too. Especially those that don't own the ships they sailed in on. Nobody wants to leave. They work at whatever they can to earn a grubstake, so they can rush to the next strike. Everyone dreams of becoming rich with the next find."

"Glad I got me a job all lined up," I said.

"Who'd you say you were working for?"

"The California Stage Company out in Sacramento."

"Frank and Jim are good boys, but if they don't treat you right, you come work for me. Business is booming, and I can always use a good driver," John said, sticking his hand out to me. "Look me up when next you're in town."

"Will do," I said, giving his hand a firm shake. "Sure to be passing through at one time or the other. Glad I got to know you, John."

"Same here, Charley."

By the time John and I parted company, the first of the small boats and big-bellied canoes were alongside. I decided to stay put and watch the unloading awhile before going below to fetch my bags. Figured I might dicker a cheaper price from one of the later boats.

Men smaller than me with long, black braids down their backs clambered up the side of our steamer and over the rail while their partners stayed below in their dinghy to keep it close to the side of the steamer. I watched as two boats vied for the same spot. The nearest boatman rolled to his knees in the center of his craft and used his oar to poke the boat that was trying to nudge him out of the way. One quick jab sent the other boatman overboard, ending the struggle.

The slitted black eyes of those who had climbed on deck darted from one passenger to the next. I figured they were looking for the richly dressed, or the easily duped. One China man near me grabbed the carpetbag of a stout man and threw it overboard. I glanced over the rail to see where it would land. Outstretched hands snatched it out of the air and stowed the bag in the rear of the boat. The passenger ranted and gestured, but the porter stared him down. I could have sworn the China man was laughing behind those flat eyes of his. I figured to be careful in any dealings with them when the time came. I couldn't help but laugh at the stout man, one I remember as being a jackass while aboard. He clambered over the side to struggle down a rope ladder, shouting all the way that he would speak to the authorities.

The sun glistening on the water stabbed my eyes, so I turned my attention to the shore. The town of San Francisco fanned out from the bay's edge and rippled over low hills. From the middle of the bay where we had anchored, I could hear the dull roar of teamsters, the crack of bullwhips, and the hammering of new construction. The streets and walks of the young city buzzed with activity, though every road seemed to have its own logjam where drays and wagons unloaded milled lumber and supplies. Mixed with the brine of the sea, I smelled the fresh scent of pine and the tang of sawn timber along with the bitter odor of a dead fire.

"You going ashore?" Captain Patterson asked, startling me out of my wandering thoughts.

"Yes sir, just looking over the town," I said. "Was thinking I smelled a dead fire."

"You got a good nose. They had a fire wipe out about eighteen to twenty square blocks, near as I can tell. Big hullabaloo. Some think the Australians set it."

Captain Patterson turned his back to the rail and yelled to one of his men. With a glance at me, he said. "It appears nothing gets done around here without me. It was a pleasure to have you aboard, Mr. Parkhurst. Good luck."

I turned my attention back to the growing city. Everything looked unfamiliar. My heart hammered in my throat. What had I done? I was down to five hundred dollars. There was no going back. Like the gold rushers, I was going to be here for a while, prepared or not.

But unlike the rushers, I had a job waiting for me. Seein's I didn't know how long it'd be before I got back to San Francisco, I took two days to kick around town and outfit myself before heading out to Sacramento. Jim Birch warned me before I left that I would need heavy, warm clothes and a buffalo greatcoat to weather the Sierra Mountain route.

Providence seemed clean and near silent compared to this town. The streets were crammed with horses, oxen, mules, donkeys, small herds of sheep and goats, a gaggle of damn geese—one of those little bastards nipped me in the butt as I passed. I damn near wrung its neck, but caught myself and gave the little girl herding them a peppermint instead. Then there were the humans, people of every skin and hair color, size and shape. I swear to God, I saw a woman who must've weighed in at 400 pounds. Biggest damn person I ever did see. And China men dressed in loose fitting black pants and white shirts with the front of their hair shaved, leaving long black braids hanging down their backs past their waists.

As I followed one of them China men, watching his pigtail sway, a wagon drew abreast filled with a dozen or more tiny China woman all dressed in cotton pants and shirts like the man I'd been walking behind. Most of them had a glazed, hopeless look to their dark eyes like a colicky horse. But one of them set to squawking like some poor hen trying to outrun the meat cleaver. She managed to jump off the wagon, but the look on her face as her feet hit the cobblestones drew my eyes down to see what could have caused such pain. Her short rounded feet looked like those of a rag doll. I couldn't believe what I saw. No one had feet that short. Had she lost her toes in some horrible accident?

She hobbled with outstretched arms toward a well-dressed China man who had been forced to stop a step behind me 'cause I blocked his path. She pleaded with him in her choppy sounding native tongue and fell to her knees, her dark head bowed. The words kept tumbling out.

From behind the wagon, a ship's captain dismounted from a long-legged bay to grab ahold of her. He yanked her to her feet.

"Get back into the damn wagon and stay there. You're my property until your passage is paid." He lifted her up and tossed her into the wagon as though she were nothing more'n a sack of grain then remounted his horse.

"What the hell are you doing?" I shouted at him.

"Mind your own damned business," he said, clucking his horse into a slow trot to catch up with the wagon that had lumbered off as soon as the girl's body had thumped onto the wagon's floorboards.

"You can't treat her like…" The man beside me rested a hand upon my arm as I raised my voice to roar at the retreating back of the self-satisfied bastard who moved off with the wagonload of women.

"Best do as he says, or you could find yourself shanghaied." Surprised by his British accent, I paused and almost lost him in the crowd as the surrounding masses started moving again. I grabbed his arm as he was about to cross the street.

"What did she say?"

"She said her name was Lee Lan and that while visiting relatives in Canton with her parents, someone kidnapped her off the street and shipped her here."

"But…"

"If you know what is good for you, let it be. It happens all the time in this town and others like it."

"What happens all the time?"

"She will be sold to a brothel at auction in some alley a few blocks from here for a couple of thousand dollars. This evening, because she is beautiful and her feet are bound, she will be dressed in fine silks and will begin her life as a daughter of joy; her virginity sold to the highest bidder. Some of the others less fortunate in looks will not be so lucky."

"What do you mean by her feet being bound?"

"It is customary for a girl of good birth to have her feet bound shortly after she is born so they will not grow."

"Oh, my God."

He left me standing there, horrified at what I'd learned. Again, I was a witness to slavery and cruelty, and unable to do anything about it. Finding myself shanghaied for revenge was the last thing I wanted to deal with. I stepped back into the mainstream of traffic thankful I had choices.

27

New Sights

Once again, I blended into the busy comings and goings of the
life around me. I tried to take my mind off those poor
women and the life that awaited them. I kept feeling I'd let them
down, though to this day, I can't figure what I could've done to
help them short of buying them myself. And, though I had some
money, I couldn't afford to buy a slave to give her freedom,
especially since I just got here and was running low on funds.

It ground my oats the way women were treated—how others
stood by and allowed such low-down behavior. Why did I have to
live the life of a man in order to do what I wanted? To make my
own decisions?

My first night in town, I decided to join the nightlife seein's
how I wouldn't be back to San Francisco for a while and probably
wouldn't get any sleep even if I tried. I stayed on the outskirts of
things and watched. There had to be a saloon on damn near every
street corner. I saw men, in from their diggings, gamble their hard
earned gold and lose. I saw others led down blind alleys by
groping dance hall gals who'd walk out minutes later without them
followed by some big muscled feller stuffing a small sack of gold

into his pocket and slicking back his hair with the palms of his hands readying for the next unlucky soul. I pulled my jacket closed. What little I had left, I wanted to keep.

I saw drunken brawls and sober fist-fights. Dance hall girls working the boards and birds of the evening working the men, me included. Geez, for the love of me, I couldn't understand why. I sure ain't pretty to look at—leastways not in my opinion. When soft hands started stroking me, I would move on to the next saloon to watch what happened there.

The crack of a whip drew me to a couple of drivers that were betting on their skill with a blacksnake whip. To win, all one had to do was slice an envelope in two from fifteen feet. I picked up a few bucks showing them how it's done. Then some damn drunk upped the ante to cutting a cigar clenched between a man's teeth. It didn't bother me none so long as I didn't have to hold the damn thing in my teeth. Had I been on the other end, I would've refused. Nobody was sober, including me. As it turned out, I won a few more bucks, till some damn fool had one too many snorts of whiskey and cut the cheek of the poor sod holding the cigar. All hell broke loose in a fistfight. I fought my way out of the saloon and moved on.

As dawn crept over the city, I went back to my room at the hotel and caught some shuteye. When I woke a few hours later, I stopped in many stores looking for things I needed. Prices were higher than migrating geese. No wonder no one could afford to outfit themselves for the goldfields unless they were already richer than King Solomon. I was damn glad I only had to buy some heavy clothes as Jim suggested.

I got myself a pair of dark blue embroidered leather gloves. They had only one pair my size on hand, or I would've gotten another. I bought two pair of dark blue fine merino wool trousers and a couple of them indigo-blue denims that Strauss feller was making. I noticed that drivers wore the denims over their good woolen trousers for warmth but rolled up four to six inches so's the quality wool ones showed. I hired a China man to make up a half-a-dozen white, box-pleated shirts, and send them on to me in care of the California Stage Company in Sacramento. Went to the haberdashery, got me a wide-brimmed Texas hat to keep the sun out of my eyes. Then paid dearly for a pair of fine leather boots and a buffalo greatcoat for warmth. I figured I was set to face the cold reaches of the Sierra Mountains and shapeless enough while wearing my new clothes not to draw attention to my gender.

The sound of gunfire exploding every few minutes got me to thinking. Decided I better buy me a new gun while I was in town. From what I'd seen of San Francisco, I figured the rest of California could only be rougher, especially since the word about them gold rush claim-jumpers was that they'd shoot first and maybe worry when the smoked cleared. Heard stagecoaches said to carry gold shipments were held up regular-like, too, so I bought a Colt Navy .38 pistol and plenty of ammunition to tide me over. Figured I had some practicing to do when I got settled in.

I made it an early night, retiring to my room after a big meal in the hotel's dining room. The food was good, fancy in fact. Had me a pan-fried steak with onions, a mound of mashed potatoes, and fancy green beans with slivers of almonds in them all slathered with rich brown gravy. Then I topped it off with coffee and fresh, sun-sweet strawberries piled on a wedge of cake sopped in fresh cream. It was almost as good as Tilly's cooking. I wondered whether I would ever get back east again to taste her chicken and dumplings and thick apple pie topped with sweet crumbs again. Doubt saddened me.

I ordered up a bath, seein's how I didn't know when I would have the opportunity for another. I swirled and sipped a glass of Monongahela while my bath was brought up. The shaving mirror caught my eye, and I tilted it to take a look, something I didn't do too often. Still weren't much to look at. My thirty-nine years were showing in crow's-feet, sagging cheeks, and grey hair. Nothing that was big earlier on had got any smaller. Same wide jaw and big ears. They hadn't changed none. Guess I ought to be grateful. Them ugly parts made my act convincing.

That honest to goodness real sit-down bath felt mighty good, and when the water got chilly, I climbed out and fell into bed.

Since the night was no less quiet than the previous one, I slept as best I could between nerve-jarring explosions of noise below. Dawn was a long time in coming, but eight o'clock saw me climbing into the stage bound for Sacramento and my new life.

After finding a boarding house not far from the stage office, I headed over to the California Stage Company and found Frank Stevens pouring over schedules and bills of lading.

"Charley." He wrung my hand and thumped my back with his big hands. "Glad you came. Was happy as hell to hear you were coming aboard when Jim's letter arrived two weeks ago."

"Glad to be here. He must've wrote the night we talked. It took me a few weeks to settle my affairs."

Frank was generally quieter when Jim was around. Those two were a study of differences. Frank's dark brown eyes watched the world from a boyish face underlined with a close cropped beard and dark brown hair. But it was Jim's handsome face and outgoing enthusiasm that brought in the business. When the two were together, Frank let Jim do all the talking, but it was Frank's get-the-job-done manner that kept the stage line moving.

"When do you want to start?"

"This afternoon."

Frank threw back his head and laughed. "That's what I always liked about you Charley, you were never a shirker. Tomorrow you ride the Placerville run to get the lay of the land. Get a good look at the Sierras while you're there. You'll be going over the hump one day soon."

"What time does the coach leave?"

"Seven sharp," he said. "How about dinner tonight to catch up on what's been going on back home?"

"Sounds good," I said. We decided on a place and time for dinner, and I left him to his schedules.

Driving stage in the West was different than back East. Tougher. I still drove Concords, but they were pulled by mustangs, a wilder breed than the blooded horses I was used to, but no less spirited, just weren't trained as well—they learned on the move. As did most whips, I kept my right foot on the break, and when I needed to rein a command, I would slow the coach to take up the slack in the ribbons before turning the team. They came to understand my voice commands and sharp whistles, and would respond as though we were all thinking the same thoughts. I weren't one to lay a whip to a horse as a general rule. It was the sound that got their attention when they were tired and their minds wandered. We learned to work together, and I was as much a member of the team as any of my six-up. We generally got so's we respected one another.

Sacramento was the greatest stagecoach hub in the world and the California Stage Company its biggest stage and mail line. The company owned two hundred coaches and wagons, about fifteen-hundred horses, and hundreds of men to work the routes. We could brag having twenty-eight daily routes covering some two thousand miles of rough roads. Them roads had me chawing t'bacca inside a month. The bumps and ruts were enough to jar the teeth right out of your head. Better to have something soft between your teeth than to crack them hitting a rut going full tilt. Kept my mouth from drying out, too. We drove in all kinds of weather bare to the sky and whatever fell through it. The summer sun sucked you dry, the wind-whipped grit wore away your skin, dried out your nose and mouth so's you could hardly breathe. I wore a bandana across my face and my hat brim pulled low, but by the end of a day's run my lids gritted over my eyes so bad I could hardly see. Had a good stiff whiskey or two at the end of the day to clear my gullet. And that was the good weather.

The rest of the year, rain and snow and sleet froze your bones so's you were sure you'd never warm up again till you hit hell. A snort of whiskey now and then helped. Some drivers drank steady, but they're the ones that'd have accidents, wreck their coaches, and injure their passengers. Not me, no sir, with me, safety came first. I left my drinking to my off-time in the evenings and even then not much as a general rule. Still needed several shots on occasion to get to sleep on the nights my daughter filled my thoughts, that is, if I had the evening off. I could make good money driving double runs, which I did off and on. Sometimes, I would cover a hundred miles in twenty-four hours. Course, when I got back to my bunk, I would sleep long and hard without dreams of Mattie.

There weren't much companionship up top neither. Sure, sometimes I had someone riding shotgun, or a passenger riding cheap to the next way station. But for the most part, it was a lonesome job that tired your bones so they ached pretty near all the time—that was the start of the rheumatism that finally wore me down so's I had to retire from the ribbons years later.

Sure as Frank said, I was driving over the Sierras, the "hump" they called it, in no time at all. The temperature in the high mountains was cool most of the year and damn cold the rest, so I was real glad I had my wool trousers and buffalo greatcoat for warmth. Still, I don't think God made a prettier place on earth than California's mountain country.

My eyes feasted on such grand scenery as to make your heart ache with the beauty of it all. Clear skies in such shades of blue a woman would want a dress made of any one of them colors and feel like the Queen of Sheba wearing it. And at night, those same skies turned coal black and glittered with sparks as pretty as dawn-lit dew drops. So many stars filled the night sky they lit my way many a time. And when the moon rose silver-full and crisp, the night became bright as day, a hunter's paradise for the puma and wolves that roamed the wooded lands at the knees of the Sierras.

I missed my mountains whenever the company changed my run to the flat lands of central California. Saw my Sierras off in the distance now and then, but that weren't the same as pulling out of a home station at dawn as the mist rose from Lake Tahoe, or from the valleys snuggled between the toes of the mountains. I missed the majesty of the crags, the orange and gold and purple and pink colors the morning and evening sun gave their slopes, and their stark snow covered ruggedness at high noon that damn near blinded you and made the trail interesting come winter.

I spent many a run on the flats thinking on the glory of the mountains; the rivers that threw themselves off cliffs with a roar to become a veil of mist as it fell hundreds of feet to the valley below, the whisper of the wind through the pines, and the clapping of gold aspen leaves at their last hurrah before winter set in. There were times when driving the flats that the sun beat down on me so hard that I felt sapped of all spit and sweat. At those times, I thought on the bitter cold of the mountains trying to remember what it felt like.

It was a warm day in June that had my mind wandering over the Sierras, thinking on their cool, crisp air that I drove right smack into being robbed.

Stages don't just carry passengers, they carry the United States mail and oftentimes gold or large payrolls for the army and such in their treasure boxes. Course, we generally didn't know what was in the box, and if we did, we kept mum about it, but somehow road agents managed to get the inside story, or get lucky.

I was on a run between Stockton and Mariposa with a coach full of passengers and a heavy treasure box, my mind wandering like I said, when five men stepped in front of my Concord as my team started into a sharp bend on a narrow road cut into the side of a hill.

"Hold up," a muffled voice ordered through a flour sack with three jagged holes cut out of it.

I had no room to maneuver my team, so I had to pull up.

A jackass braying laugh from the leader made the hair on the back of my neck stand on end. Dark little pig eyes stared at me through the holes over a cocked shotgun aimed at my chest.

"Get that box down here, I say." I recognized a New England accent. The leader of the gang was beefy through his chest and belly and wore sugar sacks over his boots. "I'm not waiting much longer before I blow a hole through you. You're wasting my valuable spending time." Another jackass braying laugh had my skin crawling as I reached into the boot under my seat and felt my holstered handgun.

Did I have enough room to pull the gun, spin, aim, and shoot?

No. The belt was wrapped over the handle of the gun so's it wouldn't slide out of the holster. Shit.

I'd never come close to being robbed before, so I guess I'd gotten lazy, figuring it wouldn't happen to me. I yanked out the ironbound oak chest containing the valuables entrusted to me.

Someone laughed behind his mask. "Yeah, we're going to spend that money soon's we get it. Ain't we boss?"

"Shut up, you moron," the leader said.

One of the two men standing at the head of my team eased his way alongside the horses keeping his gun pointed at me until he yanked open the coach door and aimed at my passengers.

"Just slowly and carefully place yo' valuables in this here hat," a deep gravelly voice said. "Everything'll be fine, if you all do as I say, nice and easy."

I sure wished at that moment that I'd kept my gun handy. Didn't generally hold with killing people, but for the bastards that were robbing us, I would have made an exception.

I dropped the box over the side of the coach. We all heard the rich sound of coins slapping together. Two of the henchmen hurried to the box, each grabbed a handle and stepped away from the wheels of my coach. The man heading the team darted to the side.

"Get on out of here," their leader shouted, waving us on with the nose of his shotgun.

The coach door slammed shut after a polite "thank you, ladies and gents."

I started up my team and moved them out slow, continuing to round the tight bend we'd begun. Once more, that moronic laugh floated back to me. In a flash, I knew the bastard. I stood in my box and took a quick look back. The voice was deeper, but I remembered that damn laugh. The robbers were in the midst of pulling off their masks, and I caught a glimpse of the leader's profile. Yup, it was him. Now more'n ever, I wished I had my gun handy. I had my six-up to handle in the turn and my passengers to think about, but I swore I would never drive coach without wearing my gun 'cause if I ever saw that bastard again, I would plant him in the ground if it were the last thing on this earth I ever did.

Though I hadn't thought about him for many years, I recognized the dark piggy eyes, the thick, beefy torso, and most of all the jackass braying laugh of Billy Todd, the bastard from the orphanage who kilt my best friend.

From that day on, I looked for Billy Todd everywhere I went. Nothing. Didn't hear his name, didn't see hide nor hair of him till I put something together in my mind. Heard tell of a bandit they were calling Sugarfoot 'cause he wrapped his boots in sugar sacks before a job. Most figured he had bought himself a fancy pair of boots with his ill-gotten money and was afraid someone would recognize his boots during a hold up. Still the same sneaky snake he ever was.

Six months crept along while I kept my eyes and ears wide open, hoping to find Billy Todd and make him pay for Fish's death. I asked around, describing him the best I could, especially that damn laugh of his. Got so's I figured he and his gang must ride a fair piece before pulling a job 'cause nobody I spoke to seemed to recognize him or his laugh. I even stepped into sheriff's offices to look over the wanted posters wherever I had a coach stop and a few minutes to spare.

But, as luck would have it, he found me. Yup, him and his gang held me up a second time. But this time I was ready for him. I saw it coming as his boys stepped out into the road in front of my six-up, and him standing off to the side of the road with sugar sacks covering his boots. They were getting sloppy 'cause I weren't heading into a sharp turn on a narrow road like I was last time. I cracked my whip, stepping up my team. Billy Todd's boys had to step back or get run over. I pulled out my six-shooter and blew a hole through Billy Todd's chest just right of center. The force of my shot threw him backward. His head snapped back, flinging off the loose-fitting mask. He dropped his shotgun. As I drew abreast of him, I looked him in the eye.

"That's for Fish, you stinking bastard. Die. Hell is waiting for you." I saw a spark of recognition in his eyes. He looked mortal wounded.

I shoved the Navy Colt into my holster and cracked my blacksnake whip. The team leapt forward. Within a half a dozen strides, we were away at a gallop. The robbers fired off a few shots, but no one was hurt.

I reported the hold up to the sheriff as was my job, and waited for word on the outcome.

Next day, the sheriff came back to town with Billy Todd's corpse draped over a pack mule. The sheriff had found him in a gulch not far from where I told him we were held up.

I was damn glad I kilt him and gladder he recognized me before he died.

28
Proud and Independent

W e drivers had more than our fair share of excitement on our runs—washouts, landslides, downed trees, oncoming coaches on narrow, no-pass roads. You name it, we had to get over it, around it, or through it.

I'd heard tales of accidents, seen a few bad ones, but the one I remember most I didn't see. Just heard about it the night after it happened while playing a few hands of poker with a couple of whips. A driver I didn't know well pulled up a chair and hunkered down, slopping his glass of whiskey and knocking his bottle into the table as he sat.

"Rough run?" I asked.

"Worst."

"Tell us."

"Had me one of them twenty passenger coaches rounding that damn tight curve at the head of Lynch Hill. Damn cut ain't nothing much more'n a trail along the edge of that mountain."

We nodded. I'd driven that trail, my hubs scraping the upside of the grade while I kept my eyes on the down side to make sure the wheels were on solid ground. It takes a lot of grit to keep your horses calm while your heart's pounding in your throat. I found a good wad of chewing t'bacca helped me through times like those.

"My hubs were grinding away at the upside when along came a couple of wild hogs. They started down the side of the mountain a slipping and a sliding, sending rocks and slides of dirt down toward my team."

I just knew what was coming 'fore he said it. Horses ain't stupid. Those on the near side know that there's a damn steep drop alongside them, and one wrong move will put them over the edge. But the horses on the off side ain't so sure about the drop, but they are sure that there's something coming at them from the right. Something big 'cause it's moving rocks and dirt down on them. They can't see out of the corner of their eye 'cause of their blinder flaps, they're guessing something along the lines of a puma, 'cause puma like to jump on a poor unsuspecting horse's back and snap his neck. Being mustangs, they've seen it happen. They draw the air in through their flaring nostrils, searching for the dreaded scent. Terror runs through the entire team setting them to rearing and stomping.

"Well, the off horses started dancing with worry hearing the ruckus above them," the driver said. "Then those dumb hogs, six of them there were, slipped and slid their way right smack dab into the middle of my six-up sending them a kicking and a hopping as though they were standing on red-hot coals." He shook his head, his blue eyes glassy as he relived what he was telling us. He poured himself another shot, and downed it before continuing. The game forgotten, the boys and I just stared at him suffering. He took a deep breath and started up again.

"Though the near leader tried to hold the line, she lost her footing over the downside and dragged the rest of the team over with her. I jumped as the coach followed them." Tears slid down his weathered cheeks.

"The gulch was more'n one hundred and fifty feet. The coach kept rolling and spitting out passengers. The horses rolled one over the other, legs going every which way. When the dust settled, nothing moved but the busted wheels slowly spinning in the air above the overturned coach.

"The live horses neighed in pain. I lost my gun when I jumped. Had to borrow a passenger's six gun to shoot the last four alive. All of 'em had busted legs.

"Five people died outright." He started rocking back and forth on his chair as we watched in sickened horror for him to tell the rest.

"The passengers were all hurt. Busted arms—legs—ribs. Those that could helped others less able while I hoofed it back to the last swing station for help." All of us at the table lowered our eyes glad it weren't us.

"The bitching part was that when all was said and done, there was only one damn dead hog. Dirty, good for nothing rooters."

"Lose your job?" I asked.

"Naw, When I told'em at the station what happened, they said it couldn't be helped, but I got to change runs. I'll see that in my mind for the rest of my days. I don't ever want to drive that run again. Ain't got the stomach for it." He slid back his chair, nodded his head and left.

None of us had the heart to play poker after that, so we called it a night. I knew I would keep seeing that accident in my mind's eye for a long while. Was damn glad it weren't me. Thought about it a lot though. Could've happened to anyone, it weren't the driver's fault like the stationmaster said. But I learned a lesson from it just the same. From there on, I swept my eyes along the upside of every mountain I crossed. No damn hogs were going to upset my team. I was going to shoot them before they had the chance to stampede my six-up off the road. I wanted to stay alive and keep my passengers and horses safe.

Course, every time someone made a comment about my excellent driving record within my hearing, my chest swelled with pride. Couldn't help myself. I was able to do what few men could do. And for that, I worked harder to keep my record clean and damn near impossible to match. Even so, one day when I was full of myself and in a hell-bent of a hurry, I took a corner too fast and flipped my Concord. Had no passengers aboard, thank God, but I scraped up my coach, upset my team, and busted my ribs, to say nothing of my pride. Never saw a doctor about it though. Didn't want anyone to know I weren't what I appeared to be, so I wrapped my ribs tight with long strips of sheeting and moved as gentle-like as I could for a couple of months until the pain lessened and the bones mended, which weren't helped by the bouncing I took day after day over rough roads. Breathing was painful, slinging passenger's bags into the boot or up top damn near made me pass out a time or two, but I did it with no one being the wiser.

Over time, my pride healed, too. So, when an upstart challenged me to a test of skill. I took him on. Couldn't help myself.

"Hey, Charley," he says to me. "I hear you're a pretty good reinsman."

"Yup," I said, taking a dislike to the little cock-bird as he strutted up and thumbed back his hat.

"You ever hear of the Dollar Toss?"

I decided to act dumb, so I shook my head no.

"Well ya see, it's like this, the idea is for a driver to get his team a going down Main Street like he was ending his run, and pull up with a flourish like we professionals do when..."

The idea that the little brat considered himself a professional almost made me laugh. What a little Bantam rooster.

"...then some feller tosses a silver dollar into the road and the driver has to run both wheels of his coach over the coin driving full tilt. You understand, old man?"

That did it. Old, was I? I decided right then I was wringing every cent he had out of him and next year's wages besides. That boy needed a lesson in manners. I had that skill under my belt long before his mama was wiping his bottom. What he was describing was the best test of skill there was for a whip, and the hardest to win for many. A driver that got one wheel over the coin considered himself in fine form. But I'd passed Eb's "silver run" test back in Worcester as he was bringing me along. And, well, maybe I was getting on up there in years, but that didn't mean the upstart was going to get away with being disrespectful.

"I think so," I answered. "You run it first." As he started walking away, I challenged him to a wager. "Twenty-five cent cigars for every successful pass I make running both wheels over the dollar."

"You're on," the cocky little bastard said, coming back to shake my hand to seal the wager as though my word weren't good enough. Oh, he was going to pay big.

I called to a couple of the whips about to enter the Wet Your Whistle saloon. "You boys ever see this snot-nosed kid around before?"

"Yeah," one said. "His name's Dobbs, Willy Dobbs."

"Been challenging anyone who'll take him on," another said.

"He's not in your league, Charley."

"Yeah, few are," one admitted.

After that comment, I could feel myself getting prideful again, and I thought, calm down woman, remember the damn coach you rolled. Don't let it go to your head, especially now you got people watching. Your reputation could end up at the bottom of the shit heap.

"Think it'd be a good idea if you boys did the judging," I said.

"Yeah."

"Right."

"Sure."

"Proud to," they answered.

Willy woke up his team, got them prancing with worry. He trotted them down the road and turned them around. I knew right off that he weren't going to make it. He hadn't left himself enough room to line them up proper-like. Willy snapped his whip over the ears of his leaders, causing them to leap, leaving the swing team a step behind and the wheelers confused. Not a good start, but he got them going.

Pete Hill, the tallest of the four-man judging team and a fair driver himself, tossed the dollar out far into the street as Willy came on. It was a good throw. Pete gave him plenty of time and room to rein his team for the approach.

"Near miss," Pete yelled at the retreating coach.

"Again," came Willy's reply.

Dobbs turned his team too fast and slid his coach. Again, he was too close, but Pete gave him plenty of time and plenty of room with his second toss, and again, Willy missed.

"Again," he called back as he flew past.

On his third try, he rolled the right rear wheel over the dollar but not the front. Rules were that you had three tries to get both wheels over or you'd lose. If you got two solid runs and missed one you could go twice more for three out of five, but it had to be both wheels over the coin. Course, you get both wheels over every time, you can keep driving till you miss or quit, and clean the pockets of your challenger, which is what I planned to do.

"That's all you got," one of my other judges shouted. Willy reined in his team, tied off his reins on the brake, and jumped down.

"Only got one wheel, boy," Pete called out as Willy drew near. Not taking our word for it, he checked the tracks before strutting over.

"Let's see you do better," he challenged.

By now, the townsfolk had started congregating, and I heard voices raising my name. Saw mothers clutch their children's arms in tight fists, so they wouldn't get too near the fun and get hurt.

"Show 'em how it's done, Charley."

"Got a wager on ya, Charley."

It had been at least twenty-five years since I'd done this drill, so I reminded myself not to get too cocky.

I woke my team up and trotted them down the street a hundred yards further than Willy had and turned them around at a slow trot. When I had them pulling their equal share at a decent clip, I asked for more with a crack of my whip over their heads. My beauties responded, as I knew they would, and over we went.

"Two wheels," I heard Pete shout after me. I lifted my arm in the air and circled above my head, telling him I would be back for another run. Actually, I'd already won the wager, but I was intent on showing that little rooster what was what.

Now it's easier for a driver to aim at a toss when he aligns his coach wheels on the driver's side, but Eb and I had practiced on both sides. I centered myself in the driver's box for my second run. I guess it was the pride that made me do it, but I aligned the run for my off side and made my pass.

"Two wheels," Pete called out again. The folks on the sidelines applauded my pass and money changed hands. I repeated my performance another three times before I slowed my coach to a stop in front of the saloon, tied off and climbed down.

"Now I could go on," I said, striding up to Dobbs "but I would rather not wear out my team teaching a young upstart like you his manners. You owe me five cigars; them twenty-five ones mind you, not no cheap ones."

The children in the crowd sidled over to me for a handout of sweets like I generally gave out when I drove into town.

"You were lucky is all," Willy said. "I ain't got no money to buy no twenty-five cent cigars for no old-timer."

"We don't cotton to welshers 'round here," Pete said, grabbing Willy's arm and slamming him into the wall of the saloon. Another man reached for Willy's free arm and pinned it to the wall. I grabbed Pete's elbow as he was about to haul off and flatten the boy's face.

"Boys, not here. Not in front of the kids." I handed out what sweets I had on me and shooed the children on home.

"Listen here," I said when the last kid was out of sight. "Pete's right, we don't like welshers, not only around here, but all over. If you don't pay up, you'll regret it for the rest of your life, 'cause it'll latch onto your reputation and follow you wherever you go."

"Better pay up, boy," Pete said. "Charley's right, the decision you make now will last a lifetime."

I looked at Pete and the stranger holding the boy's arm. "You can let him go. It's his decision.

"Pay me by night's end, boy, or live with the name Willy the Welsh for the rest of your life."

Willy turned away with shoulders hunched, shoving his fists deep in the pockets of his coat, but later that night he looked me up in the saloon and slapped five quarters down saying, "Buy 'em yourself, old man," and stomped away. I never saw the boy again, but though he paid up, I still always think of him as Willy the Welsh.

29

Them Mormon Women

I learned long ago that it was best to be nice to my customers. Eb said time and again, "You want a job, you be nice. You want a successful business, you be nice. You want people to tell their friends how good a ride you gave them? Be nice." He'd started drumming that into my head early on, and I never forgot.

So, I was nice, well as nice as I could be being a woman pretending to be a man. It could get a little confusing sometimes if you let your mind wander a mite at the wrong time. Anyways, I always hoisted my passenger's bags up. Tipped my hat to the ladies when they spoke to me, making sure to yank my hat brim lower in the process so's they wouldn't get a good look-see at my face, as they were wont.

I shot the bull with the menfolk, occasionally inviting one that appeared interesting to join me up top to relieve the boredom on the next stretch of road. I liked talkers since I didn't do too much of that myself as a rule. They helped the time pass.

I enjoyed the children best. Always had sweets or little gifts tucked away in my pockets for them. They would come a running as I drove up and bounce on their toes waiting for me to step down. I would raise my arms in the air as though I was being held up by bandits. "Who wants a sweet?"

A chorus of "me's" would ring out as they clustered around.

"One for each," I said, and let them have a go at what was in my pockets. The little girls were more polite than the boys o' course, but they learned. I loved those moments.

Sometimes, when I would see a little girl with long, curly black hair, my Mattie would pop to mind. I would tot up her age in my head, and compare her to the child standing before me, then I would blink away the gathering tears and get on about my business.

I would hear comments made by female passengers and townsfolk about how nice I was to the children, but I would pay them no never mind. I loved the kids and did it for the joy of their frank desire for sweets.

One day, while in the town of Hope, I stepped back from emptying my pockets of sweets and landed on the toes of a lady passenger.

"Sorry, ma'am," I said soon as I saw the grimace of pain on her face. "I'm sorry to beat hell—sorry again, ma'am. Didn't mean to offend you with my barn talk. Are you all right?"

"Yes, I'll be fine if I can sit down for a moment." She gave me a crooked smile, and slipped her hand through my arm like them girls do that are sweet on a feller. The hackles on the back of my neck stood up.

"You drive the stagecoach with such flair," she said.

"Just doing my job, is all."

"You mustn't be so modest, Mr. Parkhurst. You set my heart to fluttering, the way you so masterfully control those great big horses." At that, I started to pry her hand off my arm.

"And so many of them, too. I declare, it's excitin' to see you pull up. I look forward to it every time your stage arrives." Just as I pealed off the one hand, the other came into play.

"In fact, I always make sure I travel in your coach, Mr. Parkhurst. I feel so safe in your capable hands."

I walked over to the bench outside the door of the stage office and stopped. She finally detached and sat. I skedaddled.

I may have seen her before, but I hadn't taken notice then. Since I made the same run every couple of days, I learned over the next few weeks that she took the coach every week to the next town to shop or visit. I didn't know which. I did my best to stay away from her. I didn't look at her direct—I'd learned to spot her from the corner of my eye and look the other way quick, and climb aboard my coach before she got to me. That worked for two trips.

Then I learned two things I didn't want to know. She was Mormon. And she had a Mormon friend in the next town. Now I had them traveling with me both ways and making eyes at me. Seemed to have one or the other of them every damn trip.

I'm uglier than sin and generally twice as dirty. Them being religious and all, I couldn't understand for the life of me why they were looking me over. Though I don't usually cuss in front of womenfolk, I started cussing to keep them at bay when I saw them sashaying towards me like a span of mares in season. Damn!

Only place I felt safe in Hope was the Step-on-In Saloon. Generally, I was of a mind to bed down early in the town livery, maybe read awhile if I had light. But I began spending more time in the Step-on-In drinking and gambling to be safe from the reaches of them Mormon women.

As it happened, I was holding my first good hand of Draw Poker—One-eyed Jacks Wild that Wednesday night—when a man entered the saloon, almost brushing the top of the doorway. Dressed in black broadcloth with a wide, flat-brimmed hat, he drew my eye as he removed the hat and strode to the bar. He waved the keep over, then began slowly rotating the brim between his long fingers.

"You in or out, Charley?"

I dragged my eyes from the silver-winged dark hair to look at the cards I'd been dealt. I threw a quarter into the pot in the center of the table and glanced back at the best-looking man I ever saw on either side of the country.

A deep mellow voice washed over me. "Charley Parkhurst around tonight?"

"Hey, Parky, someone here to see ya," the keep said, pointing towards our table.

My eyes dipped back to my cards and my heart started to thud.

"Charley Parkhurst?" the rich gravy-like voice poured across our poker table. I looked up and saw him staring at one of the other players. Something deep inside of me made me want that voice talking to me.

"I'm Parkhurst," I said. I sounded short of breath, but it may have only been the blood rushing in my ears. "What can I do for you?" I couldn't quite look him in the eye. He was too damn handsome. I was afraid my bones would melt right there at the table in front of him and the other four rounding out the game.

"I would like to speak with you, if I may."

Oh God, that wonderful voice had manners behind it. I don't think any man had ever spoken to me with manners before. My eyes flashed up to his and dipped back to my cards.

"Your bet, Charley," the dealer said.

As I recollect, I was holding a royal flush in spades, but my insides couldn't concentrate on the cards. My brain was crackling, and my eyes, though looking at the cards in my hand, were seeing the pair of hazel-green eyes I'd just looked into.

"Raise you ten dollars," I said, pushing a stack of silver dollars toward the pot.

"My name is Granger. Titus Granger," the voice said.

"Too rich for me," one of the players said.

"Me, too."

"I'm out."

"I guess it's just you 'n me, Charley. I call," the dealer said, sliding his silver toward the pile. "And raise you twenty."

"Be with you in a minute, Mr. Granger," I said. "Got some business to attend to here first."

"So I see," the voice said, sounding less rich and more wry.

I'd been dealt this hand, no draw. I weren't about to lose it, but I didn't have but eighteen on me. The dealer was counting on that. "Jim, lend me two, will you?"

"I'm all out, Charley. Sorry."

"Ned? You know I'm good for it."

"I'm slapping wood myself. I gotta call it a night." Ned said, scraping his chair away from the table.

I glanced at the last man at the table. He had a pile of coins in front of him, and small eyes, and those small eyes were staring straight at the pot of silver in the center of the table. He didn't so much as glance in my direction, hearing what I'd said to the others.

"Well, I guess I got to..."

Two silver dollars plinked on the table and rolled toward the pot. I glanced up. Golden voice had covered me. I pushed my eighteen forward. "Okay, let's see what you've got."

With a smirk, the dealer placed his cards on the table one at a time. My eyes sped over the smudged faces of the cards.

Seven spades.

Seven diamonds.

Seven clubs.

My chest began to ache. There were two one-eyed jacks in a deck of cards. One black, which I held in my hand, and one red.

He placed the seven of hearts on the table. Filling out four of a kind.

His smirk slid into a winning grin. Only five of a kind using a one-eyed jack could beat out my Royal Flush. Shit!

He slapped the jack of diamonds down on the table and started reaching for the pot.

"That ain't a one-eyed jack," I said, rising from my seat. "The red one-eyed jack is a heart." The others faded away from the table, one knocking over a chair in his haste.

The grin slid off the dealer's face, sharpening it to a look of hatred. He stopped reaching for the pot and straightened. Without looking at the card in question, he said, "My mistake," and turned away, grabbing his coat off the back of the chair.

The bastard was figuring on my being too drunk to notice!

"Mr. Parkhurst?"

"Yes, Mr. Granger," I said, yanking the chair under me again. "Pull up a seat." I poured myself a shot of Monongahela and downed it as the voice sat. I motioned to pour him a drink, but he shook his head. I poured myself another to sip while he talked.

I singled three silver dollars out of the pot and slid them toward Mr. Granger, and pulled the rest toward me, sliding them off the edge of the table into my poke. I glanced into his hazel-green eyes. "Thanks..." I blinked twice, "for coming through for me. Appreciate it."

"I figured you were good for it. Been asking about you around town. You have a good reputation, one of honesty and integrity. Otherwise, I wouldn't be here."

"What can I do for you, Mr. Granger?" I nodded, taking a sip of whiskey.

"Marry my daughter."

The whiskey shot out of my mouth in a spray. "What?!"

"My daughter wants to marry you. And, having asked around as I said, and looked into your financial capabilities, I've decided she's had worse hare-brained ideas than this."

I think I must've sat there with my mouth hanging open like a dolt, 'cause I knew my mind weren't working all that good just then.

"Of course, I would like Mary-Elizabeth to marry someone closer to her own age. Someone who would always be there for her. To protect her and care for her."

I couldn't bring myself to say anything. All I kept thinking was, "oh, no, oh, no." But that soon turned into "oh, shit, oh, shit," and the sweat began to gather on my forehead, dampening the brim of my hat.

"But she and Barbara Downs are set on marrying you. I'm sure you're aware that we Mormons believe in taking more than one wife." His voice rose making his statement a question.

"I'm Presbyterian. We only marry one man to one woman."

"That's all right. We accept other enlightened ones into our church."

I couldn't find anything to say. I felt as though I weren't a part of this conversation, much less the center of it. In a detached way, I felt disappointed he was married.

"They're the best of friends and believe they can manage home and hearth together with you as their head."

I glanced in his direction from under the brim of my hat. A small smile played at the corners of his mouth, but those hazel-green eyes of his were brimming with laughter.

"'Sweetly' was the word she used." He paused then nodded his head. "Yes, 'sweetly' it was."

I could have sworn I heard a low chuckle at the end of that bit. Now the sweat started to trickle between my breasts.

"Barbara's staying with us this evening. Her father will surely approach you himself on this subject soon."

When I didn't say anything, he continued, "I believe they're at home right now planning their nuptials. You know how young women get. Well, then again, maybe you don't. Though I'm not a wagering man, I would bet on that, Mr. Parkhurst. They are quite intent on landing you as their matrimonial prize."

That was it! I couldn't take no more. I was past finding something polite to say and getting derailed every time he opened his mouth to make one further point. I slapped the table with the flat of my hand, "What is it about me that them women find so damn interesting?"

"I'm sure I don't know, Mr. Parkhurst." Titus Granger said with an outright chuckle. "So, what is your answer to be? What do I go home and tell my daughter?"

"Anything you want providing it's no." I knocked back my shot of whiskey and shot up from the table. I strode out of the saloon without a backward glance and knew if I ever heard that rich voice again, I would head out the other way at a dead run.

Sunrise had me hanging around the back door to the stage office with saddlebags in hand waiting for the stationmaster. I'd tossed and turned like a rabbit on a spit all night and felt all achy and cranky from listening for a soft footstep and the rustle of skirts. Hadn't even stopped for breakfast. I wanted out.

When I heard the sound of boots scraping the stage office floor, I pounded on the back door. The turn of the latch sounded like a judge's reprieve from the noose.

"Gus, you got to get me on the stage out of here, least as far as the next swing station," I said, bursting through the door like a horse with its tail on fire. "You got to change my run."

30
A Trip Home

T ime for a change, is all," I said when I'd calmed down some.
That's how those sudden-like changes spun my life around.
Two Mormon women with a marriage idea floating around in their
heads. Women!

"You serious?" Gus asked.

I gave him one of my looks.

"I got to get a gold shipment to New York City," he said.
"It's not in the direction you want to head out, and it ain't a
driving job since we don't have any routes east of here, but I
would see it as a special favor to me if you'd messenger it all the
way for me. I been worrit about who to send, and I trust you,
Charley, like nobody else."

I stared at him for a couple of minutes.

Now seein's I was strong for my size, having had to wrangle
horses and passenger luggage pretty much all my life, it wouldn't
be hard to keep a real close eye on that chest of gold and heft it
from one stage run to the next till it got to New York City. Pay
wouldn't be as good as when I drove, but I'd be able to sit back

and relax, even catch up on my sleep, if all was quiet like I expected.

"You'll earn messenger fees of course, and the line will pay your return trip to Hope. I'll even throw in passage to California, if you're still of a mind to change your run when you get back."

Gus's request had me heading in the wrong direction, but the idea set a little excitement going in me. Said he trusted me more'n anyone he had working for him, which tickled my pride. But the center of the thing that decided me to go was that I would have the chance to visit Eb and Tilly again.

"Might even pick up some driver pay along the way, if you've a mind," Gus said, still trying to wheedle me into the job. "Wouldn't be no hair off our hides."

Seein's the Balchs were the only family I'd ever been a part of, and seein's how we were all getting on in years, this job would give me a chance to see them one last time. When I left Providence, I figured I would never set eyes on them two again. We swore we would write, but over the years, we'd lost touch. I moved around a lot, and there weren't much to say in a letter what with me looking at the rump end of a six-up all day. Course, there were times when I would miss getting a letter all together. I knew that 'cause there'd be holes in the news I did get referring to something told in another letter I didn't get.

I looked up at Gus, I could tell he was in a lather wanting me to take the job.

"You got yourself a deal. When do I leave and from where?"

"Today. The treasure box is due in this morning."

All I can summon to mind about that run into New York City is sleeping in the coach with my head banging against the wall; that is, when there was room for me inside, or jawing with the drivers while sitting up top to get a breath of fresh air. And slinging that damn heavy chest from one coach to the next.

There weren't so much as a whisper of a robbery, or any sign of something near exciting to happen. It was the kind of run a driver likes, and that was fine with me. I figured that if anything happened to threaten my trunk of gold, I would have to shoot the bastard, or die in the attempt. I weren't fond of the idea of being on the receiving end of a bullet.

Not one for big cities, I delivered the gold, got my receipt, and headed to the northern docks for a ferry to Providence, figuring I would sleep on the packet. Had to get off on Block Island to change ferries, but a day after riding into New York City, I was once again in Providence. It weren't the same town I remembered. Lordy, no. It bustled like the city I'd left behind the day before. Nothing looked familiar at first. There were more buildings, some I got a crook in my neck looking at. More people, but nobody I knew. Coaches, carriages, gigs, wagons, drays, and more people on horseback. The names of the streets hadn't changed, though there were more of them.

I made my way down Benefit Street, excitement rising within me like a bubbling pot of coffee. I hadn't telegraphed ahead to let them know I was coming. I was picturing in my mind their surprise when I entered the inn and bellowed Tilly's name. Which is what I did.

"Eb and Tilly don't own the place any more," a fat man said, wiping down the bar with a dirty cloth. Tilly would never have allowed anything to get that dirty much less continued to use it.

I stood in the middle of the common room feeling like some other person. Eb and Tilly didn't own the Franklin Inn or the What Cheer? How can that be? I looked around. I was in the right place. It weren't as tidy as Tilly would have kept it, but it was the same place I'd eaten in many times over the years between the time we left Worcester, and I left for Georgia, then California. My gut felt hollow.

"Hey, mister," the fat man now stood before me. "You all right? Have a seat." He pointed me to a small table by the window, one I'd sat at many times. He ran the cloth over the table, pushing crumbs to the floor. Tilly would have a fit. But Tilly weren't there.

"What do you want?"

"Huh?"

"What do you want to eat?"

"Oh, ah, give me a plate of your lunch special and coffee."

"We don't got no lunch special," he said. "Chicken or ham today."

"Chicken."

"Coming right up. Bertha," he yelled. "Chicken plate, coffee."

I looked out the window without seeing what was there. I felt like a balloon floating on the wind. Where were they? Where did Eb and Tilly go? A part of me had been tethered to the Balchs and this place all along, but now I'd come unmoored, and I felt damn uneasy.

The smell of chicken drew my attention back to the table. I looked at the half chicken wallowing in greasy gravy, still expecting to see Tilly's mouth-watering chicken and dumplings. I couldn't seem to get it in my head that Tilly weren't there any more.

Someone beside me cleared their throat.

"Charley, is that you?"

I looked up. "Bertha?" I don't know why I hadn't put it together when the barkeep shouted her name along with my order a few minutes ago, but there she was, a bit rounder than I remembered. A busted front tooth now marred her good-natured smile. "God, it's good to see you."

"I almost didn't recognize you."

"Glad you spoke up. I just heard Eb and Tilly don't own the place anymore."

"It's good to see your face again, too, Charley. I used to have a crush on you years back."

"Now ain't you glad you didn't get hitched up with me seein's how I turned out uglier than a summer cow pie?"

"Naw, go on, you ain't that bad. You sure used to cut a fine figure with that coach you drove." Bertha slid into the chair across from me. "How was Californy? Did you dig up a lot of gold?"

"No. Pretty much stuck to driving coach or hauling freight out to the fields. I sloshed a pan or two out of curiosity, but I never saw gold that way."

"Pity, you could've been rich."

"A lot of people went, but many more died than got rich."

"Oh."

"Say, what happened to Eb and Tilly?"

"Eb up and died back in the winter of '61—"

"Eb—dead?" I felt as though someone had punched me in the gut.

"Yeah, got sick in the lungs. Tilly sold out after Eb passed and went to live with some relative or other in New York state somewheres."

My mind couldn't take it all in. Tilly gone, too? "You know where exactly?"

"No, she wrote you about it. I remember how disappointed she was that she didn't hear back from you."

"Her letters must've gotten lost. I didn't know."

"Bertha." The barkeep bellowed. "You got people to feed."

"I got to go," Bertha said. "Been nice talking to you, Charley. You planning to stay around here now?"

"No, California is my home these days." I was disappointed she had to get back to work. I'd hoped to get a line on others I'd known in town, but after eating only about half the food set before me, I paid the bill and left the inn. I went out back to give the stables a look-see. Eb had always had his stableboys keep the place neat and clean, but now this, too, had the same run down look as the inn. Eb would have been sick to see his business in such shape.

Tears burned my eyes. The loss of both Eb and Tilly washed over me. I felt guilty as hell, too, that I hadn't continued writing even when no letters came my way. I should have known better being a stage driver, the U.S. Mail gets stolen pretty near every time a stage gets robbed. I kicked the dust, sending up a cloud of pent up anger. I should have known.

I returned to the street and started walking. I didn't know where I was going, but I knew I couldn't spend another minute there. It was too empty. Maybe I would run into somebody who knew where Tilly was, but I doubted it. A coach driver and an innkeeper didn't share the same off-hours company, especially since we were of a different age and appeared to be the opposite gender.

I found myself in the part of town where old and new shops lined the streets and figured to pick up a few things to take back with me, prices being cheaper here in the East. I bought myself a dark blue suit for dressing nice, two pair of fancy navy blue, fringed driving gloves complete with embroidered backs the way I like them, a dozen pair of socks, a few secondhand books along with Horatio Alger's new novel, Ragged Dick, and a new pair of fancy, ready-made boots. I managed to mash all of it into my canvas sack except the suit and boots. I put the suit packages in the box with my well-worn boots to carry under my arm.

Stupid move that. Wearing new boots when I had a lot of walking to do. It was their prettiness that done me in. Had a stitched pattern all the way up the shaft. That womanly wanting of pretties crept up on me from time to time. Couldn't seem to walk away without buying them.

After getting reacquainted with the layout of the town, I found myself leaning against the wall of Abernathy's Emporium chawing a fresh plug of t'bacca and wondering where I was going to bunk for the night, or whether I should head back to the ferry.

So, there I stood dressed in my now second-best clothes right down to my fancy new gloves and boots, when who the hell should come parading past as though the king and queen of Portugal but Dom Ramirez with his daughter on his arm. Dom in a black suit and tie with a fresh white shirt, and his daughter set to sail in fluttering white ruffles down her sleeves and skirt. Dom, he didn't seem to see me at all, but his daughter now, she saw me. A sneer crossed her pretty face, and she pulled aside her skirts as she passed so's not to brush up against me, as though I was covered in spring cow shit or something.

I ain't proud of what I done, but it was out before I thought on it. I spat t'bacca juice down the back of her bustled skirts and muttered, "Prissy bitch." Who the hell was she to look down on me like that? I earned my way in life and earned the respect of everyone who knew me and then some.

Dom heard what I said, and he turned on me with his mouth open to say what was on his mind, and by the look on his face, it weren't going to be nice—he recognized me and snapped his jaw shut. Before I could take it all in, he and his brat were sailing on down the walk again. They got to Abernathy's door and she fluttered in, head held high, with t'bacca spittle running down her sails. I started to chuckle to myself when I see Ramirez heading back up the walk toward me. He stopped in front of me, his black eyes bore into mine. There weren't any sparkle to them as there once was.

His expression reminded me of my father's, a past caring gaze that exposed the dead man inside. The lines chiseled into his once handsome face made him look old and worn. His clothes bespoke money.

"You look like hell," he said.

"You look as prissy as she does."

He glanced toward Abernathy's. "My daughter, Catarina."

"Why ain't her mamma taking her around to the shops?"

"She died."

"When?"

"Last year." He nodded, his face ashen. "My son, too. Influenza."

"Sorry."

"I come a long way since we knew each other," he said, throwing his shoulders back.

"So have I," I said, standing straighter. I weren't going to let this dandified jackass think he was better'n me. My chin jutted forward. My need to punch his face for not being there with me when Mattie died; for leaving me as he did flooded through me. My fingers curled into fists.

"I got lucky in marriage," he said with a slow shake of his head. His shoulders drooped again as though he no longer had any spirit left in him. "Constança, she came from a wealthy family. I learned much from them."

I snorted. "Some folks get money thrown at them, I reckon. I earned mine."

Don nodded his head in silence for a moment. "I not see you for what—fifteen, sixteen years now. Right here outside Abernathy's, yes?"

I could only nod, my throat had closed at the remembrance of that moment.

"And our child?" he asked in a tone so low, I could barely hear him.

"Dead."

His dark eyes searched mine. "At birth?"

I bit the inside of my lip to keep from crying, took a deep breath, and said, "Her name was Mathilde Winifred Parkhurst. Mattie died the summer she was two. Snakebite. Down in Georgia."

Dom stared down at the wooden walkway shaking his head. "I'm sorry."

"She never knew a father's love, but she had adopted aunts and uncles, and a mother who loved her and grieved mightily when she died."

What little color Dom had drained from his face. He kept staring at the ground with his hands deep in his pickets. I felt pity for him. Truth be told, he hadn't fared all that much better than me.

He took a deep breath and finally looked me in the eye. "I'm sorry for everything. For getting you pregnant. For leaving you as I did. For never knowing our daughter. I was young and full of myself."

What he had said was such a surprise, it drained the anger right out of me. All I could seem to do was give him a small nod of my head, which he returned before walking away.

I turned on my heel and headed home. Home to California.

31

Home Again

On the way back to central California, I delivered the gold receipt to Gus, said my goodbyes, and headed out on the same coach I'd come in on.

I was sick of hearing about the War Between the States now that it was over. Everybody had something to say, generally it was something mean. Nobody would gentle down and see anybody else's view, just kept yelling at one another. Unfortunately, my friend, Frank Woodward and I were no exception.

An old-time cotton southerner, Frank was one of them who couldn't seem to get over the outcome of the war. He was a pleasant sort even while drinking unless a wrong word was spoken. A wrong word being the War—that being the War of Northern Aggression as he called it. The South—especially Reconstruction. The Chinese, the freedmen, or women. Any one of them subjects would get him going like a runaway team.

With that said, from time to time Frank and I would get into a "discussion" at the mention of one of them wrong words, though I generally stayed well away from that last one. Though we were friends for nigh-on twenty years, he had no idea I was a woman.

He'd be furious as a hornet-stung mustang if he knew, and would probably take a shot at me seein's how every woman he ever knew "done him wrong."

But I remember well the discussion we got into over labor and states rights one time that drove me to make a rather surprising decision.

"God made the niggers and the Chinks to be slaves," Frank said. "They're property, bought and paid for, or least ways they oughta be. Why the hell can't the damn government leave things as they are? Them slanty-eyed Chink bastards are taking up jobs here like the freed niggers are back East. Jobs Californians need."

"They're human beings," I said. "They're people like us."

"The hell they are."

"I've seen both the Negroes and the Chinese treated worse than stray curs. Nobody should be treated that way. I don't cotton to the idea of slavery at all."

"That might be rightly so, but it is still a man's decision to do with his property as he sees fit."

"Bullshit!"

"States got the same rights," Frank said.

"No, they don't. What good is it to have a couple of dozen small states fighting among themselves like some of them European countries? Them southern states got to join the union again."

"It's our right of freedom. We fought a war with England so's we could be free, not so's we can be ruled by the North. The South will never unite." Frank's jaw clamped shut, his lips pursed tight, and I didn't hear another word out of him, nor could I get a word into him. He had shut me out as though I didn't exist anymore, the stubborn old mule.

I was afraid he was right about the Southern states refusing to ratify the fourteenth amendment to join up with the North again. Many of the fellers I knew driving stage were from the South. They spouted the same rights to freedom ideas whenever the subject came up, but what they hid behind was a deep down bitterness about losing the war, and seeing the Chinese work jobs they felt Californians should have. They hated the North for winning the war. They hated the Chinese for bringing the railroad. In some ways, I couldn't blame them, what with all the Reconstruction horror stories we heard, and the choking off of the stagecoach business that the railroad would bring.

I felt sorry for the South. Felt sorry for the Chinese, too, they worked damn hard for the little they got.

After them arguments with Frank, I would wonder how Freddie and her boys made out after the war. We'd lost touch after she'd paid off the land I gave her, and I came West. And I would wonder about that black woman back in Georgia and her four mulatto daughters, and whether the one she was expecting at the time of the auction was a girl or a boy. I would think, too, about that little China doll I saw in San Francisco when I first arrived, wondered whether she was still alive. All this thinking made me melancholy as hell. What was it all for? It seemed to me that women got the worst treatment and had the least opportunity to defend themselves. None of us had the vote, probably wouldn't for a long time to come, seein's how the men were running the world, and rather poorly I might add. It appeared to me to be time for the women to take over and show them how it could be done with a whole lot less fuss and a whole lot more caring and compassion. So I decided to do something about it.

The morning of April 25, 1867, I climbed the stairs to the second floor of the brick flatiron building between Main and Willow Streets and walked into the Santa Cruz County Hall of Records to register to vote.

The small bespectacled clerk toted a large black bound book from the top of a file cabinet to the long counter that divided the room. The place smelled of old paper. Wooden cabinets and stacks of paper crowded the room and muffled the slap of the book as it hit the counter. The name engraved on a chunk of wood atop the desk bespoke the clerk's name and title. Mr. Hugo Reeves flipped open the cover with a hollow snap and said, "Name?"

"Parkhurst."

He referred to a list of numbers in the front of the book before sliding his forefinger along the alphabetically tabbed short end of the pages. When he came to the "P," he flopped the pages over to reveal a large, columned page with only two entries filled in.

Mr. Reeves dipped his pen and wrote the number 1039 and Parkhurst in the next column before looking at me expectantly.

"What's your full name?"

"Charley Darkey Parkhurst." He wrote Charles Durkey, but I weren't about to take issue with him. Sweat had busted out on my upper lip.

"Age?"

"Fifty-five."

"Where were you born?"

"Lebanon, New Hampshire." The room was quiet but for the scratch of his pen and my heart thumping in my ears. I was surprised at how calm my voice sounded.

"Where do you reside?"

"Soquel."

After writing the town's name, he skipped a few blank columns and wrote the date.

"Do you solemnly swear that the information you have given me is accurate and true?"

Oh, shit. The sweat trickled down the middle of my back as though I stood in a steamy bath house. "Yup," I said, swallowing the lump in my throat. After all I didn't lie—exactly. He never asked whether I was a man.

As Reeves wrote "sworn" in the next column, I asked, "Do I have to do anything else?"

"No, that's all," he said, slapping the register closed. "See you come election time. We oughta be set up in the new courthouse by then."

"Right," I said. Feeling a bit giddy, I walked out into the sunshine with a smirk on my face. I, a woman, was going to vote for who I wanted as President of these United States in the next election and those damned Democrats were going to be defeated if I had anything to say about it.

Women less able to take care of themselves than me played upon my mind some. Most times, I could do nothing about helping them. After all, if I got myself into trouble trying to help someone else, I would be no help to anybody. The words of the China man I met my first day in San Francisco echoed through my mind many times when I was about to put my nose in another woman's trouble: "You could find yourself shanghaied." Didn't want that— ever. I liked being independent. It meant the world to me. But I figured it meant a whole lot to other women, too, so, when I heard that my neighbor, Widder Johnson, and her daughter were being evicted 'cause they couldn't pay their mortgage and taxes, I stuck my neck out and, yup, there was a backlash. The way it played out was this.

I was riding past her house one morning on my way into town when I heard this pitiful wailing coming from her tidy home. The house weren't much more'n a clapboard cabin, a step or two above a shack. Her husband, a man of about thirty, had keeled over dead of a heart attack three years before while plowing his field for spring planting and had left her a big mortgage debt and pitiful little in the way of money. She'd sold off the farmland, but managed to keep the house, such as it was, to live in with her pretty daughter. The widder worked hard. She kept the place neat and took in mending and laundry when she could as a way of making ends meet. I spoke with her a couple of times, and she never once complained about hard times. So, it was a surprise to me to see the sheriff step out the front door, shaking his head.

"What brings you out this way, Angus?" I called to him as he mounted his blue roan mare and rode toward me. "What did you go and do to the widder that's got her crying?"

"Aw, Charley, there be days I hate my job and this be one of them. You ken the new bank manager, Tobias Blackwell? The portly man that's so full of his own self-importance it looks like he's a going to bust his buttons."

"Yup, I've seen him about. Didn't cotton to him either, I take it?"

Now Tobias Blackwell was still considered "new" though he had arrived to the town and the position of bank manager some five years before, but 'cause he didn't fit in, and was not liked by most, he hadn't become "townsfolk" yet. At the rate he was going, he weren't going to make it neither, not with that attitude he toted around.

"Right you are. He's gone and foreclosed on the Widder Johnson. She's got to be out within the week."

"Bastard." I said. "Where's she going to go?"

"Don't know. She don't either. She has no family hereabouts. Her husband's family haven't lifted a finger to help her since he died. Shameful that is, but what's a body to do?

"There you have it. It's my job, and there be days I hate it."

"How much she owe?" I asked.

"Six hundred."

"She must've seen it coming. Couldn't have known otherwise."

"She's a church-going woman. It's my guess she was trusting in the Lord and hoping for a miracle," he said.

"It's been my experience miracles don't happen unless someone makes them happen."

"Right you are. That bank manager is going to need a miracle, too," Angus said with a chuckle and a shake of his head. "He's pining to become a member of the Order of Odd Fellows, and he ain't ever going to make it with his stingy ways. He's been asking to join for the past four years, I hear."

"Why won't they let him in?"

"He's got it all wrong, a body's got to be asked to join."

"What are they all about, those Odd Fellows?" I asked.

"They're do-gooders. They started up a home for old folks over in Sacramento. And they're all about love, friendship and truth, or so I hear from my brother-in-law who's a member of the local chapter. He don't much care for Blackwell either. Nobody does."

The sheriff and I hit town and went our separate ways. I waited four days to see what would happen, hoping those Odd Fellows would pitch in for the widder, but I didn't hear a thing.

Then I made a decision.

For all the times I'd wanted to help, but backed down 'cause I couldn't afford to get involved, I decided to help the Widder Johnson.

32

Sticking My Neck Out

I groomed and pulled on my blue suit from Providence to go into town. When I walked into the bank and asked to see the manager, I was told to take a seat.

I could see Blackwell on the other side of the room cussing out one of the clerks. I was pretty sure he'd seen me come in, so I waited. He mumbled something to his secretary about not wanting to be disturbed and went into his office, shutting the door with a snap that echoed throughout the building.

I waited.

I studied the high ceiling with its carved tiles and counted them. Five hundred of them there were. Since I weren't good at my multiplication tables when I was at the orphanage, I had to multiply smaller quantities of ceiling tiles and add them together. I did that once before I approached the secretary again to ask to see Blackwell. The man flushed when I reminded him, but refused to disturb his boss, stating what I'd already heard Blackwell say.

I sat down and recounted the ceiling tiles. Watched town folk come in, do business and leave. Some spoke with me for a few minutes, others waved their hello. While my mood changed from amiable to angry, I counted the large marble blocks that made the floor. When I'd done that twice, I decided I'd had enough of Blackwell's play for power. While sitting there, I'd figured out what the bastard was doing. He was making me sit there, hat in hand so to speak, to await his pleasure 'cause he figured I had come to ask for a loan. I felt like a mustang tied to a post in the middle of a corral with only myself to fight with.

I got up, straightened my suit, and marched past the secretary straight into the manager's office without knocking.

"Who the hell are you, and how dare you walk in here without being announced by my secretary? Connors," Blackwell roared. "Connors, get in here." The entire bank could not have helped but hear. I walked to the oversized walnut desk and confronted the obese prig straight on.

"My name is Charley Parkhurst. I have waited over two hours to speak with you," I said, barely able to hold back the rage that had boiled up inside me.

"Loan applicants are to wait until called upon," he said. "Connors, show this man out."

I shook my arm out of Connors' dutiful but light grasp. "I am not a loan applicant, you horse's ass. I am here to pay off a loan, not to apply for one."

"I don't know you. You don't have a loan with this bank."

"Everyone else in town knows me and any one of them would vouch for me if necessary. And the loan is not mine, but that of the Widder Johnson."

"Well, now," Blackwell's flabby cheeks quivered as he stood. I continued to look him straight in the eye though he was a few inches taller than me. I think he may have tried standing on the balls of his feet to look down on me. "Connors, get me the Johnson files. Have a seat, Parkhurst."

I noticed the lack of "Mr." in front of my name. Blackwell weren't about to give an inch. He remained standing after I'd taken a seat. I continued to look him in the eye with all the anger I felt until he took his seat after Connors brought the requested file.

Blackwell shuffled through the neatly stacked papers, acting like he was important and that the finding of the exact amount of money owed would require a long detailed reckoning, but I would've bet the number was right there on top, and he was showing off.

"Ah, yes, six hundred and five dollars and sixty-seven cents," he said.

The look he gave me clearly spoke his doubt that I could pay. I pulled out my poke and counted out six-hundred and six dollars in gold and silver. When I looked up Blackwell was slack-jawed. That there made the whole transaction worth it.

"You now owe me thirty-three cents," I said.

"Yes, of course, Mr. Parkhurst. Connors, bring Mr. Parkhurst his change and write him a receipt."

"As for the deed—"

"I'll have that made up right away, Mr. Parkhurst."

"It is to be made out to Mrs. Johnson and delivered to her. She is not to know who paid her debt. Is that understood?"

His mouth actually hung open at that point. I almost laughed out loud.

"How can she be beholding to you if she doesn't know?"

"I am not doing this so Mrs. Johnson will be beholding to me, you old goat. She is a good and respectable woman. You mind that, Blackwell."

"Yes, yes, of course she is."

"I expect the deed delivered this afternoon. She has suffered over this long enough." I walked to the door and drew it wide open before continuing in a voice loud enough for all in the bank to hear. "You will see that it's done, Blackwell?"

"Yes, yes, of course."

Connors handed me a receipt, and I left the bank feeling a bit better after putting Blackwell in his place.

The following day, I rode by the Johnson home and was glad to see her out sweeping the doorstep, which gave me the reason I needed to stop for a bit of a chat. The news spilled right out of her. She told me the whole story with such joy on her face that I felt real pleased with myself, not that I let it show, mind you, but I was damn glad I did what I'd done.

About a month later, Sheriff Angus's brother-in-law, Jake Irelan came to see me. I didn't know the man well at the time, him being a doctor and all, so was surprised to have him climb off his thick-boned chestnut at my door and heartily shake my hand as though we'd been friends for many years. After the opening niceties he was off and running.

"Mr. Parkhurst," he said. "You've heard of the Independent Order of Odd Fellows haven't you?"

"Yes, I have. Won't you come in?"

"We are a charity organization under the guidance of the California Lodge No. 1 in San Francisco and chartered by the grand lodge in Philadelphia. You've seen it haven't you? Our headquarters in San Francisco?"

I nodded. I'd seen it all right. You couldn't miss the huge building on the corner of Seventh and Market Streets, with its spikes and spires.

"Would you like a drink?" I asked.

"Sure, sure," he said. "Along with the Masons, we built the first hospital in San Francisco."

"Heard that," I said, handing him a glass of Monongahela.

"We are also known as the Three Link Fraternity. Each link stands for a concept we hold at heart, Friendship, Love, and Truth. We are a proud organization of men, proud of our accomplishments and the generosity of our members. We are spreading all over the state, all over the country in fact."

"Please have a seat," I said, pointing my hand to one of the rough hewn chairs at the hearth.

"Our fraternity looks after the less fortunate—widows, orphans, fellow members who have come upon hard times. We like to say it is our duty to relieve the distressed, educate the orphan, and bury the dead.

"We at the Odd Fellowship in Soquel have heard of your largess in helping Mrs. Johnson out of her difficulty awhile back, and I'm here at the behest of the Fellowship to invite you to join us as a member."

"How did you find out about Widder Johnson?" I asked, shooting up from my chair, my voice rude and commanding. "No one was to know that I had anything to do with that. I told Blackwell to keep it under his hat. Damn him."

"As you may already be aware, Mr. Parkhurst, Tobias Blackwell is a toady. He has wanted to be inducted into our fraternity for quite some time and approached me with the information that he paid off Mrs. Johnson's mortgage, thinking perhaps that it would be his ticket into our organization."

"What?!" I shouted so damn loud Doc Irelan jumped in his seat. "That bastard!"

"Now, now, Mr. Parkhurst. We Odd Fellows have straightened this out. What Blackwell doesn't know is that his secretary is a brother, and as soon as Connors heard of his boss's allegation, he put us on the straight of the matter right away."

"Blackwell used my secrecy against me. He has no honor," I said. "Why the hell is he running a bank?"

"Actually, he isn't any longer. The owners of the bank are also Odd Fellows and have since discharged him for his deceit and lack of integrity. His self-righteousness has never stood him in good stead with the people of the community. His discharge was long overdue and welcomed by all but himself, I'm sure."

"I would wager you're right. But why didn't the Odd Fellows help the Widder Johnson?" I asked.

"We had just cleaned out our coffers helping another neighbor in distress," Doc Irelan said. "Otherwise, we would have. But I can't divulge who we helped. I'm sure you understand that for the sake of the organization and the party receiving our assistance, we never discuss such matters. We prefer our recipients maintain their dignity."

"What do I have to do as a member?"

"Well, that's quite easy, in fact. We gather monthly at the lodge at which time we hold our business meetings and spend time enjoying the company of like-minded men. The cost to our members is five dollars per meeting. The money we garner goes toward the doing of our good works."

I reached over to shake Doc's hand, "I would be proud to be a member," I said. "I admire what you do."

And so I became a member of the Independent Order of Odd Fellows, and managed to live through helping someone without getting myself shanghaied.

The national election between Ulysses S. Grant of Civil War fame and Horatio Seymour of New York took place a few months later. Again, I got dressed in my best suit and rode on over to Tom Mann's hotel to vote.

I stood in line awaiting my chance to mark my ballot feeling good, though a little nervous. I talked to the fellers in line with me and those passing by, some of them newfound brothers, which gave me a feeling of belonging I liked.

The man standing behind me must have come straight from a saloon. I'd watched him stagger across the street, listing in the direction of the hotel. I'd seen him around. Had a reputation for starting trouble, so I started up a conversation with the feller ahead of me. I didn't want no trouble from no drunk.

"Hey, ain't you that stage driver everyone talks about?" Prideful devil that I am, I generally like being recognized for the work I do. But there was a belligerent whine to the man's voice that made my skin twitch like a horse trying to get rid of a biting fly, so I acted like I didn't hear him.

As each man gave his name, the clerk checked it against the voter register and wrote a "v" in the book, then called for the next in line. I was next but one.

"Hey, I say, ain't you that stage driver I keep hearing about?"

Behind me, the man's over-loud voice was an annoyance I couldn't ignore. I could feel my cheeks begin to flush and sweat to gather on my upper lip.

"You taking to me?" I asked over my shoulder.

"Yeah, you with the build of a woman—fat ass, narrow shoulders, and no beard."

"No need to get insulting. Can't help the way I'm made." Worry sweat dampened my body making my clothes stick to me. Turning away, I crossed my arms and tried to look bored.

"Look, she even blushes." His loud voice echoed through the building drawing attention.

"Next."

I was next. I rubbed my gloved hand across my upper lip and gave my name.

"You sure—" the drunk said. I gave him a sharp look.

The clerk found my name in the register, and made his mark before looking me fully in the face. "This man bothering you, Mr. Parkhurst? I could get the sheriff if you want. Angus?" he said, waving the sheriff over before I had a chance to reply. A few fellers behind us moved closer to find out what was going on.

"Something wrong here?" Angus asked.

By now nervous sweat poured out of my body and trickled where my clothes weren't already sticking to me.

"No, no, there ain't nothing wrong," I said. I put a grin on my face that felt like I'd just tasted fresh horse droppings. "This here feller's just poking fun is all. He don't mean no harm."

"You registered to vote here?" the clerk asked the drunk.

The drunk looked around appearing a little befuddled. I moved off and entered one of the tiny cloth-sided voting booths that lined the large courtroom. I pulled out my handkerchief and wiped my face and neck dry. I listened to the continuing conversation at the table.

"I was just saying—"

"I asked you whether you were registered here. You're holding up the line."

"C'mon with me," Angus said.

"But I—"

"Next."

The echoing voices of the sheriff and the drunk moved away. I gripped the voter stand to steady myself, taking several deep breaths to calm down and cool my hot cheeks.

I marked my ballot.

I marked it for Sarah Jean who had no way of defending herself from the unwanted attentions of her stepfather, and the degradation of the pregnancy that resulted.

I marked it for the slave mother and her four daughters I saw auctioned off on my way to Georgia back when I was pregnant with my Mattie.

I marked it for the little China girl shanghaied from her family and shipped to San Francisco, and sold into sex slavery.

I marked it for the widders and the downtrodden women I'd seen.

And I marked it for myself and other women like me who had big dreams, plenty of grit, and wanted more than the written and unwritten laws said we could.

33
What to Do

I was on a stage run between San Francisco and San Jose when one of my leaders cast a loose shoe as we were heading into Redwood. We were ahead of schedule and approaching town at an easy trot, so I pulled them up. I checked the mare over and walked back to pick up the shoe. It weren't bent much, so after unloading my Concord in town, I headed down to the blacksmith shop, hoping the smith would reset the shoe right away.

The smith weren't in.

"He left yesterday," his young apprentice said, a lad of about ten years. "He told me to keep the embers alive because he's expecting to get some work done when he gets home tomorrow. Said I's to tell anyone needing work that he'll take care of it first thing he gets home."

"Well, boy," I said. "I got a mare that needs a shoe reset, and a coach full of passengers that need to get to San Jose. The mare can't go no further without chipping up her hoof to beat hell along the way, and I got no time to lollygag around here waiting for tomorrow. Fire up that forge. I'll reset her."

The boy shot me a look of distrust. "Know whacha doin', Mister?"

"Yup," I said. "The horseman who brought me up taught me." I cross-tied the mare and threw some coke on the embers and stirred a bit to get the fire going, then stuck the shoe in the forge to warm up. "Work the bellows for me, would you?"

Without a word, the boy started pumping.

The mare was a new addition to the team and skittish. Since she was lightweight and willing, I'd teamed her with a steady gelding and put her up front. She was doing pretty well though she needed to be trained up a bit yet. But here in the forge, she kept dancing side-to-side, so's I couldn't pick up her left hind hoof to save my soul. I tried speaking softly to soothe her. Tried humming, hoping that would calm her. She weren't listening no how, so I finally lost patience and smacked her rump. Fact is, nothing seemed to work, so I decided to let her dance while I straightened the shoe. After about fifteen minutes of pounding it straight, I flung it into the water barrel for tempering and cooling, and approached the mare again. She still fidgeted as though she had bats for brains.

"Come here, boy," I said. "We need to give her something else to think about." I pulled the mare's upper lip through the looped rope of a twitch and twisted the handle before handing the tool to the boy. "Hold this and keep it tight."

I slid my hand down the mare's neck, along her sweated chestnut body, over her hip, and down her hind leg, crooning all the while. As soon as I slid my fingers along her tendons, she side-stepped away. I started petting her again at the hip and worked my way down. She backed away, tightening the cross-ties to the point I knew she'd leap forward if I continued. Straightening, I told the boy, "Stand to the side so she can't slam into you. Keep the twitch tight. We're in for a long haul. She don't want to be shod."

The boy moved aside, gave the twitch another half-turn, and nodded his head for me to start again.

I pulled her forward to take the strain off the ropes and started running my hand down her sweated neck, along her body, then down her leg, pinching her tendon just above the fetlock to get her to pick up her hoof. She brought it up high and fast.

"Come on, bring it down, girl," I said. "Let me have it, I ain't going to hurt you none." She relaxed her leg enough that I was able to pull her hoof between my thighs like a vise, leaving both hands free to work. It looked to me like whoever set the shoe hadn't clinched the nails tight enough. Even so, she would need to be re-shod all around soon. As I cleaned the underside of her hoof, she jerked her leg back, but didn't manage to pull it away. I finished cleaning out her hoof and ran the rasp over the bottom of it until it looked level, then let go of her leg.

"You're doing good, kid. Take the twitch off and rub her nose while I reheat this shoe." When it was glowing orange, I approached the mare holding the shoe with a pair of tongs. "No need to twitch her yet," I told the boy. "We'll see whether she can behave without it."

She let me pick up her leg and singe her hoof to check the setting of the shoe. I praised her as I let her leg go. I threw the shoe back in the water for a few minutes, and while it cooled, I took up her hoof once more to file down a high spot on its underside.

When I set to work nailing the cooled shoe on her hoof, she blew up and had to be twitched again. But I managed to get the shoe nailed with the help of the boy, and was rasping the outer edges of her hoof to match the shape of the shoe when she jerked her hoof, and I dropped the metal rasp. It smacked against a metal bin nearby with a loud clang.

All hell broke loose.

Everything happened so damn fast, I didn't know what happened for two days.

I vaguely remember being woke up by a man calling my name and peering real close at my face. When I opened my eye, he started talking. I didn't hear a word he said.

What I do remember after coming awake was a feeling of such pain that I thought a bolt of lightning had struck my left eye and ricocheted around in my brain before coming out the base of my skull.

After the man quit jawing, he give me a shot, and I knew nothing more for two days.

"Charley?

"Charley, wake up.

"Talk to me, Charley."

Didn't want to. Too hard. Felt like I was crawling out of a deep, black well. All I wanted was sleep. But the gruff voice kept nagging.

"Come on, Charley, wake up."

I groaned to be let alone. Hands kept shaking me. The damn voice wouldn't shut up.

"'Tis time to rise and shine."

That did it. Nobody tells me to rise and shine if they want to live. I started to sit up, reaching for my gun. That move was a mistake. I started sinking into the dark again, but hands washed my face with cold water and the voice kept pestering.

"Come on, Charley, wake up. Atsa girl."

Atsa girl? Whoa, that snapped me awake.

I opened my eye and tried to focus, but I kept losing the will to stay awake.

"There ye are," an Irish voice said. "Stay with me now."

"What the hell happened?"

"Horse kicked ye in the face."

"Got to get my passengers to San Jose."

"Charley, I stitched ye up, but I couldna save…I'm sorry. The eye was too mashed, I had to remove… I stitched the lid closed."

I touched the bandage covering my left eye. Another lightening-ing bolt sliced through my head.

"Oh, God, give me something for the pain."

"Can't. Ye been out cold for two days on morphine. Can't give ye much more. It'll do ye harm it will. Morphine'll make an addict of ye, if we're not careful. Like them China folk and their opium."

"Who the hell are you?"

"Doc Murphy."

"Where am I?"

"Redwood."

"The mare?"

"Now what would I be knowin' about a mare?"

"It was a mare that kicked me."

"That was some blow for a woman to take."

Between the vicious pain and the morphine dopiness in my head, all I could think was that I'd avoided doctors all my life so's I could keep my secret safe and now this. Would this one keep his mouth shut? "Please don't say anything about me being a woman."

"How long ye been keepin' this a secret?"

"Since I was a kid."

"I was the one to undress ye, so I know ye spent some time as a woman. As a mother, in fact."

His words sent pain knifing through both my eyes.

"If I can't have some of that morphine, how am I going to get rid of the pain?"

"Couple of shots of whiskey oughta do it. It's the best advice I can give ye other than changin' yer line of work and actin' like a respectable woman."

"Ain't giving up my horses."

"Ye'll have pain in that eye for the rest of ye'r life."

"Won't give up driving."

"Ye can put cold compresses on it, which should give ye some relief. Ice or snow'll work best."

"I got to get back to work," I said, swinging my legs over the side of the bed.

"This isn't the time to be thinking on that."

"Why the hell not?"

I got silence in answer to my question.

"You telling me I can't drive a six-up no more?" My voice rose along with my panic.

"Lay back now and rest," Doc said. "No need to get all riled. We'll talk later."

"The hell we will. I want to know now…" My gut heaved. The doc was lucky there weren't much in it since he was standing right in front of me, holding me upright on the side of the bed.

"Charley, ye've lost yer depth perception."

"My what? I thought I lost my eye."

"Both yer eyes work together tellin' yer brain where yer at. Do ye understand?"

I shook my head with my eye closed so my gut wouldn't lurch again. A low groan rolled up my throat. Though I was doing my best to be tough, I felt like a mostly run-over frog.

"Suppose yer walkin' along and there's a door half open. Ye walk toward the doorway thinkin' its open with yer right eye, but yer blind side doesn't see the edge of the door. There's a damn good chance ye'll walk smack dab into it because ye don't have two eyes workin' together anymore."

My jaw set in determination. I would figure it out as I went.

"Rest now," he said, easing me back into the soft mattress. "If ye have trouble gettin' to sleep tonight, I'll give ye one more shot of morphine so ye get a good rest. But do the best ye can for the rest of the day without it."

"Doc?"

"What?"

"The boy?"

"Ye be askin' after the smith's apprentice?" Doc chuckled and shook his head. "He don't want to be a blacksmith no more, but he's fine."

Fear kept me awake; fear and pain. My good eye traveled along the rose vines of the papered bedroom walls as I thought about what I should do. I couldn't imagine not working horses. Horses were my life. Coaching saved me after Mattie died; I wouldn't know what to do without them.

I closed my good eye, not 'cause I was tired, but 'cause it, too, ached bad.

All told, I stayed at Doc Murphy's house a week. He brought my food up from the kitchen and left strict instructions with his housekeeper that I was not to be bothered. I appreciated what he done, knowing he disapproved of me pretending to be a man.

While at Doc's, I came to learn what he meant by that depth perception he'd been talking about. I kept bumping into the small table and chair that rounded out the guest room's furniture. When I looked out the window, the scenery looked flat. Tried reading the newspaper Doc brought up, but I kept losing track of the lines I was trying to read. By and by, I got better at reading, but my eye would ache after awhile, and I would have to quit.

Before I left, Doc fitted me with a black eye patch. I looked in the mirror and didn't recognize the man staring back at me. I'd become what I pretended to be. I'd never been pretty to start with, but this was downright ugly. There was no trace of a woman in what I saw. I wondered what my Mattie would think of her Mama now.

34
Come a Long Way

A fter leaving Doc Murphy's, I sent word to the stage office that I would be taking some time off to heal, and climbed on the next coach out of Redwood. I headed back to Searsville in San Mateo County where I was bunking at the time.

"Jee-hosephat is that you, Charley?" Hank Monk said as I stepped off the coach. "I heard you got a bit stove in, but son of a bitch, your eye."

"Yup, seein's how it still hurts like hell, I'm going to let you buy me a drink." Hank and me knew each other from way back. We met when we were both working for the Central Overland. Before the hair-raising, noggin-bumping ride he gave Horace Greeley of the New York Tribune back in the spring of '59. Hank and me spent some of our off time together. He never guessed I was a woman, even though we shared a buffalo robe one night on a camping trip in the high Sierras. I still chuckle when I think on it.

"Charley's back." I heard one kid shout from across the street. A passel of children called my name as they ran at me.

"Wow, Charley what happened to your eye?"

"Horse kicked me," I said. "What could you kids possibly want from an old-timer like me?"

"Sweets," a tiny blue-eyed girl said with a big smile.

I smiled back best I could. "Help yourselves," I said, holding up my arms so they could reach into my pockets. My heart sang for the first time in a long while. I'd been afraid the kids wouldn't come around now that I looked uglier than sin wearing that damn eye patch.

"Come on, Charley, first bottle's on me." Hank thumped my shoulder and drew me into the nearest saloon. "Glad to see you up and about. Heard the mare went berserk and busted a leg so's they had to shoot her."

"Wish it had been me that pulled the trigger," I said, knocking back my first shot and pouring another. "I'm mighty thankful the boy holding the twitch didn't get hurt. He weren't much more'n ten and a runt to boot." I snapped back two more shots to quiet the pain.

"Jee-hosephat," Hank said, rubbing his hands over his face as though trying to clear his thoughts. "Can you still drive?"

"Don't know."

"What you planning on doing?"

"I'm no better now than when I commenced. Pay's small and work's heavy. I'm getting old. Rheumatism's chawing at my bones. There ain't nobody to look out for us old used-up stage drivers. I'll kick the bucket one of these days, and that'll be the last of old Charley."

"You got some good years in you yet."

"Hope you're right, Hank. Pain's pestering my head, I guess I ain't thinking straight. Figured I would pack up and spend a few weeks up in the mountains. Get used to…I don't know, seeing half as much, I guess." I tried to sound as though it weren't worrying me to death. "Going to head out to Mariposa; heard about a grove of trees bigger'n any brick and mortar building made." I needed time to think, to get myself sorted out. Back at the doc's I'd been too closed in to think right. I needed to spend some time in my Sierras.

My thoughts had gotten blacker each day since trying to shoe that mare. I'd had an idea slip through my mind that had scared me real good. I thought to put a gun to my head. I'd managed to set it aside, but I knew it was still there, waiting. Waiting to see whether I could get back to driving a six-up. I knew there were other things I could do. Could run a swing station for one stage line or another, could probably raise cattle or chickens or something. I knew before this happened that I couldn't drive a stage forever, my bones wouldn't take it. I would have to step down at some point and still bring in the bacon until they planted my sorry ass in the ground. But I wanted to make that choice. My life had gotten to be wait and see since the batty-brained bitch bashed my eye, and I didn't like that one damn bit. I liked knowing where I was headed and when I had to get there.

Next day, I saddled Chester—this being the third Chester of my acquaintance—and headed south, rounding San Francisco bay before heading east-southeast across the wide flatlands of mid-California toward Mariposa and the Sierras. Had a bit of a time keeping my seat when I swung into the saddle that first time. Kept sliding to one side. Seems my eye had to do something with sitting straight, too. I took it easy that first day out so I could regain my natural balance on horseback.

I had bought me a Molly mule for toting and had her lead wrapped around my saddle horn. She carried my stock of food and such, and weren't happy about the idea. Liked to have taken a chunk out of my leg there that first day. But she and I had us a bit of a "discussion" about good manners, and she came away with the corrected notion that it weren't polite to bite me. After that, we got along fine.

The lowlands and the hills along the coast were easy riding and within a few days the Great Central Valley lay before me, but it would be many days ride before I got to where I was headed. I figured to restock my supplies in Mariposa before heading up into the Sierras to see the big trees I'd heard tell of during my stage runs between there and Stockton.

I had over three hundred miles to go until I reached the mountains with only me for company. My thoughts dwelled in all the tarry crannies of my mind where my darkest memories hid. I would find myself thinking on my Mattie and tears would stream from one eye. Then I would find myself thinking about Fish and how Billy Todd got away with his murder. Then on how Dom up and left me. Then of the look of pain on Tilly's face and the anger on Eb's as I told them I was leaving for Georgia. Then I would find myself thinking about Mattie again. I couldn't seem to pull my mind away from the black periods of my life for any length of time. I began looking at my Colt as a way to escape.

But I kept it holstered and rode on.

A body can see the Sierras out ahead and think to reach them by nightfall and still ride hard two, maybe three days before climbing the foothills. I drove them mountains many times, and still got struck all of a heap with wonder every time I saw them. On a clear winter's day, I've seen their snow caps look like the froth of giant sea waves, the mountains looking to be as blue as the ocean reflecting a cloudless sky.

The Great Central Valley carpeted in lush grass spread before me further than a couple of days' ride. It'd be a good spot to fatten up herds of cattle and raise horses. It was a long haul, but peaceful as well as beautiful. Though I kept wishing I had both eyes to enjoy it, yet was I glad I could see and weren't blind. I still had my independence. Still had choices.

Next morning as I headed east, the sun peeked over the mountains, turning the rising mist to rainbow colored streams of light as they slipped between the tall Ponderosa pines on the far side of the river. The light tickled the rippling waters, turning each wavelet into a bright sparkle. It looked as though the Creator cracked opened a door in heaven to sneak a peek at the beauty He'd created. I watched until my good eye ached, and the rainbow beams faded.

Later that day, I crossed the Merced Falls toll bridge at the upper end of the dam water. James McCoy, the toll keeper, came out and charged ten cents for me and Chester to cross. Had to throw in another nickel for the damn mule. Well, I started getting on about the rates when he pulls out a cigar and hands it to me, then invites me to step down to wet my whistle. Course, I paid for my drinks and spent a pleasant half hour catching up on the local gossip since I'd last been on the stage run to these parts. It made a nice break in my ride.

I arrived in Mariposa early that afternoon, stocked up on some whiskey, plug t'bacca, staples and canned goods.

"Say, you know where them big trees are I hear about?" I asked the feller behind the counter. "I got me a yen to see them for myself."

"You mean the giant sequoia?"

"That'll be them."

"Them beauts grow two-hundred, two-hundred-fifty feet tall. What a sight. Me and the missus visit every chance we get."

"Whoa! That tall, huh? I'll be damned. Point the way."

"They're thirty miles due east of here. Gee, since you're heading in that direction, you ought to see the big valley while you're up there, too. It's a bit further north, but well worth the time." He went on to tell me what to look for in the way of landmarks and such, and a little history about the place. I rode out about mid-afternoon and camped a couple of miles outside of town.

I awoke in a sweat the next morning. I worked at keeping my worries at bay, but they caught up with me most nights in my dreams. I'd wake up at odd times with bile rising in my throat, the blood rushing in my ears, breathing fast and shallow. If it was close to dawn, I'd get up and start my day just to keep my thoughts centered on things I had to do.

I covered the remaining twenty-five miles that day, arriving at the grove late in the afternoon. The last six or seven miles was a steep climb, but well worth it. There was no mistaking that stand of trees for any other. Them sequoia grew into the sky head and shoulders above the tall Ponderosa and the sweet smelling Jeffrey pines with each sequoia standing apart, its toes covered with brown needles and burs. There were few sapling offspring and even less bramble. One looked to have been struck by lightening; its top bare of needles, pointing blackened branches to the clear blue heavens. Two-hundred and fifty feet straight up looked awfully tall to my one eye. I paced one off that had fallen to the ground and was crumbling back into the earth—two-forty it was. Seemed shorter laying on its side then them standing straight. Paced around the base of the tallest one I saw; it must have been at least thirty feet round. I had never seen such a forest. Walking through the grove for three days gave me such a peaceful feeling I didn't want to leave. All that time looking up into them trees seemed to help strengthen my eye, too. I even slept better at night. But on the fourth morning, upon waking to the cry of a Steller's jay instead of a nightmare, I headed north.

"I'm a tellin' you," the feller back at the general store in Mariposa had said. "You ain't going to want to leave that valley. Me and the missus spend time up there every summer. Can't get enough of it."

"He's right. It keeps drawing us back. Wait till you see the falls and the cliffs," the wife said.

They told me the valley I was headed for was called either Uzumati meaning "grizzly bear" in the native Miwok speak, or Yochemate, which meant, "some among them are killers." Most folks, they said, slurred the two words together and called it Yosemite. A valley that most spoke of with awe and claimed it to be the prettiest place on earth. Hard in my estimation to imagine something that could compare to the giant trees, but I went for a look-see just the same.

This place was doing me good. Each day I felt stronger as I clawed away from the black thoughts and gathered the beauty into my mind. My heart drank in the great wonders that I saw, like the Monongahela I downed after a dusty coach run. I'd decided that with this much beauty, I didn't want to die just yet.

The Yosemite Valley was more beautiful than a fresh flower tipped with morning dew and sunshine. The mountains that walled in the valley glowed at dawn and sunset as though they were pure gold. Rivers flowed off the tops of great granite walls, turning to spray before thundering to earth, some to continue spewing off cliffs a second and a third time before roaring into the Merced River hundreds of feet below leaving a rainbow in their wake that thrilled my eye. I saw a long narrow cascade of water turn to molten fire in the setting sun one evening. The sheer beauty of it all made my heart ache with pleasure. And hard as it may be to imagine, the beauty doubled as the mountains reflected themselves off the still waters on the valley floor.

I made my way further down the valley before making my base camp 'cause at each bend of the river, a new view of the valley drew me on. While my eye guzzled the scenery and my thoughts wandered, a ruckus exploded at my left side catching me off-guard.

The damn mule began hopping around like a jackrabbit. I reached for my gun. The stupid mule sidestepped behind Chester. The lead rope rammed up under Chester's tail and the gelding went berserk. I got dumped in the dust. The horse and the mule galloped off in opposite directions.

And there I sat, spitting and fuming, when I hear the low growl of a puma. My eye raked the ground around me. Another growl sent the hair on the back of my neck on end and drew my eye to a ledge somewhere above my head. Ten feet? Twenty? Couldn't judge it right with only one eye. But I caught sight of a pair of fawn colored eyes glaring down at me from a sand-colored face. The puma gathered its quarters to pounce, its muscles rippling under its tawny hide. I dug in my holster for my .38, but it weren't there. I chanced taking my eye off the cat and thought I saw the gun several feet away. I lunged to my right and groped for it. When my sweaty hand felt cold steel, I grabbed ahold. As I drew it into my trembling hands, I fumbled getting it settled in my palm so's I could shoot. I aimed over my head but away from the puma and pulled the trigger twice, hoping the noise would scare it away. It snarled at me. Afraid to take my eye off the cat long enough to get to my feet, I decided that it looked close enough for me to shoot it dead.

I aimed and shot. Twice. I missed the cat, but chipped granite under the ledge.

The huge cat screamed, sending shivers down my back.

Sleek muscles rippled as the great cat bunched to pounce.

I dug my heels into the dirt and scooted backward on my ass closer to the base of the sheer rock wall so the cat would have to jump over me exposing its underbelly, giving me more time to aim and shoot. I held my Colt in both hands waiting for it. I only had two shots left. I had to make them count, or I'd be that animal's next meal.

As the puma lunged, I spent my last two bullets as it flew over my head. I saw its body flinch just before it hit the ground. Must have nicked it, but without a backward glance, the cat disappeared behind some large boulders.

Was I in worse danger now that it was wounded? Or would it stay clear of me and my camp? I worried whether a wounded puma just might hunt me instead of staying clear.

I reloaded my gun, panting and furious, while scanning the area all around me for sign of the cat's return.

"Bastard, you come after me, I'll shoot you." Air rasped through my fear-constricted throat. I holstered my gun, then bent over to throw up behind a nearby Ponderosa pine. When I quit heaving, I took off my gloves to wipe my mouth then stuffed my hands under my armpits to stop them from shaking. I leaned against the pine, my legs too unsteady to hold me up. Tears began to flood my eye at such a rate I figured I would be blubbering like a little kid within seconds. I leaned over behind the tree again and hawked to clear the bile out of my craw.

What was I doing out in the wilderness when I couldn't protect myself, couldn't hit anything I aimed at?

I picked up my hat, dusted myself off and rammed it back on my head. I pulled the Colt out of its worn leather holster again, tilting it this way and that to watch the sun play along its well-oiled, blue steel barrel. It felt hot and heavy in my hands. Maybe I should end it all here where no one would find my remains. My reputation as a coachman would remain untarnished, and no one would know what happened to me, or much care.

I gazed up at the cloudless sky through the tears in my remaining eye, looking for answers. I thought about the times I'd had it rough and considered them against the rest of my life. Each time I'd hit a slump, I'd always managed to pull myself out and things got better, or at least returned to normal. And I'd always liked normal when it included driving a six-horse team pulling a coach full of passengers. Meeting my deadlines. Maintaining my reputation of being the safest driver in California. Over all, my life was—good. Not easy, but good. I liked being independent.

No, I would have to learn to shoot and drive all over again.

With no cat in sight, I holstered my Colt and dragged the tears off my right cheek with the sleeve of my coat. Tugging on my gloves, I headed in the direction Chester had hightailed; the blood still pounding in my ears. Fear and the uncertainty of my life as a whip gnawed a hole in my middle as I went to find my horse.

I found the gelding a quarter of a mile down the trail, grazing. He generally came to my whistle, but not that day. My guess is he thought I got him into that mess, so I deserved the walk and owed him an apology to boot. I rubbed his forehead a few minutes as much for my comfort as his before climbing on. Then, in a quieter frame of mind, we walked back down the valley to see where the dumb mule had hied herself off to. We caught up with her about a mile down the trail and it took Chester and me fifteen minutes to grab ahold of her lead. Guess she thought I needed to pay the price of getting her all het up, too.

That night I set up my base camp at the point where the Merced wound north and joined a smaller creek. Behind me lay the three-tiered waterfall, and in any direction I looked, there were huge granite cliffs that must have been made when the earth was born. Nothing I had ever seen until then, or since, has matched the grandness of that valley and those giant sequoia trees.

The next day, I shot a mule deer with my rifle. It was not a clean kill. Had to track it and finish him off with my skinning knife, a fact that galled worse than a saddle sore. I hate to see any animal hurt, unless o' course, it's a snake. I managed to sling the dressed-out deer across the back of the mule after much sidestepping on her part due to the smell of blood, and a few, well, more'n a few, cuss words from me. But I got the carcass back to camp and cut me a juicy steak for dinner. While sitting at the fire enjoying my steak and licking venison juice from my fingers that evening, I heard the scream of a terrified woman that made the hair on the back of my neck stand straight up.

Chester and the mule snorted and yanked back on their tether, dark eyes encircled by their whites. The tether held. The Molly brayed. Chester danced side to side. It took me a moment to recognize the sound that had sent a thrill of fear through all of us.

The puma.

"It'll be all right," I said, approaching the nervous animals and running a hand down each of their necks to soothe and reassure them. "I think it's far enough away that it won't bother us." The sound of my voice kept me company, but it also helped to calm the anxious animals. "But I better get that carcass cached just the same. Fresh blood might draw her attention." Though I knew the cat would probably not approach me, or the fire I had going, still I didn't know how hungry she was. Didn't want her spooking my animals either.

Soon as I finished my steak, I tied the carcass by the hind legs and threw the rope over a high limb. I tied the rope around the tree trunk, leaving the deer hanging some fifteen feet off the ground making it not impossible exactly, but less easy for the puma or a bear wandering about to help themselves to a free meal.

Next day, I jerked most of the meat and stored it higher in a tree a short way from camp. Didn't want no varmints stealing my vittles, or getting ideas about my stock being easy pickings. What was left of the deer, I hauled a couple of miles away and left for them that were hungry.

Over the next week, I practiced my shooting. Since I'd packed plenty of ammunition and canned goods in from Mariposa—I liked canned peaches to finish off my dinner—I used the empty tins for target practice. I had to take aim with more care now that I only had my right eye. Course, I never was a shootist to begin with as some claimed to be. In fact, I didn't want to be, but damn, I did want to hit what I was aiming at especially when it was deadly, like a rattler, or that damn puma. So I kept practicing. The crack of my gunfire snapped echoes off the surrounding granite, scaring the game for miles around. Didn't hear the puma again after that.

When I got good with the cans lined up on a tree branch, I jury-rigged a couple of them so's they'd swing in the breeze. And, as I got to hitting most of what I was shooting at, I moved on to hunting rattlesnakes so's I could wipe them off the face of the earth. I circled camp each day searching for the slithery bastards and every one I saw, I would shoot. At first, most of them slithered away, a few with chunks out of their hides, I'm glad to say. After awhile, I got so it'd take only one shot and they didn't have a head left to strike with. I just had to take time with my aim, but I learned to focus along my gun sites and get what I was aiming at. With the one eye, I now preferred shooting with my rifle, as I could hold it to my shoulder and sight along the barrel.

I spent hours each day riding through the valley and exploring trails that branched off from the broad valley floor. Gray squirrels chattered at me from the limbs of black oak and dogwood as I passed, and a time or two, I spotted the reddish-brown of a bobcat slinking off into the woods as I approached.

One afternoon, I heard a deep-chested roaring off to the west and put Chester into a lope toward the bellowing. I pulled him up about a quarter mile short of two black bears fighting in a meadow and watched them have at it. Ten minutes after we drew up, the larger of the two, having at least seventy-five to a hundred pounds on the younger bear, held his ground as the other loped off. Weren't sure what caused the ruckus. I didn't see any female close by, so maybe it was about territory, or maybe it was 'cause they were male and needed to test their mettle. Lord knows.

My thoughts growled as loud and mean over the next few days. Didn't matter that I'd already proved myself a whip on both coasts of the United States, I'd have to prove myself all over again. I packed up and headed east-northeast, working my way out of the Yosemite Valley. Round and round the questions went like a mustang trapped in a boxed canyon with a puma sitting at the open end, waiting. My mind kept brewing about how I was going to pick up those six ribbons and take up where I left off.

35
A Long Way to Go

T wo weeks later, I rode down off the mountains through Tioga
Pass with a plan and that damned mule. There were still
times she'd forget our original agreement that she weren't to bite
me, but other than those ornery days of hers, we got along well
enough that I was still glad to have her do my toting.

I headed east, aiming to join the Wells Fargo outfit over in
Council Bluffs, Iowa. Figured I needed a change of scenery. Back
when I'd run into Hank Monk, he had made mention of Ben
Holladay's call for whips for his Midwest and Sierra runs. Seein's
how Holladay lost help regular-like, what with the Indians stirring
up trouble, killing and scalping people, it weren't a wonder he was
coming up short of drivers. It took extra nerve to drive stage when
you might have to fight to stay alive. I had the nerve, I just needed
the job.

I set myself to learn to drive all over again.

I rented a team from a feller out in the new state of Nevada
and put them and myself through the lessons Eb taught me back in
Worcester. Much was second nature, but I had some trouble
making smooth left turns. I practiced them left turns till that team

would veer toward a left turn, even if I hadn't planned on going that way. Learned to use my ears more than I had before. Wheels sounded different from one road surface to the next, iron rims grit on dirt, clatter on cobblestone, and thunder over hard-pack or solid rock, and whisper over grass. Went back to making those circles and figure eights Eb used to have me do. Over the few days I had that team, I walked circles, trotted circles, even called them up into a lope to do circles. Mostly to the left in the beginning.

Then I rented two spans. Now some call this a four-in-hand, but that's for when they be pulling a fancy coach. Since they were a little further out in front, my circles had to be bigger, but I followed the same practices I'd put the last team through. There weren't any six-ups for rent seein's how they were for Concords and the like.

I got a few lucky breaks as I headed east. Helped one woman whose husband got himself kilt over a gold strike squabble. It was near on a week 'fore word reached town that she was a widow. She hired me soon after to drive her across Nevada to Salt Lake City where she had family. Had me pegged for a woman the second day out. Like I said before, women look at men differently than men look at other men. She didn't mind I was a woman. Asked me about my life and the loss of my eye. Was rather impressed with what I'd done for myself. Said she wished she could do the same, but I doubted it. She weren't the type that'd feel comfortable-like being self-sufficient. She was friendly and liked to chatter and weren't particularly interested if she got an answer or not to what she was saying, which let me think my thoughts as I wanted. Having company helped the time pass.

Out of Salt Lake, I drove a load of freight for a church train, one of them down-and-back runs them Mormons make to pick up fellow church members and bring them back to their Salt Lake community. When I explained I was only going east, they assured me they'd have drivers for the return trip, so I earned my way east through Utah, Wyoming and Nebraska territories to the Missouri River at Omaha where they were to pick up their next batch of settlers. From there all I had to do was cross the Missouri into Council Bluffs, Iowa, and get me a job with the Wells Fargo line.

I knew I had driving a team of four down solid, but a six-up was still a horse of another breed. Well, I guessed, I would have to bullshit my way through that one. It weren't like I'd never driven a six-up before.

Ben Holladay was hiring to fill the ranks of those who'd been either scalped, or had lost their nerve. Had a long line of fellers wanting to be stage drivers. I didn't count them, but there must've been more then fifty men fixing to work for Wells Fargo that day. I gave my name and took a seat in the back of the hall to await my turn and listen to what was going on. There sat Ben at the head of the packed hiring hall shouting, "Next?"

The name-taker would call out the next man's name on the list. And that feller would walk up to the table, sometimes hat in hand, generally not, and Ben would start asking his weeding-out questions.

"Drive coach before?

"How long?

"Who'd you work for?

"Ever hear of Johnson's Cutoff up in the Sierras?

"How close to the edge of a cut with a thousand feet drop on one side and a wall of dirt on the other would you drive my coach, if you had a deadline to meet?"

Well, I got to tell you. I ain't ever heard such bullshitters in all my born days. Some of them boastful men bragged that they'd drive "with only half the wheel on solid ground." No dag-blamed fool would do such a thing. But Ben, he'd listen to them and tell them to sit down when he was done asking his questions.

I got to tell you, I was beginning to worry that this Holladay feller was actually thinking of hiring one of these crazy liars. It got to be my turn, and I headed for the door.

"Hey, where you going?" Holladay yells after me. "Don't you want a job?"

I pulled out a plug of t'bacca and cut me a fresh chaw before answering. I folded my jackknife, slipped it in my pocket, and said, "Sure I want a job, but not working for you Mr. Holladay. I would stay as far away from the edge of that ledge as the coach hubs on the upside would let me." I opened the door about to leave. A loud crack echoed through the hall as Holladay slapped the table with the flat of his hand.

"By Gar, you're the man I want," he yelled. "What's your name?"

I closed the door with no small measure of relief.

"Charley Parkhurst, sir." A low buzz filled the room. Some of the men started talking amongst themselves darting glances in my direction.

"You the Parkhurst that got those passengers over the flooded Tuolumne River before the bridge collapsed?"

"Yes, sir."

"I heard about you," Ben said, coming up the isle toward me. He put his hand on my shoulder. "Nice piece of driving, Charley. Step outside with me for a minute, would you?"

Ben made it sound as though I drove a loaded six-up over that damn bridge, but I'd been too worried. It'd been raining pretty steady for a couple of days. The swollen Tuolumne raged, tumbling boulders as though they were horse droppings. My leaders stopped dead soon as their hooves hit the bridge and wouldn't budge. I cracked the whip over their heads once, but they still wouldn't move. Got down and walked out onto the bridge. Seemed solid. Looked over the side at the white water; bridge seemed sound. Went back and grabbed the reins of the leaders, thinking to walk them across, but they'd have nothing doing. Kept tossing their heads and stepping back, crowding the swing team, making them nervous, too. Seein's how there was no way to turn around so's we could head back, I unloaded the passengers and had them walk across the bridge in the pouring rain. Heard a lot of muttering over that, but I told them it was for their own safety. Once they were over, I could see the bridge begin to sway a mite and knew I would have to get the rig across mighty quick. No amount of coaxing would do. I climbed onto the bench. Cut myself a new chaw of t'bacca and bit down. Uncoiled my blacksnake whip and cracked it behind the ears of each one of my team. Leaders still wouldn't move till the swing team and wheelers crowded them onto the bridge. Once the whole team was on, they hurried, taking small steps as though hobbled. Soon as we reached firm ground on the other side, the bridge busted into kindling and rushed down the Tuolumne. The team stomped and skittered as the ashen passengers climbed back into the coach without a word, and we headed out.

Ben and I stepped into the bright September sun. The cool breeze that hit my face felt real good after the blush of recognition. Getting noticed always made me nervous and started me sweating.

"Have you driven a six-up with one eye, Charley?" he asked, searching my good eye for the blink of a lie.

"No." My planned lie died in my throat. "I been practicing with a double-span," I said. "But I been driving a six-up since I were seventeen years old. I can still drive, Mr. Holladay. Give me a chance."

"I admire your sand, Charley. Heard a lot of good about your driving, but I got my passengers to think of."

"I would never endanger any passengers, Mr. Holladay. Let me prove to you that I can still drive."

"How?"

"Let me hitch a six-up and show you."

"We don't have any serious obstacles here. The driving conditions I'm concerned about you'd face on the run up in the mountains. Anything can happen in the spur of the moment. I ain't questioning your reputation, Charley, I'm questioning your ability to see well enough to avoid danger."

"You ever seen a man run over a silver dollar with both wheels of a coach moving full tilt?" I asked.

"I heard it can be done, but I ain't seen it myself."

"If you're willing, that will be my test. I'll do it as many times as you want. Your call." I yanked at the cuffs of my driving gloves. My heart was thudding at the risk I was about to take. I didn't know the horses I would be driving, and I hadn't done a silver run since I had shown Willy the Welsh what was what some fifteen, maybe twenty years ago. Back then, I had the use of both eyes.

Holladay gave me a long searching look. "All right. Give it a go. Hitch the six in the corral to the mud wagon out back. Their run is coming up in under an hour. That should give you enough time."

As I took off for the corral, I heard Holladay yell into the hall, "Hey, boys, you might want to see this."

It ain't easy hitching a team you don't know. Course, I could match them by size, the wheelers being the largest, the leaders being the lightest weight, with the swing team being the middle range. But in a team of six horses that work well together, each horse has its preferred place in the hitch. Each is used to the position they work in with the rest of the team. My belly knotted as one wheeler refused to take the bit. When a seventeen-hand horse decides he don't want to take the bit into his mouth, and puts his head in the clouds, someone my size has a fight on her hands. The more time it took to harness the entire team, the less time I would have to prove myself, and the more I thought about it, the more I sweated. Damn!

Holladay rounded the back corner of the hall as I was hitching the near leader to the mud wagon. "You coming?"

I could feel the heat rise to my cheeks in embarrassment. "Yes," I shouted. "I'm a coming."

"Old Caesar give you a hard time with the bit?" Holladay asked as he climbed into the driver's box next to me.

"He tried."

"I got some of the boys strung out along the road, so we can do this in one pass," he said.

"I was hoping to get the feel of the team before we started."

"Don't have the time, Charley. Dust is rising in the east. Stage is ahead of schedule. We got to do this now if it's going to get done."

"Yes, sir." We rounded the hiring hall at a trot.

"Each man will toss his dollar so you can see it land. I told'em all to play fair."

Over a half mile stretch, there were five men spaced some-what evenly apart. I barely had time to get the team pulling together before the first throw. The wheelers and swing teams were in the traces, but the leaders were fractious. They kept leaning into each other. I'd misguessed which side to hitch them on.

I caught a flash of silver as the sun glinted off the first throw. The near mare weren't paying attention to me.

"Missed," the thrower yelled.

I cracked the whip over the mare's head to get her attention and let her know I weren't fooling around.

"Get along, my beauties." Talking cheerful-like, I let the rest of the team know I weren't angry with them. The mare started to straighten out.

I saw the flash of the second throw. I knew without looking that the front wheel missed.

"Hit one," yelled the rider.

We had rolled over it with the rear wheel.

Close weren't good enough. I'd said both wheels.

After retrieving their coin, the riders fell in behind us at a gallop a whooping and a hollering, trying to shake up the team and make them harder to handle, less easy to guide with the ribbons. But it had the reverse effect on the leaders. The hollering put them solidly into the traces. Now we were all working together.

Toss three.

The flash of silver fell on the left side of the road. My bad side. I leaned into Ben to get a better look, and squeezed my left hand to adjust my team to hit it with the near wagon wheels.

"Hit two."

Was it luck? Could I do it two more times?

Toss four.

The toss was early. I saw the flash of silver, but couldn't make out where it landed. It weren't as far to the left this time. It looked to be center. Too much depended on me seein' where that coin lay. I stood, something I never did; a driver could get hisself bounced out of the driver's box with one on'ry rock half-hidden in the dirt. I spied my target and sat. It was on my side of the road this time. I gave a slight tug with my right wrist. The team stepped to the right.

"Hit two."

I had less than a moment to talk myself down from getting cocky as the rush of pride tore through me. I'd done it again, but I still had one more to go. My team started to slow. I needed them in the traces to get the quick response I needed from the twitch of a finger should I have to adjust their heading.

"Get along, my beauties."

Toss five.

I had just enough time to crack the whip once to shape them up. I felt my six-up step into the bit just as I saw the coin hit center for sure this time. It was a shorter run than the others. I had less time to correct my team's approach. I gave a gentle tug with my left arm. My beauties swung a horse width to the left.

"Hit two."

Relief and pride flashed through me. I'd done it!

Ben Holladay thumped me on the back as I turned the team around. "You're hired. I ain't ever seen nobody do what you just did. Mister, you can work for me any time. Boys," he yelled. "Hiring's done for the day."

We headed back to the barn. I pulled up to the hiring hall door with a flourish like I'd always done at the end of my stage runs. All five men tossed their coins in the driver's box along with their congratulations and admiration. I admit to sitting pretty tall that afternoon. I couldn't stop grinning. I was back driving a six-up again; doing what I loved. I knew my Mattie would have been proud of her mama.

That day, when I was back in top form—that's how I want to be remembered. I don't want to dwell on the aches and pains of rheumatism, or the viciousness of the cancer that took hold of my mouth and throat here at the end. Don't want to be remembered as a complaining old coot by my friends Frank and the Harmons who took good care of me these last few weeks.

Ever since leaving the orphanage, I went after what I wanted. And, for the most part, I don't regret doing what I done. Found life to be quirky as a new-broke mustang though. When I got things I wanted, like driving coach for a rich family, I found I didn't want that, I wanted adventure. Yet, when I gave birth to the daughter I didn't want, I loved her best of all and would've given my life to spare hers.

Life ain't like driving a six-up. You don't get to take hold and make it go where you want every time. Life's more like the road. Can't ever be sure what you're going to find round the bend. Might be a rockslide blocking the road, or maybe a beautiful sunset that makes you glad to be alive. All I know is they're both on the same road. And, man or woman, you got to be willing to face one to get to the other.

After the End

C harley never told Frank her secret because as she said, "Frank hates women. Some female broke his heart when he was young, and he's never forgiven her, or any other woman. Don't think he even liked his Ma much. Frank's an old bach' and likes thinking we're alike. Wouldn't hurt the old bird for nothing, he's been a big help to me these past few years taking care of my stock whilst I was away. I'm looking to him to see me through till the cancer wins out."

I had guessed Charley's true gender shortly after we met, and when I verified the fact by asking her, she made me swear not to bandy it about till after she was gone.

In the end, it was O'Neill that told Frank.

I stayed inside to prepare the body, but I heard every word.

"He was a what?!" Frank bellowed.

"Charley was a woman."

"I would've knowed."

"She bound her breasts, Frank. By the looks of it, she gave birth at some point in her life, too."

"Concarn it all. Don't that beat hell. All these years, I thought I had a friend and the damn bitch was laughing at me."

"Now, Frank, Charley wasn't like that."

"Made a horse's ass out of me, she did, front of the whole town."

"Doubt many knew. I imagine there'll be quite a few surprised neighbors hereabouts."

When I stepped out onto the porch a while later, Frank sat rocking back and forth crazy fast like a youngster would, his anger-clouded face flashed me a look to kill. "You're laughing at me, too, and don't tell me you ain't."

"I would never do that Frank," I said. "Charley was my friend, and I promised not to tell a soul."

"You knew?"

"Yes, I guessed some time ago."

"Son of a bitch!"

"After I knew, I asked whether I could write down her stories," I said, handing him the leather bound journal of Charley's life. "Thought maybe you'd like to read what she was about all these years. But, before you get started with that, let's open Charley's trunk. She told me some weeks ago, when she knew she was going to die of the cancer, that she wanted me to open the trunk with you. She didn't say what was in it, but I'm hoping her suit's in there, so we can put her to rest in it. I have her all washed, but I want to dress her before she stiffens."

Frank brought out the small trunk and dusted it off with his handkerchief, his face still showing traces of resentment, but not the consuming anger of a few minutes earlier. We looked at each other, and I could see in his eyes a spark of curiosity that met the excitement I felt at the prospect of delving into who knew what kinds of telltale treasures of such an interesting life.

First thing to meet our eyes were two envelopes, one addressed to Frank, and the other to me. We tore them open and read in silence. To this day, I don't know what Frank's contained, but my letter thanked me for all I had done for her over the years, which certainly wasn't much considering how independent she had always been. And another sheet of paper contained Charley's will, leaving a sum total of $600.00 to twelve-year old, Georgie Harmon. It stated that the money was in the care of the merchant

Otto A. Stoesser, Sr. in Watsonville, and would be handed over upon the delivery of the letter.

Charley's generosity brought tears to my eyes. Blinking them away, I put the letter aside and delved further into the trunk. The next items were what I'd been looking for, Charley's going-to-court suit, the one she had bought in Providence. She'd had several lawsuits over the past few years between herself and Frederick A. Hihn and had always dressed for the occasion. As I removed the neatly folded suit, a large swath of red caught my eye. I put the suit aside and withdrew Charley's red dress. She never mentioned that she had kept it all those years. And beneath that lay a baby's shoe. Mattie's. I put both in Charley's casket just before Mr. O'Neill nailed it shut.

My heart felt like a boulder lodged in my chest. Feelings of emptiness and regret washed over me. Along with Frank, I'd lost a good friend. One I'd known only a few years, yet, I was glad I had the privilege of knowing her. As I thought of her loss, and my loss of her friendship, I could no longer hold back my tears. Like she said, "I went after what I wanted, and I don't regret doing what I done."

I hope I can say the same when my life is over.

Author's Note

Any work of historical fiction is a work of imagination based on as much fact as can be learned, along with the legends and myths found surrounding the person, place or incident. The author takes this linear life or timeframe, and massages it to conform to established and expected literary structure, to furnish the reader with believable drama that hopefully delights the imagination and feeds the soul. With this in mind, the author hopes the reader will enjoy the story and forgive any historical gaps the reader may perceive.

Additional copies of
Charley's Choice
may be purchased through:
www.BuyBooksOnTheWeb.com
and
www.fernjhill.com

Visit the author's web site for:

The historical facts and legends about
Charley Darkey Parkhurst

A study guide for *Charley's Choice*

Signed copies of *Charley's Choice*

31919620R00162

Made in the USA
Middletown, DE
16 May 2016